Mortar and Murder

"With plot twists that curve and loop . . . this story offers handy renovation tips, historical data, and a colorful painting of the Maine landscape." —Examiner.com

"Mystery author Jennie Bentley has nailed together another great mystery with *Mortar and Murder*." —*Fresh Fiction*

Plaster and Poison

"A delightful small-town Maine sleuth . . . Solid and entertaining." —*Midwest Book Review*

"[A] thrilling story that keeps the readers guessing and turning pages." —*Fresh Fiction*

"A believable and beguiling mystery. Each novel in the series delights and the third installment only raises the stakes." —Examiner.com

"A pull-no-punches mystery." —*The Mystery Gazette*

"This is one solidly built mystery . . . Attractive characters and a beautiful setting round out this wonderful read."
—*RT Book Reviews*

D0816041

continued . . .

Spackled and Spooked

"Smooth, clever, and witty. This series is a winner!"
—*Once Upon a Romance*

"Bound to be another winner for this talented author. Home-renovation buffs will appreciate the wealth of detail."
—Examiner.com

"I hope the series continues." —*Gumshoe Reviews*

Fatal Fixer-Upper

"An ingeniously plotted murder mystery with several prime suspects and a nail-biting conclusion."
—*The Tennessean*

"A great whodunit . . . Fans will enjoy this fine cozy."
—*Midwest Book Review*

"Smartly blends investigative drama, sexual tension, and romantic comedy elements, and marks the start of what looks like an outstanding series of Avery Baker cases."
—*The Nashville City Paper*

"Polished writing and well-paced story. I was hooked . . . from page one." —*Cozy Library*

"There's a new contender in the do-it-yourself home-renovation mystery field . . . An enjoyable beginning to a series." —*Bangor Daily News*

"A strong debut mystery . . . Do-it-yourselfers will find much to enjoy." —*The Mystery Reader*

FLIPPED
OUT

JENNIE BENTLEY

BERKLEY PRIME CRIME, NEW YORK

THE BERKLEY PUBLISHING GROUP
Published by the Penguin Group
Penguin Group (USA) Inc.
375 Hudson Street, New York, New York 10014, USA
Penguin Group (Canada), 90 Eglinton Avenue East, Suite 700, Toronto, Ontario M4P 2Y3, Canada
(a division of Pearson Penguin Canada Inc.)
Penguin Books Ltd., 80 Strand, London WC2R 0RL, England
Penguin Group Ireland, 25 St. Stephen's Green, Dublin 2, Ireland (a division of Penguin Books Ltd.)
Penguin Group (Australia), 250 Camberwell Road, Camberwell, Victoria 3124, Australia
(a division of Pearson Australia Group Pty. Ltd.)
Penguin Books India Pvt. Ltd., 11 Community Centre, Panchsheel Park, New Delhi—110 017, India
Penguin Group (NZ), 67 Apollo Drive, Rosedale, Auckland 0632, New Zealand
(a division of Pearson New Zealand Ltd.)
Penguin Books (South Africa) (Pty.) Ltd., 24 Sturdee Avenue, Rosebank, Johannesburg 2196,
South Africa

Penguin Books Ltd., Registered Offices: 80 Strand, London WC2R 0RL, England

This is a work of fiction. Names, characters, places, and incidents either are the product of the author's imagination or are used fictitiously, and any resemblance to actual persons, living or dead, business establishments, events, or locales is entirely coincidental. The publisher does not have any control over and does not assume any responsibility for author or third-party websites or their content.

PUBLISHER'S NOTE: Neither the publisher nor the author is engaged in rendering professional advice or services to the individual reader. The ideas, projects, and suggestions contained in this book are not intended as a substitute for consulting with a professional. Neither the author nor the publisher shall be liable or responsible for any loss or damage allegedly arising from any information or suggestion in this book.

FLIPPED OUT

A Berkley Prime Crime Book / published by arrangement with the author

PRINTING HISTORY
Berkley Prime Crime mass-market edition / October 2011

Copyright © 2011 by Penguin Group (USA) Inc.
Cover design by Rita Frangie.
Cover illustration by Jennifer Taylor / Paperdog Studio.
Interior text design by Laura K. Corless.

ISBN: 978-0-425-24407-4

BERKLEY® PRIME CRIME
Berkley Prime Crime Books are published by The Berkley Publishing Group,
a division of Penguin Group (USA) Inc.,
375 Hudson Street, New York, New York 10014.
BERKLEY® PRIME CRIME and the PRIME CRIME logo are trademarks of Penguin Group (USA) Inc.

PRINTED IN THE UNITED STATES OF AMERICA

10   9   8   7   6   5   4   3   2   1

— Acknowledgments —

As always, great big thanks, hugs, and kisses to the following wonderful people, without whom I would not be here, doing what I'm doing:

My brilliant agent, Stephany Evans, for sticking with me through it all; my wonderful editor, Jessica Wade, for letting me continue the journey with Avery and Derek; the Penguin design team: artist Jennifer Taylor for another gorgeous cover illustration, and designers Rita Frangie and Laura K. Corless, for making the book beautiful inside and out; my hardworking publicist with the Penguin Group, Kaitlyn Kennedy, without whom this book would be nowhere; my beta reader, critique partner, and internet buddy, Jamie Livingston-Dierks, for always being there for me and always being a source of laughter, inspiration, and good advice; my Sisters and Brothers in Crime, my fellow ITW Debut Authors, my fellow Romance Writers of America and Music City Romance Writers, and assorted writer friends I don't necessarily have any organizations in common with, but who have somehow impacted my life and my writing anyway; everyone who's bought a copy of *Fatal Fixer-Upper*, *Spackled and Spooked*, *Plaster and Poison*, or *Mortar and Murder* sometime in the past three years, especially those of you who liked the stories, and even more especially those of you who told someone about them; my non-writer friends— yes, I do have a few; and my family, especially my husband and my two boys, who have learned to accept the fact that I spend much of my time in a world far removed from theirs, where they can't join me, and who love me anyway; and last but certainly not least, Faye of the Cali Ponds.

Around the time when I started writing this book, the first and second of May 2010, Nashville was hit by record amounts of rain and severe flooding. A few intrepid local writers started an internet auction called Do the Write Thing for Nashville, and in a few weeks, raised more than $75,000 for flood relief. One of the many generous souls who supported the effort was Faye, who outbid everyone for the chance to name a character in my next book.

Faye, meet Fae. And Aurora. And Cali. I hope you'll be pleased with what I did with the names you gave me.

xoxo

—1—

When my stepfather, Noel, asked my boyfriend, Derek, and me to participate in an episode of a renovation show his TV network produces, I didn't think it would be a problem. Derek and I had renovated four houses together, starting with the 1870s Second Empire Victorian I had inherited from my great-aunt Inga a year earlier. After that, we had bought and restored a supposedly haunted midcentury ranch, and then turned a decrepit carriage house at the back of my friend Kate's property into a romantic retreat for two just in time for her wedding to Waterfield Chief of Police Wayne Rasmussen. For the past few months, we had worked our fingers to the bone on a 1783 center-chimney Colonial on Rowanberry Island. By the time the TV crew was set to arrive on the coast of Maine, it was mid-July, but contrary to my first blithe impression, there was indeed a problem.

"There's no way!" I told Derek, and not for the first time. "No way at all we can renovate a whole house in a week!"

When Noel first approached me about taking part in a renovation show, I hadn't realized we'd be dealing with a time constraint. There are so many shows out there, with so many gimmicks, that I figured we'd be redoing something small, like a kitchen or bathroom. Something we could easily do in the five days the crew would be in town. But as it turned out, the program we would be participating in was called *Flipped Out!*, and for good reason.

Anyone who has ever renovated a house can tell you it's not usually a quick and easy process. As Derek had warned me during the very first conversation we'd ever had, more than a year ago now, it always takes longer and costs more than you think it will.

And that's OK most of the time. When you're just working for yourself and not on a schedule, it isn't the end of the world if it takes you a few extra days, or even a few extra weeks, to finish the job.

This time, that wouldn't be a possibility. The television crew would arrive in Waterfield Sunday night and would depart again the following Saturday morning, and we'd be expected to finish a whole house by the time they left. They'd shoot "before" footage bright and early on Monday morning, and God help us if they couldn't shoot "after" footage at the end of the day on Friday. When I'd asked Noel what would happen if we weren't finished by Friday night, his answer had been, "Just make sure you are."

"We're gonna be fine," Derek said now, in answer to my lament. "Don't worry, Tink. I've got it covered." He grabbed his hamburger in both hands and took a bite.

We were sitting in a booth at the Waymouth Tavern, a restaurant on the outskirts of Waterfield. An imitation Tiffany lamp burned above our heads, and out the window, we had a view of the Atlantic Ocean and a few of the islands dotting the coast of Maine. Rowanberry was one of them, although it was too dark by now to see anything but a low shape in the water with some lights on one end, where the little village was.

My name isn't Tink, by the way; it's Avery. Avery Marie Baker. Tink, or Tinkerbell, is Derek's nickname for me. It started out as sort of a joke, supposedly because I'm little and cunning—Maine-ish for cute—with lots of bright yellow hair I keep piled on top of my head when I'm working. And also because (Derek said) I pout a lot. At that time, I daresay I did: This was just after we met, and we spent our days butting heads over how to renovate my great-aunt Inga's house. Derek, being a traditionalist and a restorer at heart, wanted to keep as many of the original features as possible. I—native New Yorker and educated textile designer—wanted to squeeze in as many modern amenities as I could.

He'd won, of course. He'd made a convincing case for preservation and authenticity, and besides, I have a hard time saying no to him. It's those blue eyes, and that lazy grin, and just the whole adorable package.

I'm crazy about him. That's why I ended up staying in Waterfield and going into business with him instead of selling Aunt Inga's house for a tidy profit and scurrying back to Manhattan at the end of last summer.

At the moment, he wasn't endearing himself to me, however, and yes, I'm sure I was pouting. The one-week time limit for renovating the little cottage on Cabot Street was freaking me out, and he wasn't giving me the sympathy I craved.

"Derek." I pulled the plate with the rest of his supper out of reach, thereby forcing him to look at me. "How can you tell me not to worry and that you've got it covered? How do you expect us to be able to do all the work in five days and not lose our minds? Just not sleep?"

"That's one possibility." Derek reached across the table to put his burger back on the plate before pulling it toward him. He has longer arms than I do. I sighed. He added, "I'm serious, Avery. We'll be fine. All the materials are bought, and we've got a schedule laid out day by day, if not hour by hour. We know exactly what we're supposed to be doing at any given time."

"That's true," I admitted. We'd spent the past week preparing so we'd be ready to launch into action tomorrow morning, as soon as the crew had arrived and had shot their "before" footage of the cottage.

The house we were renovating was a little 1930s cottage, roughly eleven hundred square feet, with two bedrooms and one bath, a living room, a dining room, a kitchen, and a tiny laundry. The current owner had been using it as a rental, and as a result, it was pretty basic, with few or no frills. It was also a little beat up. But it had lovely oak hardwood floors—or would have, after we had applied three or four coats of polyurethane to them. The ceilings were fairly tall, and whoever owned the house in the 1970s had resisted the temptation to spray them with texture back when popcorn ceilings were all the rage. Scraping texture off a ceiling isn't a big deal—all it takes is a spray bottle full of water, a putty knife, and stamina—but it's messy and time consuming, and again, time would be at a premium this week.

In the living room there was a gorgeous natural-stone fireplace that had never been painted—no paint we had to strip, yet another reason to rejoice. It's a crime to paint natural stone, but that doesn't stop some people. And there were wonderful casement windows on either side of the chimney. They'd been painted shut, the way many old windows are, but we had taken the time to break the seal and force them open as part of the prep work. The kitchen was original but well made, and as I'd learned when we renovated Aunt Inga's house and Derek had insisted on keeping the old kitchen cabinets, they could be made to look wonderful. The current owner had covered the outside of the house with vinyl siding, which wouldn't have been my choice, but it had been done recently enough that the vinyl was still fairly clean, and it meant we wouldn't have to paint the exterior. A good hose-down with a power washer would do wonders. And the curb appeal was outstanding, with a pretty little porch with stacked-stone pillars and an original front door with matching sidelights. Drab now, but it would be cute as a button when we were finished. All in all, we would have had to look long and hard for a better candidate for a quick flip.

Still, five days wasn't much time to get the job done.

"We'll have help," Derek said between bites of burger.

"Are you sure they'll come through? Kate's gonna be busy with the B and B, isn't she? She'll have a full house."

Kate McGillicutty-Rasmussen was my first friend in Waterfield. She owns the Waterfield Inn, the B&B where I'd stayed my first night in town and where the television crew would be staying during the five or six days they'd be here, as well.

"She'll find the time," Derek said. "She owes us; we renovated the carriage house in record time last year. And Shannon and Josh are both out of school for the summer, so they'll be available as well."

Shannon McGillicutty, Kate's daughter, and Josh Rasmussen, Wayne's son, were students at local Barnham College. They were excited about the idea that they could do a few hours' manual labor in exchange for getting their faces on television.

Derek continued, "Cora said she'll be on hand whenever we need her, and Beatrice is back in town, too."

Cora is Derek's stepmother, and Beatrice is her youngest daughter. Bea and her husband, Steve, divided their time between Boston, where Steve was transitioning out of a job with a big law firm, and Waterfield, where he was starting a small practice of his own. Cora is fantastic in the garden, and although Beatrice is mostly a math whiz, I knew we'd be able to find something she could do to help. After all, another pair of hands is another pair of hands.

"Between all of us," Derek said, "we'll get it done." He took another big bite of burger, seemingly not the least bit worried. I picked at my crab cakes.

"It's just a very short time and a whole lot of work."

"Not that much," Derek said. "It's mostly all cosmetic. Slapping lipstick on the pig. Dressing it up for the cameras. New paint, a couple of coats of poly on the floors, new kitchen counter, new tile in the bathroom. You'll be surprised at how fast the work will go."

"If you say so." Although I probably wouldn't feel calm again until next week, when this whole ordeal was over. The house on Cabot was a great little cottage, it would be tons of fun to redo; I just wished we could really do it right and give it the time we should, instead of being in and out in five days flat.

Derek pulled his plate back across the table, put the burger on it, and started chomping on fries. I played with my crab cakes while sneaking glances past him to a romantic table for two where the other reason I wasn't looking forward to the coming week sat.

Top-producing Realtor Melissa James was currently sharing a toast with Tony "the Tiger" Micelli, ace on-air reporter for Portland's Channel Eight News.

Melissa is Derek's ex-wife. They married young, while he was still in medical school. When he decided—after four years of education and four of residency, plus a year of working with his dad, Waterfield GP Benjamin Ellis—that he didn't want to be a doctor after all, Melissa dumped him. Then she took up with my distant cousin Ray Stenham. That relationship had ended six months ago, and since then, Melissa had been on the prowl. I'd been a little worried that she might want Derek back, but lately she'd spent much of her time in the company of Tony the Tiger, so I was keeping my fingers crossed that that relationship would work out. Given the champagne toast and the steamy looks, not to mention the little velvet box I thought I saw sitting on the table, it looked like the chances were pretty good.

They hadn't noticed us come in, and I had breathed a sigh of relief, but I should have known it was too good to last. They finished their meal before us, and as they made their way toward the door, Melissa looked over and saw us. And tugged Tony's sleeve before heading in our direction.

"Oh, hell," I said.

"What?"

"She's coming this way. I was hoping they wouldn't notice us."

Derek glanced over his shoulder and saw the two of them bearing down on us. "Be nice, Avery."

"When am I not nice?" I wanted to know.

He opened his mouth to answer, but before he could, a manicured hand with long pink talons landed on his shoulder. It may have been my imagination that turned the gesture into more of a caress, but I don't think so. Melissa enjoys rubbing my nose in the fact that she spent five years married to my boyfriend.

"Hello, Avery." She showed me all her blindingly white teeth in a smile of false warmth before she turned her attention to Derek. "Hello, Derek."

I don't think I imagined the way her smile changed. Not to mention her voice. She was practically purring.

"Hey, Melissa." Derek's didn't. He doesn't want Melissa back, and he's made that clear. I just don't like the way she's all over him. He doesn't belong to her anymore, and she gave up the right to pet him when she dumped him for Ray Stenham.

Derek greeted Tony the Tiger. "Micelli."

Tony nodded back. "Ellis."

He's a good-looking guy. Tony, I mean. Derek is gorgeous: six feet tall, with hair that's a shade closer to blond than brown, at least in the summer, and those melting blue eyes with crinkles at the corners. But Tony's quite all right, if you like the type. A half dozen years older than Derek's thirty-five, and sort of slick. Black hair and hooded brown eyes, olive complexion, always very nicely dressed. My boyfriend is happiest in faded Levi's and worn T-shirts, while even Tony's golf shirts are ironed and his jeans have creases down the front. He and Melissa make a lovely couple: She's always decked out to the nines, too. Tonight's outfit was a flirty Zac Posen skirt and blouse, with gold sandals and matching jewelry. Including the obscenely large stone weighing down the ring finger of her left hand.

"You two all ready?" she wanted to know, absently massaging Derek's shoulder and making the lima-bean-sized diamond sparkle in the light from the Tiffany lamps.

"We're ready for an offer on the house on Rowanberry Island. Any activity?" I smiled insincerely.

After our usual Realtor, Irina Rozhdestvensky, had married a few months ago and become too busy with her new husband to tend to her career, we'd had to fall back on Melissa to market and sell our latest renovation project. It was over my strenuous objections, since I had spent the past year actively trying to avoid doing business with her. But she *was* the premier real estate agent in Waterfield, and probably in all of down east Maine, and when she cornered Derek and told him we needed someone with real experience to handle the sale of what had turned out to be a half-million-dollar historic waterfront property, he had been unable to say no. The house had been on the market for a couple of weeks now, but she hadn't pulled a buyer out of a hat. I couldn't resist bringing it up, even though I knew it was unreasonable to expect to get an offer so soon.

Melissa widened her fabulous violet blue eyes innocently. "I told you it would take time, Avery."

She had. I guess buyers with that kind of money don't grow on trees.

"What I meant," she added, "was whether you were ready for tomorrow."

The house we were flipping for the cameras belonged to Tony Micelli. When Melissa found out about Noel and the TV show, and that we needed a project to work on for a week, preferably without having to actually buy it first, since most of our money was tied up in the house on Rowanberry Island, she'd suggested Tony's place. He'd owned it for years, had in fact grown up in it, and had been using it as rental property for a while now. The tenants—a couple of students from Barnham College—had graduated and left town at the end of the semester, and now Tony recognized the opportunity to give his property a cheap facelift before cashing out. Having the house featured on television would likely bring any selling price up, and he had a girlfriend who could market it for him. Besides that, he'd probably enjoy having Derek—his girlfriend's ex-husband—doing the manual labor.

The sticky "ex" situation had been the biggest consideration in whether or not we wanted to take on the project. I'd wanted to say no when Melissa came to us—to Derek—with the idea of using Tony's house for our project. I didn't want to deal with her any more than I had to, and the idea that Tony would be hanging over our shoulders, making condescending comments and ordering Derek around, seemed reason enough to stay clear. But Derek said he couldn't care less what Tony did; he liked the house, he thought it would fit our needs, and besides, he was used to dealing with demanding personalities—after all, he'd been married to Melissa for five years. And it was just for a few weeks: one before the shoot, one during, and one after, to tie up any loose ends. So I'd relented. I still wasn't thrilled about having to deal with them both, but I could cope. At least I thought so.

"As ready as we'll ever be," Derek answered, sending me a smile across the table.

I smiled back. Melissa smiled, too, tightly, and dropped her hand from Derek's shoulder, albeit not without a last little stroke. "Has the crew arrived?"

"I assume so. If something had happened, I'm sure Kate would have called."

"They'll be at the house in the morning?"

"Bright and early," Derek said.

"Wonderful." Melissa glanced at Tony. "We might stop by, if you don't mind. To meet everyone."

Her tone indicated that we'd better not. Mind.

"Sure," Derek said. "It's your house. Not like we want to keep you out."

Speak for yourself, I thought.

"Tony's been in broadcasting for twenty years, you know. It's quite possible he already knows some of the crew." She used the hand with the ring to smooth her sleek, moonlight-pale hair behind one ear. By now, I was sure she was trying to draw attention to it, but I wasn't going to give her the satisfaction of hearing me ask. And Derek, bless him, was oblivious. Of course, he'd had his back to them and hadn't seen the champagne toast or the little velvet box.

"Television is a small world," Tony said in his well-modulated reporter's voice. "I know a lot of people. Twenty-plus years in the business, a body gets around." He passed a hand over his jet-black hair while smiling complacently at Melissa. "Are you ready to go, Missy?"

Melissa nodded. He took her elbow, and they moved away between the tables.

"I always feel like there's a smell of sulfur in the air whenever she's been around," I told Derek, sotto voce, as soon as they were out of range.

His lips quirked even as he checked to make sure Melissa and Tony were too far away to have heard me. "I think that's her perfume."

It was my turn to smother a giggle. "They'll be breathing down our necks for the next week, you know. Melissa might even offer to get her hands dirty, just to get more face time."

"I'm sure Tony has better things to do than hang around our project," Derek answered. "He'll have to cover the news for channel eight. I'm sure something will happen this week that'll capture the public's imagination and keep him busy. As for Melissa, don't worry about her. She might drop by to get her face and name on TV, but she won't try to do any of your work. Too afraid to break a nail."

He polished off the rest of his burger.

I looked down at my own hands. I've never been able to grow my nails long, and with all the manual labor that I do, no polish would last beyond a day before peeling off anyway. So I keep my nails short and natural. On my hands, anyway. I do tend to go a little crazy on my toes, however. At the moment, they were lime green with pink tips to match my sundress, which had a border of green and brown palm trees against a pink sky marching around the hem.

"Are you ready?" Derek asked.

I looked back up at him. "To go home?"

"I was thinking more of tomorrow. Are you ready to tackle the work and the TV crew? Get out in front of the cameras and get your groove on?" He grinned.

I shrugged. I was feeling a little apprehensive about appearing on TV—nobody wants to look bad or sound stupid in front of a national audience—but on the other hand, I was looking forward to doing the work, and the exposure would be good. Between our own projects, while we wait for one house to sell so we can buy another, we sometimes have to take on jobs for other people to make ends meet. A TV appearance might mean more exciting opportunities, instead of just spending our time painting other people's walls and sanding other people's floors.

"Always looking on the bright side," Derek said when I pointed this out.

"It beats always expecting the worst, doesn't it?"

"That it does. And on that note . . ." He lifted his glass. "Here's to us, and to another great project."

I lifted mine, too. "A great project without any skeletons in the basement, or for that matter, any hidden rooms or dark family secrets."

"Or dead bodies," Derek said, since we'd found one or two of those every time we'd taken on a new project.

"I'll drink to that."

We clinked our glasses together and did.

The camera crew arrived on Cabot Street bright and early the next morning. Derek and I were waiting on the porch steps, each gripping our paper cup of coffee, when the white van pulled up to the curb.

The van was unmarked. I guess I'd expected something like the Channel Eight News van, with its colorful logo and slogan and Tony and his coanchors' faces depicted many times life size on the side, but when I thought about it, I realized that that didn't make sense. The crew was based in California and wouldn't have driven all the way to Maine; they had probably rented a van at the airport to haul all their gear up here.

The driver was a lean, sallow man with a narrow face, dark hair in need of a cut, and sad, droopy eyes like a bloodhound. A pair of ill-fitting khakis hung low on his hips, and on his feet were heavy boots with thick soles. Next to him in the passenger seat sat a blond woman in her early forties wearing a businesslike gray pantsuit. She looked expensive. Back in New York, I'm not sure I would have thought so, but here in Waterfield, she stood out. It was another reminder how much my life and my perceptions had changed over the past year.

The back of the van held three other people, all dressed in jeans and T-shirts: one woman, two men. The woman was barely out of her teens and had a tangle of long, black hair pulled up into two bunches, one above each ear, as well as piercings in her nose, her eyebrow, her ears, her navel, and possibly a few other places that weren't visible at the moment. She was chewing bubblegum, and as she stepped out on the sidewalk and pivoted slowly, looking around, she blew a big, pink bubble, popped it, and did it again.

Of the two men, one was a few years younger than me, just on the underside of thirty, and the other in his midfifties at a guess. He had thinning, gray hair and a beard, plus a stomach that curved the blue T-shirt he wore under a many-pocketed safari-type vest. The younger man was unnaturally handsome, like a soap opera actor or model. His jeans were a touch too snug, and his black T-shirt clung tightly to his chest. The brown leather of his cowboy boots was a perfect match for the glossy brown curls framing a face that could have graced the cover of *People* magazine's "most beautiful" issue.

Derek snorted derisively.

I grinned.

The well-dressed woman looked at us, then came up the walk on pointy stilettos. "You must be the talent."

Derek got to his feet and extended a hand. "Derek Ellis." He indicated me. "This is Avery Baker."

"I'm Nina Andrews." She extended her hand. Her grip was no-nonsense, and so was the look in her eyes, although I noticed what appeared to be stress lines around her mouth and across her forehead. "I'm the director. This is the rest of the crew." She turned to the van. "Fae, our PA. That's F-A-E, like the fairy. No *y*, in case you ever have a need to spell it. Ted, the grip and gaffer. He does the lighting and other technical set up."

Ted was the driver, the skinny guy with the sallow complexion. He had opened the back of the van and was busy hauling plastic crates full of cords and equipment out of the vehicle and onto the sidewalk, and he must have been stronger than he looked, because the big crates didn't seem to trouble him.

"Wilson is the camera operator"—the older guy with the vest; he was helping Ted unload the van—"and this is Adam."

Her voice changed ever so slightly when she said Adam's name, although that could have been because Adam himself came up to stand next to her right then.

Up close, he was almost too pretty. Perfect nose, perfect skin, dark blue eyes with long lashes, pink lips that missed being too full by a hair, and white teeth so straight and even they couldn't possibly be real.

He took my hand in both of his, just holding it and not shaking, while he gave me a melting smile and a long, appreciative look from under his lashes. "I'm Adam Ramsey. Nice to meet you."

"Avery Baker. Likewise." I twitched my hand out of his. I was Derek's girlfriend and had no business holding hands with anyone else, and despite his obvious attributes, Adam didn't appeal to me. He had this veneer of high gloss that made him look sort of waxed. And the charm was too practiced, too calculated. He reminded me of my ex-boyfriend Philippe, the reproduction furniture maker I had worked for in New York. Philippe had been all about appearances, and I was willing to bet Adam was, too. He wasn't pleased to meet me; he was just oozing charm because I was female and that was what he did. Nina must be used to it, because she didn't bat an eye.

Next to me, Derek flashed a grin full of teeth and warning. "I'm Derek Ellis. Avery's boyfriend. She and I will be doing the renovating." He gave Adam's hand a good squeeze.

"Adam's our runner," Nina said as Adam stuffed his hands into his pockets. "He does a little of this and a little of that, wherever he's needed. Right now, he should be over there with Ted and Wilson, unloading the van." She glanced at him.

Unabashed, Adam saluted. "Sure, Neen." He winked at me before he turned on his cowboy-booted heel and sauntered toward the van. About halfway down the garden path, he passed Fae, and he must have said something to her, because she giggled and twisted her neck to look at him over her shoulder, her cheeks almost as pink as the bubblegum.

Nina narrowed her eyes, but when Fae stopped beside her, she performed the next round of introductions without comment. "Fae, this is the talent, Derek and Avery. Fae is our PA, or production assistant. She takes care of any paperwork, legal permits, motel reservations, that sort of thing."

"Nice to meet you, Fae," I said. Derek just smiled. Fae lowered her eyes, blushing again. Given the many body piercings and the amount of skin showing between the low-slung jeans and cropped top, I'd have thought she'd be harder and more sophisticated, but she actually seemed like sort of a nice girl.

"Speaking of motel reservations," Derek said, "you're staying at the Waterfield Inn, correct?"

Nina nodded. "Mr. Carrick said we had to. That he and Mrs. Carrick stayed there when they were in town for Christmas." She looked at me. "Rosemary Carrick is your mother, isn't she?"

I nodded. "She and Noel got married a couple of years ago. Second marriage for both of them. He's the one who suggested that Derek and I should do an episode of your show."

"If Mr. Carrick suggested it, then I'm sure it's a good

idea," Nina said loyally. "You're familiar with the Water-field Inn, I take it?"

Derek and I both nodded. "Kate McGillicutty is my best friend," I said, forgetting momentarily that she was Kate Rasmussen now.

Derek added, "The Waterfield Inn is the nicest B and B in town. You'll be comfortable there."

"We're already settled in. Flew into Logan last night and drove up." Nina smiled.

The Waterfield Inn has only four guest rooms. The big suite on the third floor where Mom and Noel had stayed when they were here in December, and three regular-sized rooms on the second floor. There were five people on the TV crew. I couldn't help wondering who was rooming with someone else. Adam and Nina? Adam and Fae?

Or maybe no one was. There were two bedrooms on the first floor of the B&B, too, behind the kitchen and dining room, in the "private" part of the house. Kate and her daughter Shannon had lived in them until Kate married Wayne and the newlyweds moved out to the renovated carriage house. Shannon was still in hers, but maybe Kate had offered the other to Fae, while Nina was in the suite and the three guys had the three second-floor rooms. The first-floor rooms weren't outfitted as guest rooms, but Fae might not mind, and she might even enjoy being next door to Shannon, who was close to her own age.

Problem solved.

While I'd been speculating on possible Hollywood hookups, Nina and Derek had moved on to the job ahead and what the next week would bring. Nina was explaining about the production schedule and why she'd prefer that he not wear the white T-shirt he had on while the cameras were rolling (too much of a contrast to his tanned face). She also said that we should avoid fabrics with patterns, like herringbone, corduroy, and pinstripes, all of which would create a wavy rainbow-colored pattern called a moiré effect on-screen. Since it was July and hot, and since most T-shirts don't come in those patterns, I didn't think we needed to worry.

She turned to me. "Red and deep orange aren't good colors for the camera, either, and it's probably best to avoid black or really dark blue, since you're relatively pale."

"Sure." I nodded obediently, although privately I thought that the list of admonitions didn't leave me with a whole lot of options. Derek and I both wear a lot of white T-shirts to work, since they're cheap and easy to replace when they get ruined. And they get ruined a lot. I'd have to pull out some of my nicer stuff this week. Which might not be a bad idea anyway, since I definitely wanted to look my best on TV.

"Nothing shapeless," Nina continued. "You know how they say the camera adds ten pounds? It's true. In life, you see not only the person but also what's around them, so they tend to appear smaller. On camera, all you see is the talent, and that means you take up more space, which makes you look bigger. So be sure to wear clothes that make you appear taller and leaner, not wider. Shapeless clothing will make you look lumpy on camera."

Derek and I both nodded solemnly, Derek not without an amused twinkle in his eyes. Neither of us are overweight, but who wants to look lumpy on every TV screen in America?

"Why don't you show me around?" She looked past us to the house. "Tell me what you're planning to do, so we can get some kind of shooting schedule together."

"Of course." He glanced at me. "You wanna do the honors, Avery?"

"You go ahead," I said. He was the contractor; I was just the lowly designer.

We did a walk-through while Derek pointed out the architectural features and explained what we planned to accomplish over the next five days.

"We'll refinish the floors, but that won't be until the end

of the week. One of the last things we do. It doesn't make
any sense to do it first and then walk on the new polyurethane for a week. Plus, polying floors takes time. A coat a
day for three days, and letting it cure. I'm sure you don't
want to wait around for that."

Nina shook her head. "I'm afraid we don't have that much
time. After this, we're going to New Hampshire for a week.
We'll wait for the first coat of poly to dry and do our final
shots of the finished product, but then we'll have to head out."

Derek nodded. "We're prepared to finish up what needs
doing next week. In the living room, we're not planning to
do much except paint the walls and refinish the floors. In
the dining room, we'll replace the chandelier and paint
and, again, do the floors. Avery will whip up some cushions for the window seat."

I nodded.

"What's your background, Avery?" Nina wanted to know
while Fae took a tighter grip on her pen.

"I'm a textile designer," I said. "Parsons School of
Design. I worked in New York for a while, first as a grunt
in the garment district and then as a designer for Philippe
Aubert Designs. Reproduction furniture. And then I inherited my aunt's house and moved to Maine. Now I work
with Derek."

Fae's pen made scratching noises on the clipboard as
she hurried to make note of all this.

"And you?" Nina turned to Derek.

"I'm a doctor," Derek said calmly. "Medical school,
residency, a year of general practice. My father's the local
GP. I decided I'd rather work on houses than people."

"Interesting." Nina glanced from him to me and back.
"And how long have you two been together?"

"We met at the beginning of last summer," Derek said.
"When Avery came up to Waterfield to work on her aunt
Inga's house."

"Derek was the handyman I hired to help me." I smiled.

"After we finished renovating my house, we decided to go into business together. So I settled down here permanently."

"Lovely." Nina smiled back. "We'll mention some of this in the introductions. Establish a rapport with the audience. They'll want to feel like they know you."

Of course.

"I've been watching your show," I said as we moved into the kitchen. "There used to be a host who did the introductions and explained the projects, didn't there?" He hadn't been among the crew we'd been introduced to, so unless he was fast asleep back at the B&B, he wasn't here.

Nina nodded as a shadow crossed her face. "Stuart. He's not with us this time."

"That's too bad. I liked him."

He'd reminded me a little of Derek. Tall, sandy-haired, easygoing. Handsome in a casual sort of way.

"We did, too," Nina said. "He had an accident a few weeks ago. On one of the work sites. Stepped on a live wire and got electrocuted." She shook her head, her face pale.

"Oh, no." Derek and I exchanged a look. "That's horrible."

Nina nodded. "Thankfully it wasn't fatal. He's still in the hospital, and probably will be for a while, but he'll survive. He'll need physical therapy for one side of his body, as well as some speech therapy. We're hoping that, over time, he'll recover fully, but I don't think he'll ever be able to come back to work with us."

"I'm sorry," I said.

Nina nodded, acknowledging the sympathy. "We haven't had a chance to replace him yet. For this episode, Adam will take over."

Adam?

"I thought you said Adam was the runner." I'd thought the runner was the junior member of a camera crew. The one who assists everyone else and does most of the grunt work.

"He is," Nina said. "But he's also had drama training, and he looks good on camera. He'll pull it off."

Of course. How hard can it be, right?

"Here's the kitchen," Derek said. "We're keeping the cabinets, since they're in good shape, but we'll paint them and add new hardware, as well as a new sink and faucet set, and a new kitchen counter. It's already been ordered. We'll pick it up in a couple of days."

Nina nodded while Fae made a note on her clipboard. "What about the floor?"

We all looked down at it: pristine but uninspiring off-white sheet vinyl.

"If we had more time," Derek said, "I'd tile, or at least lay another form of flooring over it. But it's in good shape, just a few years old, and time is of the essence, so we can just keep it and throw a couple of runners on top. It'll coordinate well with the overall look once we get the rest of it done."

"We ordered the countertop to match," I added.

The plain vanilla floor continued into the tiny utility room, where Derek explained that we'd hang some shelves and cabinets to make things look tidier. From there, we headed to the two bedrooms, which would both get new light fixtures, fresh paint, and refinished floors. We ended up in the only bathroom.

Nina looked around. "This is a big job."

She wasn't kidding. The bathroom was 1930s vintage and looked every bit its age. The tub was scratched and worn and needed reglazing, while the sink cabinet was a hideous natural oak, added sometime in the 1970s, with a molded plastic top. The floor was an interesting pattern of old-fashioned octagonal tiles, but many of them were broken and the grout was crumbling. We had decided we had to replace the floor. The white subway tile around the walls was in better condition; we planned to fill in with new tiles where the old ones were cracked, instead of tearing out and starting over. Derek had already removed the existing plumbing, preparatory to replacing the ugly vanity with a pedestal sink. That'd be in keeping with the period, plus, there was a linen closet built in beside the tub already, so the extra storage wasn't necessary. Add a new low-flush toilet, paint the walls, and we'd be good to go.

"We'll spend most of our money and efforts here," Derek said, "and on the front. First impression is the most important thing in flipping, and research shows that women buy houses based on bathrooms and kitchens, so those are where we'll focus on the inside."

Fae's pen scratched across the paper as Nina asked, "What do you plan to do outside?"

"Let me show you." He headed for the door to the outside with the three of us trailing behind. "The roof is in good shape, but it could use a scrubbing, so we'll power wash that, along with the siding. Then we'll do some landscaping to the front. Dig up an old porch swing from somewhere and paint it a cheerful color. There are a couple of good salvage stores around here that'll probably have an old swing we can buy. Avery will make some cushions to go on it. She's also got some pendants she's planning to make to hang from the porch ceiling."

"Twine pendants," I shot in. "They look a little bit like rice lamps."

"We'll paint the door and sidelights, maybe hang some shutters. Add a lot of window boxes and planters, and that should be it."

Nina smiled. "Sounds great. Did you get all that, Fae?" Fae nodded.

"Then let's put together a game plan." Nina rubbed her hands together as Adam wandered back up onto the porch, gazing around.

"What's going on?"

Nina didn't bother answering, just continued to address Derek and me. "Today, we'll want to shoot some introductory film. Get a few seconds of the harbor, of downtown, of some of the renovated and historic homes in town. To set the scene."

"Here we are," Adam said, in what was clearly intended to be a stuffy announcer's voice, "in picturesque Waterford, Maine, forty-five minutes northeast of Portland—"

"Waterfield," Fae muttered.

Nina raised her voice, perhaps to head off the argument before the children could start squabbling in earnest. "We'll do that a little later. First we'll film the house as-is and get the two of you on camera. After that you can get started on the work. Where do you want to begin?"

"I'll start with the bathroom," Derek said. We'd already discussed this and decided on the proper order of things. Day by day, hour by hour. "I'll reglaze the tub, then remove and replace the broken wall tiles, tear out the sink cabinet and toilet, and then start ripping up the tile floor. Avery's gonna start with the kitchen cabinets."

I nodded.

"Marvelous," Nina said. "Avery, your shirt will work fine for today. Derek, do you have another T-shirt you can wear? One that isn't white?"

Derek usually keeps a change of clothes in the truck. It tends to be a pair of clean jeans and a button-down shirt, so he can look fairly respectable if he has to meet a potential client directly after work, or in case we're going out to a restaurant or over to his parents' house for dinner. He shook his head.

"Maybe you can go without a shirt," Adam said, with a grin.

Nina thought for a second. "It's warm enough."

It was. July in Maine isn't as cold as one might think; the temperatures were the same as they'd been last summer, in the upper seventies. And showing footage of a bare-chested Derek might boost ratings. I know it would keep me glued to the TV screen.

Fae giggled and ducked her head, her cheeks pink.

"I'll take the truck and go get a different shirt," Derek said, "while your crew sets up. This is a small town. It won't take but a few minutes."

"I've got a couple of your shirts at the house," I suggested. "That's even closer than your place."

He nodded. "I'll be back in a few." He headed for the door.

"We'll get things ready for when he comes back," Nina said. "Adam, familiarize yourself with the house, please. Avery can show you around. Fae, with me." She didn't wait to see whether she was obeyed or not, just headed down the steps with Fae in pursuit. Adam turned to me and grinned.

—3—

Derek came back within fifteen minutes, dressed in a blue T-shirt and the same snug, faded jeans as earlier. By then, the camera crew was ready to begin shooting and I was ready to shoot Adam. He was one of those guys who was totally in love with himself and absolutely convinced of his own charm, which he turned up to scorching levels whenever he had to deal with anyone of the opposite sex. I had been right—he really was just like Philippe: slickly charming, insincere, and a great, big jerk.

When Derek walked back through the door, I excused myself from Adam and made a beeline for him. "Thank God you're back."

He put an arm around me. "Adam giving you a hard time?"

"Nothing I can't handle. But he doesn't talk about anything but himself."

"Most people like to talk about themselves."

"Most of us realize that we have to play fair and let

other people talk, too. Or we become insufferable bores. Like Adam. He told me every detail of his career, from playing Baby Jesus in the local Christmas pageant as a newborn until this point. I know way more about Adam than I ever wanted to. More than anyone should." I changed the subject. "Everything go OK?"

"All I did was go to your house to get a clean T-shirt," Derek said. "What could go wrong?"

I shrugged apologetically. "Cat attack?"

I have three. Jemmy and Inky, two full-grown Maine coon cats, were part of my inheritance from Aunt Inga. Jemmy is striped, with that distinctive, plumy, raccoonlike tail, while Inky is smoky black with bright green eyes. They're beautiful creatures, and they must have loved my great-aunt, but they mostly just tolerate me, and I've stopped trying to get them to be more affectionate. They prefer curling up with each other to curling up with me, and if that's the way they feel, there's not a lot I can do to change their minds, at least not after bribery has failed. I feed them and talk to them and take them to the vet for regular checkups, but beyond that, we've just agreed to coexist peacefully, with no special privileges on either side.

Mischa is a different story. Derek and I found him on Rowanberry Island in April, when we started renovating the Colonial house. He had taken up residence under our front porch. Over the course of the next few weeks, I coaxed him out with tuna and milk and tried to make friends with him, and then I became attached to the little guy. When we finished the renovations, he came back to the mainland with me and moved into Aunt Inga's house. He's much friendlier than Jemmy and Inky. Mischa loves being held and stroked, he sleeps in bed with me (unless Derek's there; then he gets jealous and we have to put him outside in the hall), and he screams pitifully whenever I leave him in the morning. It's been a real adjustment for

Jemmy and Inky, who have been none too happy about sharing their house and their food bowls with a young upstart. However, things are starting to iron themselves out. Mischa isn't romantically interested in Inky, so Jemmy doesn't need to posture or assert his prior claim, and since Jemmy couldn't care less about me, Mischa doesn't feel that his position as feline consort to the queen is threatened. Except by Derek. Which was why I felt the need to ask how the trip to my house had gone.

"Well," Derek said. "Yeah. There was that."

I winced and took a step back to look him up and down for damage. "He attacked you? Again?"

"He attacked my leg. Tried to climb up to my throat to claw it out. Growling the whole time." He grinned. "Good thing he's little. If he was the size of Jemmy, I'd worry."

At close to twenty pounds, Jemmy is big even for a Maine coon. Inky is smaller, around fifteen, but they're both large cats. The last time I'd taken Mischa to the vet, he'd weighed in at seven pounds, but Dr. Piedmont had warned me he wasn't finished growing yet, and to expect him to gain another few pounds. But he's part Russian blue and sleek, with shorter fur than the bushy coons, and he's still on the lean and hungry side.

"He didn't hurt you, did he?"

Derek didn't look like he was walking wounded. There were no fresh scratches on his hands or forearms, and no bloodstains on his jeans.

"I could feel his claws going into my leg when he tried to climb up, but once I sent him flying, it was no problem."

I rolled my eyes. "As if I'd believe you'd ever hurt a living creature, Mr. Hippocratic Oath."

"I'm not a doctor anymore," Derek reminded me. "Besides, doctors hurt people every day. You think it doesn't hurt someone to slice their stomach open to take out their spleen?"

"I'm sure it does. But I know you wouldn't kick a poor

defenseless kitten, even one that was trying to rip out your throat."

Derek snorted. "That kitten's about as defenseless as Attila the Hun. You should have named him that."

"He doesn't look like an Attila, even if he acts like one. Maybe I should have named him Ivan."

"That'd be fitting. Though it's too late now, yeah?"

Yeah, it was. The cat was Mischa, no matter how appropriate a name change to Attila the Hun or Ivan the Terrible would seem.

I was happy that he liked me and thrilled that he was friendlier than Jemmy and Inky and actually enjoyed being a pet, but I really couldn't have him attacking my boyfriend every time Derek came over. If he constantly contrived to launch himself at Derek and tried to hurt him, I'd have to take measures.

Making a mental note to stop by Dr. Piedmont's office and ask about options—something other than declawing— I put the cat out of my mind. Wilson had shouldered the camera and was ready to go, while Ted was messing around with wires snaking here and there across the dusty floor. Adam was rehearsing. "Hi, and welcome to *Flipped Out!* I'm Adam Ramsey." Big smile at the imaginary camera. "Hi, and welcome to *Flipped Out!* I'm Adam Ramsey," with a different inflection this time, followed by that same toothy grin. "Hi, and welcome to *Flipped Out!* . . ."

Nina and Fae had their heads together over the clipboard, bleach blond and dyed black side by side. They were almost the same height, allowing for Nina's four-inch heels, and their expressions were identical as they peered at the scrawled notes.

"Ready when you are, Neen," Wilson called. Nina held up a finger.

Wilson turned to me and Derek. "Later today we'll drive around town, get some exterior shots." He had a faint Southern drawl to his voice. "Y'all won't be needed for

that. We'll end up back here, and I'll shoot the exterior of
the house then, when the sun's high and the sky's blue."

This early, there was still a little bit of a haze in the air.

"Right now, we'll introduce the two of you and get
'before' footage of the house. Tomorrow we'll start shooting the tear-out and any work you start to do. You sure the
two of y'all 'll be able to get it all done on time?"

He looked from Derek to me and back, his eyes a bright
hazel in his lined face.

"We'll have help," Derek said. "Kate, who runs the bed
and breakfast where you're staying, will be here tomorrow
to help Avery paint the kitchen cabinets. Probably her
daughter will stop by, too. And I've got her stepson lined
up to help with the heavy lifting, as well as a few people
coming to do some landscaping."

Wilson nodded. "It's a big job."

"We've done bigger. The time is the biggest issue."

"That's why they call the show *Flipped Out!*" Wilson
said with a grin, just as Nina raised her head and her voice
to address all of us.

"Looks like we're ready to go. Will, I want you to start
over here by the door, pan the room, then focus on Adam.
You'll be next to the fireplace, Adam. You two"—she
looked at Derek and me—"head into the kitchen and get
ready to do your spiel once Adam introduces you."

"Spiel?"

"What you did for me earlier. Here's the kitchen, this is
where we'll do blah, blah, blah."

"Right." Derek managed not to wince at the "blah, blah,
blah." We ducked out of the room but stayed in the dining
room, where we'd be able to keep up with what was going on.

"And . . . action," Nina said.

I made sure to stay out of sight while Wilson panned the
living room—it wouldn't do for us to be peeking around
the archway and ruining the shot—but once Adam started
speaking, we knew Wilson had finished his pan and was

focused on Adam, so we leaned into the living room to watch.

"Hi," Adam said, grinning dementedly, "and welcome to *Flipped Out!* I'm Adam Ramsey, your host. Today we're here in Waterford, Maine—"

"Cut," Nina said. "It's Waterfield, Adam. Do it again."

Adam grimaced. Wilson went back to the doorway. Derek and I ducked out of sight, and it all started over again. And again. Adam couldn't seem to get the hang of it. He was very handsome, he probably photographed extremely well, he had a nicely modulated voice, but he couldn't remember details to save his life. If it wasn't the name of the town that slipped his mind, it was another word he mispronounced or stumbled over. After five or six takes, he had finally got the introduction and the name of the town and everything else just right, but when he moved into the kitchen to introduce Derek and me, the problems started all over again.

"Here we are with this week's team of renovators, Erik Ellis and—"

"Cut," Nina said, her voice beginning to show signs of wear around the edges. "It's Derek, Adam. Not Erik. Do it again."

Wilson looked put out. Adam looked pained. "Sorry, Neen."

Nina was making an almost visible effort to be nice. "I'm sure you are, Adam. Just do it again, please."

Wilson moved back to the doorway, Derek and I exchanged a glance, and Adam took a deep breath and blew it out again, flashing another broad smile. "Here we are with this week's team of renovators, Derek Ellis and Ivory Baker—"

"Cut," Nina said. "It's Avery, Adam. Derek and Avery. Not Erik and Ivory. Do you need a break?"

The not-so-subtle subtext was, "Take a break, Adam. And come back ready to get it right."

"Yeah," Adam said, "I think maybe I do. I'll be right back."

He left through the laundry room and headed into the backyard, where he'd probably either punch a tree to make himself feel better, or wander around for a couple of minutes, kicking at tufts of grass and muttering. Hopefully he'd come back inside in a better frame of mind. If not, there was no way we'd be able to finish the house in a week. Not if every camera appearance took Adam at least six takes.

"He's a disaster," Wilson said bluntly, not even waiting until the back door had closed completely.

Nina nodded. "But he's all we've got. For now, he'll have to do."

"You could do it." Wilson shifted his chewing gum—or maybe it was tobacco—to the other side of his mouth.

Nina smiled. "I haven't done on-camera work for years, Will. You know that."

"I also know you were great at it. Christ, Neen, anything's better than that . . . that . . ." He seemed unable to come up with a word that was bad enough to describe Adam's incompetence.

"I miss Stuart," Fae said. She and Ted had appeared in the doorway to the dining room as soon as Adam headed outside, and now she leaned there, like a wilted orchid. Derek and I exchanged a glance. It was interesting but somewhat uncomfortable to be privy to the interior workings of the camera crew. Fae added, "I wish he hadn't gotten hurt."

"We all wish he hadn't gotten hurt," Nina said. "And not just because it means we're stuck with Adam. He's got the looks, the voice, the charm. . . . How hard can it be to remember the words?" She sighed.

"At this rate, we'll be here all morning shooting the introductions."

"I can make a card," Ted suggested, his voice surprisingly deep and resonant, at odds with his weedy exterior. "With the pertinent information on it. Names, details."

"It may come to that. Or we can do the introductions as a voice-over and you can do it." Nina grinned.

Ted blushed. "No thanks. I'm happier behind the scenes."

"You'd still be behind the scenes. It's just your voice that wouldn't be."

Ted said, "Maybe Fae can do it."

The girl shook her head. "I like my job," she said.

"It'll be all right." Nina glanced toward the back door to make sure Adam hadn't come back in. "He'll get it. And after this morning, he'll have less to do. Just a question here and there to set up whatever Avery and Derek say. How are you two doing?" She turned to us.

"Fine," Derek said.

"We haven't done anything yet," I added.

"I know. And I'm sorry about that. Adam's new. He'll get it."

"Sure," Derek said. He's a nice guy, always happy to look on the bright side. This once, I wasn't able to. I doubted that Adam would get it, and I thought we'd still be standing here at five o'clock this afternoon.

Out in the living room, someone knocked on the open door, and then we heard the sound of heels clicking against the hardwood floors. "Yoo-hoo!" a musical voice called. "Anyone home?"

Nina arched her brows. "Expecting someone?"

It was Melissa, of course, closely followed by Tony the Tiger. She arrived in the doorway looking like a million bucks, dressed in another designer outfit, this one a silk dress from Roberto Cavalli, and another pair of sexy sandals. Her long, tanned legs were bare, her makeup was perfect, and every brilliant tooth was on display. So was the enormous diamond.

"Hi," she cooed, looking around the room, "I'm Melissa James. Derek and Avery's Realtor."

Behind her, Tony appeared, taking in the kitchen at a glance. He spared a nod for Wilson and one for Ted, a smile for Fae, who blushed and ducked her head, and one for me; I didn't. Then he noticed the last member of the crew.

"Nina."

For a second, Nina Andrews looked like a deer caught in the headlights. Her eyes flicked to Ted, to Melissa, to Derek and me . . . before she managed a smile. "Tony. Long time no see."

Huh, I thought.

Of course, Adam chose this exact moment to reenter the scene as well. He came through the back door from the laundry with a confident spring in his step and a cocky smile on his face. "OK, folks," he announced, "I'm ready to kick . . ."

The atmosphere, so thick you could cut it with a buzz saw, must have hit him then, because he stopped short. The self-satisfied smirk faded as he took in the newcomers. After a second, he walked over to stand beside Nina. "What's going on?"

Nina made a visible effort to gather herself. She smiled, and it looked pretty good, but only until you noticed the strain showing in the tiny lines around her eyes. "Some friends of Derek and Avery's stopped by to say hello. This is Melissa James, their Realtor, and Tony Micelli. What are you doing these days, Tony?"

"Reporting the news for Portland's channel eight," Tony said, eyeing Adam while Adam eyed him.

"Adam is the interim host of our show," Nina explained, which made Tony stare all the harder. By now, Adam had noticed Melissa and was giving her a thorough inspection, while Ted was scowling at Tony. Wilson and Fae were doing some sort of silent communication across the room.

"I guess you know each other," I said, more to drop words into the uncomfortable silence than because I needed confirmation. It was obvious that Nina and Tony knew each other, and it looked as if Ted at least knew who Tony was, although Tony didn't seem to have recognized Ted. "Tony owns this house."

"No kidding?" Ted said. Tony shook his head, looking around.

"I grew up here. Haven't lived here for years, though."

"Tony and I worked together once," Nina said to the group at large. "More than twenty years ago now. My first assignment."

Tony nodded. "Mine, too."

"It was at one of those small Midwestern stations, the ones you use as a stepping-stone to bigger and better. He moved on, and so did I." She shrugged.

"You look good, Neen," Tony said, his dark eyes appreciative. "And you're a director now. Congratulations. Of course, I always knew you'd go on to do great things."

Nina smiled back, and this time it looked more natural. "You don't look so bad yourself. Success must agree with you."

Tony preened, smoothing a hand over that slick, black hair, and then he must have noticed the way Melissa looked at him, because he reined himself in. "We don't want to interrupt anything. I'm sure you're going to be busy, since you're here just for a week. Maybe we can grab dinner one night?"

Nina's eyes flicked around the circle again, but when not even Melissa objected, she gave in to the inevitable. "That'd be nice," she said, while next to her, Adam scowled, and Ted tried to stare a hole in Tony, and Fae looked from Tony to Nina curiously.

Melissa, never one to be outdone, flashed Adam a brilliant smile. "You know, if you need someone to show you around town, I'd be happy to help. I know this place like my own backyard."

Adam smiled, obviously flattered by the attention, but it was Nina who said, "That'd be wonderful, actually. We'll be shooting some footage around town this afternoon, and if you wanted to show us some of the highlights, we wouldn't say no." She turned. "You, too, Tony. It'll be good to have someone with us who's used to camera work."

Melissa smiled, pleased. This must be exactly what she'd wanted: a chance to get her face on camera and the opportunity to hawk the benefits of living in Waterfield. Melissa won't be happy until she has turned our pretty, picturesque little town into a big city with lots of people who need the help of a Realtor.

"We just have a few more minutes here," Nina added. "You ready to do this, Adam?"

Adam nodded, determination in the line of his jaw. And whether it was because he didn't want to look like an idiot in front of Melissa, or maybe in front of Tony, or whether the walk in the garden had flipped some switch in his head, he got every word right on the first try.

"That's a wrap," Nina said, pleased, while Wilson wandered off to pan the remaining rooms with his camera, collecting "before" footage, and Ted started rolling up cables. She turned to Derek and me. "We're done here for now. We'll spend the rest of the afternoon shooting around town. Tomorrow morning, we'll be back here to film the two of you in action. Make sure you've demoed whatever you need to, and you're ready to work."

. . .

Derek and I spent the rest of the afternoon tearing things down and out. The Dumpster we'd ordered for the job had been dropped off last week, and we'd long ago started putting things into it. Derek hauled out the toilet and bathroom cabinet, and between us we removed the old kitchen counter and sink. Then Derek went at the floor tile in the bathroom with a hammer and chisel while I started removing all the kitchen cabinet doors for painting. It's one of those tedious chores that is so tempting to skip, since it's possible to paint the cabinets without removing the doors first, but the result is much better when the job is done right, so I made myself do it.

Midafternoon, Kate and Shannon stopped by to see how

things were progressing and to firm up plans for the next day. Kate had limited time to give us, as she had a house full of guests, but Shannon was fully available, since she wasn't in school over the summer and her only job was helping out at the bed and breakfast.

"We saw the TV crew filming on Main Street," Kate greeted me when they walked into the kitchen at around three o'clock.

I looked up from where I sat cross-legged on the kitchen floor wielding Derek's battery-driven screwdriver. "They were here earlier. Shot some interior footage of the house and had Adam introduce Derek and me for the camera. And then Melissa and Tony Micelli showed up."

"We saw them." Kate nodded. "Outside one of the antique stores on Main Street. Did you notice that rock on her finger? Wasn't that the biggest diamond you've ever seen in your life?"

"If it's real," Shannon said.

"I'm sure it's real," her mother answered. "Melissa wouldn't stand for anything less."

"I got a good look at it last night," I said. "Tony popped the question at the Waymouth Tavern, I think."

"Quick work. It's just over six months since they started dating."

I nodded. Derek and I had been together for more than a year, and he hadn't proposed yet. And it had taken Wayne something like five or six years to get himself engaged to Kate.

"Anyway," Kate said, "Melissa was on camera, talking to Adam Ramsey about why everyone should want to live in Waterfield, and waving that ring around. The glare almost blinded me."

Kate had moved here from Boston seven years ago, with then-thirteen-year-old Shannon, and she was no more excited than I was about Melissa's attempts to turn Waterfield into the same thing we'd both left behind.

"I figured she'd find a way to get her face on camera." I went back to unscrewing the hinges on one of the kitchen cabinet doors. "What about Tony? Was he there?"

"He was talking to Nina and to that young woman with the long, black hair and all the holes in her face," Kate said. Shannon looked at her mom and rolled her eyes.

"They're piercings, Mom. Everyone has them."

"You don't," Kate said. She didn't add, "Thank God," but I could see the words clearly in the thought bubble above her head.

Shannon shrugged. "I'm not much into body mutilation. And I don't want to be seventy years old and have to explain to my grandchildren why grandma has tattoos and piercings all over her body."

Me, either. I have pierced ears, but that's the extent of the body art so far. I prefer to make my statement with what I'm wearing instead.

Not that that aspect of my personality has had a whole lot of play lately. While I was working for Philippe, making copies of staid, boring, authentic fabrics for his reproduction furniture, I had gotten into the habit of making some slightly wilder stuff for myself, just to keep my hand in. These days, working with Derek and spending so much time in jeans and T-shirts—stuff that's easily replaced when it gets torn up or stained—it had been a long time since I'd made anything fun. Maybe I could create something funky for the cottage.

Although with only a week to do it, and all the other work we had to do, it'd have to be something simple. Simple isn't as much fun as complicated, although making something very simple look fabulous comes with some inherent challenges of its own. Roller shades for the windows, perhaps? Curtains? A long cushion and a bunch of pillows for the window seat in the dining room were already part of the plan, and as Derek had told Nina, I could whip up some pillows for the porch swing we planned to hang, as well, while I was at it. And—here was an idea—how about some gauzy curtains for the porch? Almost like mosquito netting in tropical climes; light and airy fabric suspended from a rail or rod running under the porch ceiling, pulled aside during the day—maybe even fastened with ribbons or tiebacks—but ready to be lowered when people wanted to sit on the porch at night. Mosquitoes can be bothersome in Maine in the summer, and something like that would keep them out. I don't spend a lot of time sitting on Aunt Inga's porch, since the mosquitoes like me too much for me to make my tempting self too available to the bloodsuckers. But I could imagine hanging something similar there, too, making an evening on the porch more appealing.

A shuffling noise brought me back to the present. Kate and Shannon were still standing in the doorway. Well, Kate was; Shannon was moving away to see what Derek was up to. I smiled apologetically up at Kate. "Sorry. I got distracted."

"No problem." She grinned back. "You know Shannon. She's always adored Derek. She was just waiting for an excuse to go find him."

Derek has that effect on most women, from toddlers to dignified old ladies. If it had been anyone else, I might have worried. Shannon is gorgeous, with her mother's height and centerfold figure; the kind that can stop traffic. But for all that she clearly adores Derek, I don't think she's ever harbored any fantasies in his direction. She enjoys talking and even flirting mildly with him, but he's just practice for whenever she gets serious about someone her own age.

"The crew is staying at the B and B with you," I said to Kate, and got a nod in return. "I know it's none of my business, but how are the sleeping arrangements? With five people and only four rooms . . ."

Kate grinned. "You trying to figure out who's got a relationship on the side?"

I shrugged. So sue me. The way Adam was flirting with all and sundry, surely he had to be sleeping with someone.

"As far as I know," Kate continued, "nobody does. Or if they do, they're being discreet. Nina's in the suite and Fae's in my old room. The men are on the second floor."

"That's what I thought," I said. "That you might have put your own room into service. How is everything going?"

She shrugged. "Fine, so far. No problems. They arrived late last night. They'd stopped for dinner on the way from the airport, so they just went to their rooms and to bed. Nobody sleepwalked or had nightmares. I fed them blueberry pancakes this morning. Nina picked at her food. Worried about gaining weight, I guess. Adam flirted with everyone, including me. Ted had his nose buried in a book, and Wilson was friendly."

"They seem like a nice bunch of people, for the most part."

Kate nodded. "What happened to the guy who used to host the show? Stu somebody? I hope they didn't fire him; he was great."

"Good-looking, too. And no, he didn't get fired." I told her what Nina had told me, that Stuart had had an accident a couple of weeks ago and was in the hospital. "That's why we're stuck with Adam."

Kate grinned. "Not a good experience?"

"It took an hour to film a few minutes of dialogue because Adam couldn't get the names right. He kept calling Waterfield 'Waterford,' and he called Derek 'Erik' and me 'Ivory' . . ."

"That must be a handicap if you want to be a television star," Kate said.

"Worse if you want to do theater, I'd think. That's what he told me he used to do. Hard to imagine he would have been able to memorize whole scripts and perform them every day when he can't keep a few words straight. At the rate he's going, we'll finish the renovations next December."

"Or you'll have to work twice as fast to make up for it."

"I'm working as fast as I can," I said, laying another cabinet door down on top of the stack. "You want something to do? Grab another screwdriver and start taking the hardware off those doors while I finish taking the doors off the cabinets. We have to remove the hinges and handles before we can start painting."

"Do you want me to keep the hardware?" Kate asked as she palmed a manual screwdriver off the counter and sat down next to the stack of doors.

"Stick it in a Ziploc baggie. We won't be putting it back on—updated hardware is one of those things that can really make a big difference without breaking the bank—but Derek can give it to Ian Burns, and maybe someone will want to buy it. It's classic 1930s stuff."

Ian Burns is a friend of Derek's who owns and operates an architectural salvage store in Boothbay Harbor, some forty-five minutes north of Waterfield. Derek has bought a lot of vintage fixtures and replacement parts from Ian over the years, and whenever we tore out anything we thought might interest him, we saved it.

"You got it," Kate said, and suited action to words.

—4—

The television crew came back to the house for a few minutes after their jaunt through town, sans Tony and Melissa. Tony had to go to work, Nina told me when I asked. "He's asked me to go to dinner later."

"Really?" I glanced at Kate, involuntarily. She arched a brow at me, and I knew we were thinking the same thing. This wouldn't make Melissa happy.

"He wants to catch up. A lot of water under the bridge since the last time we saw each other."

"Are you going?" Ted asked. He didn't look happy, either. Nor did Adam, although he hid it by carrying on a silent but patently obvious flirtation with Shannon. Her cheeks were flushed, although I couldn't tell whether it was from embarrassment or because she liked the attention.

"I told him I'd think about it and let him know," Nina said.

"What about Melissa?" Derek asked.

Nina turned to him. "She got a phone call. Someone wanted information about a house on an island somewhere."

"Oh." He looked at me. "I'll give her a call. See if anything's going on." He headed out the door, grabbing for his cell phone.

"You have a house on an island?" Fae asked, drifting in the direction of the outside as well. Everyone else followed, slowly.

I nodded. "It was the project we did before this one. A big 1783 center-chimney Colonial. It's on the market now. We're filling in with small projects until we can get it sold and our money out. If you get a half day off while you're here, you should take the ferry out to one of the islands and have a look around. It's nice out there."

Fae shook her head. "I'm not that big on water. Grew up in Kansas. Landlocked." She smiled sheepishly. She and Shannon looked a little like each other, I realized, both tall and pretty, with the same pale skin and dark eyes and hair, although Fae's clearly wasn't real. It was a sort of dull jet-black, not like Shannon's shiny mane of deep black cherry. And then, of course, there was the raccoon makeup and the piercings. Without all of it, her face was sweetly pretty, not as stunningly gorgeous as Shannon's.

"Tony mentioned the Something Tavern," Nina said. "Are you familiar with it?"

Kate nodded. "It's called the Waymouth Tavern. And it's up the ocean road apiece. Nice place."

"Apiece?"

"A mile or two."

"And is it formal?"

Kate shook her head. "What you're wearing is fine. Jeans are fine, too, if you want to change into something more comfortable. People in Waterfield don't stand on ceremony." She flashed that big, friendly smile. Nina looked almost offended at the suggestion that she should kick back and relax, but after a moment, she smiled back.

"That's good to know. I'll keep it in mind."

As we got out on the porch, Kate turned to the rest of

the television crew. "I'm not licensed to serve dinner, but there are several restaurants in the downtown area that you can walk to, and several more in driving distance. They all stay open pretty late in the summer. We've also got Boothbay Harbor and Portland within a forty-five minute drive in either direction. Or feel free to order a pizza or something else to be delivered. There's a list of restaurants next to the telephone in the foyer of the B and B."

Wilson replied on everyone's behalf. "We'll figure something out. Thanks."

"We'll rendezvous here at the house again tomorrow morning," Nina said, "bright and early." She glanced at Derek, who had put away his phone and was coming back up the porch steps. "Seven o'clock too early for you two?"

I grimaced. I prefer staying in bed until at least eight, but Derek's been working hard to change that. He has no problem getting up with the sun. Or staying up all night, for that matter. Or staying up all night and then getting up with the sun. It's all those years of medical school, rotations, and residency. Doctors are light sleepers, and they can easily go all day on minimal or no sleep.

"Not at all," Derek said, with a glance at me. When he saw my expression, he grinned. "It's just for a week, Avery. You can sleep next week, I promise."

"That's easy for you to say," I grumbled. "Next week, you'll come up with some other reason why I have to get up early. I know you."

Ted cleared his throat. "I may want to get here ahead of everyone and set up for the shots. Any way we can leave the place open?" He looked up and down the sleepy street. "This seems like a nice, low-crime kind of place."

Derek was already shaking his head. "Empty houses under renovation are magnets for thieves, and we've got tools and materials inside. But I'll hide the key, and whoever gets here first can open up."

"That'll work." Ted nodded. "What's a good place?"

The two of them started looking around. Shannon turned to Fae. "You wanna order a pizza and watch a movie tonight? I've got the latest Matt Damon action flick."

Fae grinned. "Sounds great."

They headed down the steps, discussing the delights of Matt Damon and the toppings for the pizza. Kate and Nina exchanged the kind of look that two mothers might, and followed.

Derek and Ted agreed to put the house key inside a chipped plaster planter full of wilted purple petunias we hadn't gotten around to moving to the Dumpster yet. As Derek tucked the key into the dirt and out of sight, I scanned the neighborhood, making sure that no one was watching.

The little cottage on Cabot Street sat surrounded by similar homes. There was a big, well-maintained Arts and Crafts bungalow down on the corner, but the rest of the houses on the block were small, all built between the early 1930s and 1945. During the Depression and the war, in times that were tough, financially and emotionally, for most people.

We were close to the edge of the Village, Waterfield's historic district. It started down by the harbor, with the late Victorian business buildings lining Main Street and a few older, historic homes interspersed: the Fraser House, a Colonial; an early saltbox or two; a few small and original Cape Cods from the early seventeen hundreds. Farther up the hill were the ornate Victorians: the big Queen Annes and Eastlakes, like Kate's bed and breakfast, and the smaller cottages, like Aunt Inga's Second Empire and the Folk Victorian Benjamin Ellis and his wife, Cora, live in. Then there are the bungalows and the rare stone or brick Tudors, along with the small cottages. Beyond where we were standing, Cabot Street petered out into suburbia, where the architecture ran to 1950s cookie-cutter tract houses, low-slung brick ranches and Brady Bunch split-levels.

There were a lot of older people in this neighborhood, people who had lived here their whole lives, whose parents may have built the very houses they were living in. There isn't a lot of turnover in a small town like Waterfield. Children take over their parents' houses, and their children take over their houses in the fullness of time. Derek would probably be expected to take over Benjamin Ellis's house when he and Cora decided they'd had enough. Derek's an only child, and the house had been in his father's family for generations. Dr. Ben had taken it over from his father when Derek's Paw-Paw Willie retired to Florida. Chances were Derek and I would end up with two houses, his and mine. Or Dr. Ben's and Aunt Inga's. That is, if we were still together at that point. It'd be a while; Dr. Ben was just over sixty.

I had no plans of going anywhere. I didn't think Derek did, either, but only time would tell. And since that thought gave me a funny feeling in the pit of my stomach, I shook it off and returned to the present.

Now that the business of the key was dispensed with, the others had started drifting toward the curb, where the television crew's van and Kate's tan station wagon were parked.

"You wanna ride with us?" I heard Shannon ask Fae. Fae glanced at the rest of the crew—maybe she was hoping Adam would tell her to come with him instead, or maybe she expected Nina to tell her she had to drive back to the bed and breakfast in the van—but when no one said anything, she nodded.

"Sure."

"Great." Shannon smiled. She must have decided that Fae needed a friend her own age while she was here, or maybe the two of them had just clicked right away, the way people sometimes do.

"We'll see you tomorrow," Kate said. "I can't get here until late morning or early afternoon. I have to clean up after breakfast and change the sheets and towels in the guest rooms before I can head out."

"That's fine." Derek put his arm around my shoulders as we wandered down the garden path toward the street in Kate's wake. "We'll take you whenever we can get you. Shannon can come out with the crew if she wants, or she can come with you later. Or Josh can pick her up; he's gonna be here in the morning."

"Is he going to help you with the tile?"

"I think I'll just have him start painting. Any idiot can roll paint." He pondered for a second and qualified the statement. "Almost any idiot."

"Josh isn't an idiot," Kate said with an amused smile.

Derek smiled back. "He's not a renovator, either. Painting is something he won't need specialized knowledge to do. I don't mind teaching people how to do this job, but this week, I just can't take the time out."

"So what are you and Wayne doing tonight?" I wanted to know. "Big plans?"

Kate shook her head. "Just dinner at home. Wayne needs to relax. He's been working long hours lately. There's always more crime in the summer, when the population doubles."

"Nothing too bad has been going on, has it?"

I couldn't recall hearing about anything terrible lately. No new murders, anyway. Not since the body we'd found in the harbor in April.

Kate shook her head. "It's mostly minor things this time of year. A lot of drunk and disorderly conduct, some fighting, one or two domestic brawls. Purse snatches and pickpockets, since people carry more money when they're on vacation. Scammers. And a whole lot of traffic tickets." She grinned. "The new radar guns are getting a workout."

"We'll keep that in mind," Derek answered, with a grin of his own.

"So what are you two planning to do tonight?"

"We'll figure something out," Derek said.

I added, "Work, most likely. I have to sew pillows and curtains. Derek has to make window boxes."

"Isn't the camera guy going to want to tape you doing those things?"

"I'll leave a seam undone for the camera," I said. "Derek can make most of the boxes and leave one for demonstration, as well."

"We'll be at Avery's house if you need us." Derek guided me toward the truck while Kate opened the door to the Volvo station wagon and slid behind the wheel. The TV van had already pulled away from the curb in the direction of the B&B.

.   .   .

It ended up being a long night. After dinner, I put together a dozen pillows from bolts of fabric I had sitting around in the spare bedroom upstairs while Derek used Aunt Inga's front porch to saw and hammer window boxes to hang outside the cottage. While he was at it, he made two planters, as well, one for each side of the front door.

"They're no different," he explained as he worked. "If you know how to make one, you can figure out how to make the other. Planters are square with legs while window boxes are rectangular. The most important thing, whether you're making a box or a planter, is to drill holes through the bottom so the water can drain out."

"Makes sense." I had taken a break from sewing and had brought Derek a cold drink to keep him going. A bottle of beer, as it happened. He doesn't care much for wine. In all the time that he was married to Melissa, she only ever succeeded in getting him to share one certain type of Bordeaux with her, he'd told me. Like Melissa, I prefer red wine to beer, but since we had to be up early tomorrow and I still had work to do tonight, I thought I'd better not indulge. I was sitting in Aunt Inga's porch swing with Mischa on my lap, sipping from a can of Diet Coke, while Derek kept working and giving me a running commentary on what he was doing. He had removed his shirt, and I stroked Mischa absently and tried not to drool too visibly as I watched him flex and bend.

Mischa was on duty, of course. I could see the determination on his little furry face and in the way the tip of his tail twitched occasionally as he watched Derek. When we walked through the door earlier, Derek with the friendly greeting, "Hello, killer," Mischa had crouched and hissed. I'd been too slow to intercept him: He had launched himself at Derek's leg, and I'd had to unhook him from the denim, claw by claw. Now he was curled up on my lap, a boneless bundle of silvery blue fur, with his eyes wide open and watching Derek's every move. Derek kept his distance; if he were to come any closer, Mischa would most likely try to eviscerate him.

"So what did you think of them all?" I asked after a moment.

Derek glanced over at me. "The crew? They seemed OK, didn't they?"

"All except Adam."

Derek lifted the bottle and toasted me with it, grinning, before he took a swallow of beer. "Nina seems nice. And she must be competent, if she's in charge."

"Funny coincidence, that she knows Tony Micelli."

"Small world." Derek nodded, putting the bottle back down on the windowsill. "Or maybe not. Television is a community. Anyone who has lasted fifteen or twenty years probably knows, or knows of, anyone else who's been around that long."

"She didn't seem too happy to see him, did she?"

Derek pondered for a moment. "Not very, no. More surprised or shocked than unhappy, though, I think. And she must have gotten over it if she agreed to have dinner with him."

"I guess so. Ted didn't seem to like him much, either."

"No," Derek said, "he didn't. Then again, you and I don't like Tony much ourselves, so I don't know that I can blame him for that."

"That's true." I had taken against Tony last autumn, when we'd found that skeleton in the crawlspace of the house on Becklea Drive, and I had overheard him wishing for a case of serial murder, with bodies buried all over the yard. John Wayne Gacy in Waterfield, Maine. I got along with him well enough, in polite, social settings and when I had to, but I didn't like him. As far as I was concerned, he and Melissa deserved each other.

"You ready to call it a night?" Derek wanted to know. "Or do you want to go back to your sewing machine for a while?"

"I probably should." But I made no move to get up, just stayed where I was, with one hand buried in Mischa's fur and the other holding the sweating can of Diet Coke, lazily pushing the swing back and forth with one foot.

Just over a year ago, I'd come here to Waterfield for the first time, only to learn when I arrived that the ancient second cousin twice removed—the "aunt" was a courtesy title—who had summoned me had died in the time it had taken me to get here.

My first impression of Waterfield was that it was hopelessly quaint, agonizingly slow-moving, and one of those places where nothing ever happened. No Balthazar coffee, no theaters or museums, no expensive boutiques, no all-night diners. The streets were winding and narrow, there was allergy-inducing vegetation everywhere, and the pace was snail-like. I couldn't wait to leave and get back to the hustle and bustle of Manhattan, back to my great job, my perfect boyfriend, and my rent-controlled apartment.

Then I ended up spending the summer in Maine, and I realized that slow-moving and quiet weren't such bad things. The air was clean, the people were friendly and they had time to stop for a talk, and of course, there was the ocean, which I can't praise highly enough. New Yorkers tend to love the ocean. And now I was living close enough to smell it whenever I took a deep breath. I never thought I'd say it, but I had no desire to go back to Manhattan. For a visit, sure, to breathe the exhaust-filled air and see the sights and visit friends, but I didn't want to move back. It was lovely here in Waterfield, peaceful and relaxing and calm. I couldn't imagine giving that up now that I had it.

"Penny for your thoughts," Derek said, watching me.

I smiled. "I was just thinking how nice it is to be here. In Maine. With you."

"That's what you were thinking?"

I nodded.

"On second thought," Derek said, putting his drill down, "I think we've both done enough for tonight. It's time to go to bed. Lose the cat, please."

"Excuse me?"

"Put him somewhere."

"Ah," I said, catching on. "I'll leave him in the laundry room. Give him a catnip toy to keep him occupied."

"Sounds good." He was already on his way toward the door. If he'd been wearing a tie—or a shirt—he'd be loosening it. "I'll see you upstairs."

"Right." I made tracks toward the utility room, carrying a complaining Mischa under one arm.

. . .

Derek didn't spend the night but headed home to his own bachelor pad an hour or so later. I tried to get him to stay, but Mischa made a ruckus in the utility room, demanding to be let out, and Derek said he needed some peace in order to sleep. I don't think he got it, because when he came to pick me up the next morning, he was bleary-eyed and grumpy. He was, however, adamant about having to get to the house on Cabot Street by seven. I managed to jump in the shower for a quick rinse, but he wouldn't even give me time to dry my hair before we left, and it was even more frizzy and unruly than usual. I planned to pile it on top of my head as soon as it was dry enough. As today was painting day, I would have had to do that in any case.

We had already picked up the paint for the kitchen cabinets. Tony had kept the kitchen the original glossy white, which has the benefit of looking traditional and crisp (and being easy to wipe clean), but I wanted something more exciting, more contemporary. If there had been time, I might have stripped the cabinets of old paint and then stained them, but since we were in a hurry, I'd have to repaint instead. And since we were working on Tony's house instead of our own, and since Melissa would be putting it on the market as soon as we were finished and it would have to appeal to a large variety of buyers, I couldn't do anything too crazy. Derek had shut down most of my brilliant ideas.

The cabinets were your basic picture-frame construction: inset panels surrounded by raised frames. Personally, I liked the idea of painting the frames white and highlighting them with metallic silver paint, and then painting pictures in the panels. A seascape, maybe. Or mountains or trees. All the way around the kitchen, one long landscape in frames. But Derek said no. And I could understand why: It would take a lot of time, which we didn't have, and it probably wouldn't appeal to everyone as much as it did to me. Tony surely wouldn't go for it. So I modified my original vision: I'd paint the frames red and black in a checkerboard pattern, and the panels white, and then stencil or freehand a pair of cherries in each. Or a tomato. Something kitchen appropriate.

Derek said no to that, too. And to everything else I suggested, until I got to the idea where I'd paint everything yellow: pale butter, two shades, frames one shade darker than the panels. That idea Derek had approved. His loft was above the hardware store in downtown, so he'd already picked up the paint, and I was ready to get started. The job wouldn't be anywhere near as exciting as I wanted it to be, but I was good to go.

In spite of running late, we beat the crew to the house.

Derek cut the engine on the truck just as the white van crested the top of the street behind us, with Ted behind the wheel like yesterday. But early as it was, Derek and I weren't the first ones here. A very expensive, flashy convertible BMW already took up prime real estate at the curb.

It didn't belong to Melissa. She drives a Mercedes in her trademark cream color. Very tasteful and elegant. This was fire-engine red, designed to be noticed, and the license plate said "GRRR." No doubt who this ride belonged to.

"Tony's up early," Derek remarked, scanning the exterior of the house and the yard. "What do you think he's doing here at this hour of the morning?"

There was no sign of Tony. "No idea. Looking for Nina?"

We both turned to Nina, who had gotten out of the van and was staring at the car, brows knitted. She was more casually dressed today, in slacks and a blouse, but with the same no-nonsense stiletto heels. She had clipped her blond hair at the nape of her neck with a barrette, and she looked polished and in control, except for the expression on her face.

"If he is, I don't think she's expecting him," I said.

"Maybe dinner last night didn't go so well."

"Maybe that's why the car is here. Maybe they had an argument on the way home, and she made him pull over so she could get out and walk the rest of the way. It's only four or five blocks from here to the B and B. And then the car wouldn't start again. Maybe Tony spent the night inside."

"On the floor?"

Oh, yeah. Maybe not.

"He's probably just looking at the progress we've made while he's waiting for us to get here," Derek said. "C'mon, Tink. Let's get this show on the road."

He leaned into the bed of the truck and handed me a gallon can of yellow paint. I started up the driveway toward the house, skirting the Dumpster. It was already half full of debris: the old sink cabinet and commode from the bathroom, the old broken tile, the old kitchen counter, a couple of rickety shelves Derek had pulled off the wall in the laundry room.

The crew straggled behind me. Fae was yawning, trying to cover it up with the clipboard. Nina walked carefully in her high heels, and she made sure no part of her touched any part of the Dumpster on her way past. Adam came next, sauntering along in another—or the same—pair of snug jeans and a tight V-neck that showed a smooth-shaven chest and a hint of man-cleavage. He looked excited about being back at work, and when he caught my eye, he winked. Wilson ambled a few steps behind, camera on his shoulder, and Ted brought up the rear, his arms full of lights and wires.

Derek reached the porch first and the petunia planter with the key. Or as it turned out, the petunia planter without the key. He stuck his hand in, fumbled around, and pulled it out, empty.

"No key?" I said.

He shook his head. "Check the door, please."

I did, with my free hand. The knob turned, and I pushed the door open. "Tony?"

There was no answer.

"This is weird," I said, my voice low.

Derek nodded, his lips tight. "Stay here. Keep the others out. I'll check the house."

Fine with me. I don't like trouble, and if Tony was inside, and something bad had happened to him, I'd so much rather have Derek deal with it.

He brushed past me and into the house. I turned to the others. "Derek's going to walk through the house and make sure everything's all right. Chances are Tony just decided to crash here for the night instead of driving back to Portland, and he's asleep on the floor in the back bedroom, but just in case something's wrong, let's all just stay out here and wait for Derek to come back."

Glances were exchanged, but no one argued. I'm not sure any of them believed me. I didn't believe it myself. There was no way Tony would have spent the night on the hard floor. Portland's only forty-five minutes away, and even if he'd been stuck in Waterfield overnight, with a car that didn't start, he could have called Melissa for a place to stay, or called another friend for a ride home, or in a pinch, found a room in a B&B or motel for the night. He would have spent the night in the front seat of the BMW before I could see him bunking on the hardwood floor of the cottage. When Derek came back out onto the porch, his face grim, my heart sank, but I wasn't surprised to hear the words.

"He's dead."

—5—

Nina turned deathly pale, and for a second, I thought she was going to faint. Ted must have thought so too, because he reached for her. But the cables got in the way, and Adam got there first, putting a muscular arm around Nina's waist. She leaned into him. Ted scowled.

I looked at Derek, helplessly. "Are you sure?"

It was a stupid question. Of course he was sure. He was a doctor; if anyone should be able to determine whether someone was dead or not, it was Derek.

He nodded. "I'm sure."

"What happened? Heart attack?" Tony was around forty. It was early for heart trouble, but not unheard of.

Derek shook his head. "He's been stabbed. Multiple times. Call Wayne. I'm gonna go back inside. Check and see what's missing."

"Why would something be missing?" I reached for my cell phone.

"It looks bare. I think the tools are gone." He didn't wait

for my answer, just disappeared back into the house. I dialed the Waterfield PD and relayed the news in a shaky voice.

Wayne must have been at home, because it was only a few minutes before he pulled up to the curb in front of the house next door. Between Tony's BMW, Derek's Ford F-150, and the news van, we took up all the available space in front of this house.

Waterfield's chief of police and Kate's husband is in his late forties, seven or eight years older than his new wife. He's tall, six-four or so, and lanky, with curly salt-and-pepper hair and soft, brown eyes that can take on the rock-hard look of pebbles when he's doing his job. He likes me, except when I meddle in his business, although he does tend to blame me for the crime wave that has swamped Waterfield since my arrival a year ago. Never mind the fact that none of the deaths, except for the first—Aunt Inga's—had anything whatsoever to do with me. I certainly wasn't responsible for any of them, and several of the victims died before I even set foot in Maine.

Wayne knows he can't possibly hold me responsible, but that doesn't stop him from giving me a hard time. That's only when it's just the two of us, among friends, of course. With the television crew in attendance, he was perfectly business-like. "Avery. Derek inside?" I nodded. "Stay out here, please."

He ducked under the lintel and into the house.

The crew watched him go past in silence. Adam still looked like he was enjoying the excitement, while Nina was pale as a ghost and kept her arms tightly crossed over her chest. I thought her hands might be shaking. She had moved away from Adam, and now Ted was standing next to her. Not speaking nor touching her, but there, in silent support. Fae had chewed all the bloodred lipstick off her bottom lip and she looked terrified, while Wilson hovered, murmuring in her ear.

"That was Police Chief Rasmussen," I said.

Wilson nodded. "We met him last night. At least some

of us did." He glanced at Nina, who wasn't looking at him. Instead, she was watching the door where Wayne had disappeared, a worried look in her eyes.

"Will we be able to shoot today?" Fae asked, her voice soft. She glanced at her coworkers and ended up looking at me. I shook my head.

"I doubt it. Every other time this has happened, the police always take most of the day to process the crime scene. I don't think we'll get back into the house until tomorrow. Maybe not until the day after." If at all, now that the owner was dead.

There was silence for a moment. Then—

"'Every other time this has happened'?" Adam quoted. "Do you have that many premeditated murders around here?"

Calling what had happened a premeditated murder seemed to be jumping to conclusions with a vengeance—I was hopeful it might turn out to be a bit of random violence, almost an accident—but I didn't contradict him. "You'd be surprised. This has happened to us twice before. Last fall we found a skeleton buried in the crawlspace of a house we were renovating outside town, and just before Christmas, when we were working on the carriage house behind the bed and breakfast, we walked in one morning and found a dead guy on the floor. Both times, it took more than a day before we were allowed to go back inside."

"I should call the office," Nina said. Her hand *was* shaking when she reached for her cell phone. "Let them know we'll have a delay." She kept talking while she pushed buttons, just as much to herself as to us, I thought. "If this doesn't get resolved quickly, we may have to abandon the project and go on to the next town. We're supposed to start shooting in New Hampshire on Monday. Hey, Murray."

She put the phone to her ear and turned away.

"Abandon the project?" Adam repeated, his expressive face a mask of horror. "We can't do that!"

Wilson responded, "It's not unprecedented. We've had to

do it before, when the delays have been too extensive. I'm sorry for you two"—here he turned to me and included the absent Derek in the apology—"but I'm sure you understand."

Did I? I mean, Tony was hardly even cold yet, and the crew was already talking about moving on to the next job? Of course, they hadn't known him like we had—not that I'd known him all that well myself, or liked him a whole lot, if it came to that—but I'll admit to being a little shocked that they were already making new plans.

But it would be rude to say so, so I didn't.

"Of course," I said. "You have to keep to a schedule. We'll just finish the house on our own time if you have to leave. We'll get paid whether we're on TV or not."

Or—would we? Tony had hired us, and the money for the project was supposed to come from Tony's pocket. If Tony was dead, would we be able to go on?

But perhaps this wasn't the right moment to dwell on that possibility. There were bigger issues going on, obviously.

"What did your boyfriend say happened?" Adam asked.

"You heard him, didn't you?" My eyes flicked, involuntarily, to the open door to the house. I couldn't see anything, but I could hear the murmur of voices, too far away to be able to make out what Derek and Wayne were saying. "He said it looked like Tony had been stabbed with something. And that some of the tools might be missing."

"A botched robbery?" Adam suggested, stopping just short of rubbing his hands together.

Wilson turned toward him. "What makes you say that?"

"Don't you remember what what's-his-name said yesterday? That houses under renovation are like magnets for thieves? Lots of tools and materials, no security."

Wilson glanced at me. "Is that true?"

"As far as I know, it is. We've never had it happen to us, but it makes sense. And Derek's been doing this job a lot longer than me; he'd know."

"So do you think this was a robbery gone wrong?"

Adam asked. "That Tommy saw someone break in, and maybe he stopped to talk to them, and they killed him?"

"Tony. His name was Tony." I shrugged. "I have no idea. It's possible. That's for the police to figure out, I guess."

"What are they doing in there?" Adam glanced at the open door.

"I'm sure they're just looking at things. Derek should be able to give Wayne the preliminary time and cause of death. The ME in Portland will have to confirm it, but it's something for Wayne to go on with. And they may be compiling a list of the tools that are missing. If any of them turn up in pawnshops or flea markets, the police may be able to track whoever pawned them. The tools won't be hard to identify; Derek puts his initials on all his tools."

The sound of a car coming up the street caused me to turn and look, and I felt my stomach drop when I recognized the cream-colored Mercedes. It pulled to the curb in front of Tony's sports car, and after a second, Melissa got out and looked around.

"Shit," Adam said, which seemed to sum up the situation admirably. "She won't be happy."

I shook my head. No, she wouldn't be. She'd be shocked and distraught and miserable. Melissa had been just about as unlucky in love as I had; before I met Derek, that is. Her marriage hadn't worked out, her relationship with Ray Stenham had gone down in flames, and now, just as she'd found Tony and gotten engaged again, her new fiancé was dead. It be enough to push anyone off the deep end. I didn't like Melissa much, but I felt sorry for her at that moment.

"Hello, everyone!" Melissa bathed us all in her brilliant smile. As usual, she looked fabulous in yet another designer skirt and wedge sandals, with sparkly stones—sapphires?—in her ears. "Hi, Avery. What's going on? What are the police doing here?"

The smile didn't waver; I guess maybe she was just expecting me to say that Wayne or his deputy, Brandon

Thomas, had stopped by to say hello and meet the television crew.

"I'm sorry," I said, feeling a little guilty about my dislike for her when I knew—and she didn't—that her fiancé had just met an untimely end. "There's been an accident."

"An accident?" She looked at us all standing there on the porch looking at her, and her smile slowly died. She turned back to me. "Derek?"

As if I'd be standing here, as relatively composed as I was, if something had happened to Derek. I shook my head. "He's fine. It's not Derek. It's Tony."

"Tony?" Her voice was strange. Not surprised at all, almost calm. It was probably denial. Or shock.

"I'm sorry." I moved to take her arm. "Here. Sit down on the steps."

But she shook me off. "I want to see him."

"I'm not sure that's a good idea—"

"I didn't ask for your permission, Avery!" She pushed past me and into the house.

"Melissa, wait!" I ran after her.

Derek and Wayne were in the kitchen, Wayne crouched next to Tony's body while Derek leaned against the kitchen cabinets, arms folded across his chest. When Melissa burst through the door, he made an abortive movement toward us, perhaps trying to forestall her, before he stopped.

She came to a halt just inside the door, as if she'd run into an invisible wall, and let out a gasp of horror. She even lifted a hand—the one with the ring—to her throat, as if she couldn't breathe. The diamond caught the sunlight coming through the kitchen window and cast it in prisms against the wall.

Not that I could blame Melissa for her dramatic reaction. It was a pretty gruesome sight, even for someone who didn't particularly like Tony. He was stretched out on the floor, with his head near the door to the utility room and his feet near the door to the dining room. His olive skin had

taken on a grayish cast. It also looked like Derek and
Wayne must have turned him over to get a better look at his
injuries. There was a huge pool of dark blood on the floor
next to him, and the entire front of his white shirt was red.
It looked as if he'd been stabbed at least a half-dozen times.

"Melissa." When Derek touched her shoulder, she turned
blindly into his arms and buried her head in his shoulder.
After a second's hesitation, he put an arm around her waist
and used the other hand to pat her back and shoulder.

I turned to Wayne. "Sorry. She pushed past me before I
could stop her."

He shrugged. "She would have insisted on seeing him
anyway, whether we'd been outside when she arrived or not."

Derek was already guiding Melissa out of the kitchen
and toward the front door, and now Wayne nodded to me.
"We need to go. I don't want anyone else to wander in and
contaminate the crime scene before Brandon gets here and
starts doing the forensic dance."

"Have you called him?"

"He's on his way. So is the van from Portland."

The medical examiner's van to carry Tony's body to the
morgue.

"Any idea what he was stabbed with?" I hadn't seen a
knife anywhere in the kitchen. I hadn't seen anything else,
for that matter. None of the tools we'd used yesterday.

Wayne shook his head. "We'll know more when Dr. Law-
rence has done her examination. For right now, we're thinking
it might be a screwdriver. Derek says there's one missing."

Surely not the battery-powered one, the one I'd used all
afternoon yesterday? My stomach twisted unpleasantly at
the thought, and I fought back a wave of nausea. The smell
in the house wasn't helping: The fresh tang of paint strip-
per and the sweet smell of sanded wood were now mixed
with the metallic scent of blood.

"Let me ask you a question, Avery," Wayne said, with a
cautious look at Derek and Melissa, who were just passing

through the front door onto the porch. He grabbed my arm and held me back. "Derek said you weren't expecting Tony this morning. That the two of you were surprised to see his car parked out front."

I nodded.

"What about Melissa? Did you know she was coming?"

I glanced up at him, surprised. "You don't think Melissa killed him, do you?"

"I'm not thinking anything," Wayne said, in blatant disregard of the truth. Of course he was thinking something, and it wasn't difficult to guess what. "When someone dies an unnatural death, we always have to look at the significant other."

"Yes, but . . . they've only been dating a few months." How significant could the relationship be in such a short amount of time? Although she *had* been wearing an engagement ring. . . .

"I noticed that," Wayne nodded when I said so. "New development?"

"The first time I saw it was Sunday night." At the Tavern, with the champagne. It sounded like a game of Clue. "And I did see them both a few times last week, while we were getting everything ready for the flip. She wasn't wearing it then."

"So fairly recent. Don't know whether that'll make the situation worse or easier for her." He gestured for me to precede him out of the house. Outside on the porch, he raised his voice to address everyone. "If I could have your attention, please?"

I moved away while everyone else turned to face Wayne. Wilson had put down the camera and was taking his turn to comfort Nina, who still looked distraught. Ted watched them, his jaw tight. Adam, meanwhile, had taken the opportunity to chat up Fae. She looked as if she really wanted him to leave her alone, but she was too polite, or perhaps just too young and afraid, to tell him to bug off. Once in a while, she'd shoot a glance at Wilson, as if looking for rescue, but he was busy and didn't notice. All conversation stopped at the sound of Wayne's voice; the only thing we could hear was Melissa snuffling into Derek's shoulder.

"I'm sorry to have to inform you that Tony Micelli is dead," Wayne said formally. "Because of the circumstances, we'll be treating the death as suspicious, and as a result, we'll have to talk to everyone associated with the victim, as well as everyone associated with the crime scene. That means all of you."

He let his gaze run over the crowd, and by now, his eyes had lost all that brown softness and were cold and hard.

"Surely you don't think one of us . . ." Adam blustered.

Wayne focused on him. "I'm not thinking anything, Mr. Ramsey. Not yet, anyway. But you were all here this morning, and you all met Tony Micelli yesterday, and you all knew where the key to the front door was hidden. . . ."

Derek must have told him those things while the two of them were inside the house together.

"But Ivory said there were tools missing. . . ." Adam protested, with a glance at me.

"Avery"—Wayne glanced at me, too, with an amused twitch of his lip he couldn't quite suppress—"is correct. However, the fact that the key was used suggests that someone who knew where it was hidden opened the door."

A babble of protest greeted this pronouncement, as everyone wanted to express their shock, outrage, and innocence, all at the same time. Wayne held up a hand. "Save it for later. You'll have a chance to tell me your side of the story."

He thought for a second. "What might be best is if I take you back to the bed and breakfast. You can wait in your rooms while I talk to each of you individually. It'll be more comfortable than cooling your heels at the police station. I'll call Kate and let her know what's going on." He reached for his phone.

"What about us?" Derek asked when Wayne had delivered

the news and Kate was prepared to play prison matron for the next few hours. "Avery and me? And Melissa?" He had his arm around her still, and she looked pale and shocked, her eyes unfocused. Her makeup was still perfect, though, so I guess all the sobbing must have been dry. Either that, or she used the most amazingly waterproof makeup the world has ever seen.

Wayne hesitated, looking at her. "I'll have to talk to all of you, especially Melissa. In your professional opinion, is she up for an interview?"

"My professional opinion isn't worth squat," Derek retorted, "since I haven't practiced medicine for six years. But in my opinion, she's in shock and probably won't be coherent until she's had some time to rest."

"Does she need to go to the hospital?"

"It might not be a bad idea to take her to see dad. Get a second opinion from someone whose medical license is actually current."

"Why don't you two do that," Wayne said. "I'll stay here until Brandon arrives, and then I'll leave him to do the evidence gathering while I go back to the B and B with the crew."

"Sure." I was a little unsure as to why he was sharing his plan as if we were working together, but maybe it was his way of telling the crew, without actually telling them, what would be going down.

"C'mon, Melissa," Derek said, helping her down the steps. "We're gonna go see Dad."

"My car . . ." Melissa stumbled when her foot hit the ground. Lurching sideways, she probably would have fallen if Derek hadn't had a good grip on her.

"It'll be safe here. The most important thing right now is to take care of you."

"Keep me updated," Wayne told me. I nodded, running after them.

$$-6-$$

Dr. Ben Ellis and his wife, Cora, live in a pristine, green-painted Folk Victorian on Chandler Street in the Village. Like a lot of houses in Waterfield, it's been in Derek's family since it was built.

When we pulled up to the curb outside the house, Derek said, "Stay there."

It brought back memories. He'd done the same thing the first time he'd brought me here. I'd had an accident during the renovation of Aunt Inga's house, had fallen down the sabotaged basement stairs, and when Derek came and found me all banged up and bruised the next morning, he had picked me up and carried me to the truck and driven me to Dr. Ben's house. When we arrived, he'd told me to stay put until he could come around the car to carry me. I, being stubborn and embarrassed and not entirely sure that *he* hadn't sabotaged the stairs—and liking being in his arms a little too much for comfort—had insisted on getting out on my own. He'd had to catch me before I fell flat on my face. This time, I did as I was told.

Between us, we got Melissa out of the truck and up the garden path to the front door. Under her own steam, with Derek supporting her on one side and me on the other. When she wobbled and Derek asked if she needed to be carried, I'd come back with a firm, "She'll be fine," before Melissa even had time to open her mouth.

On the top of the stairs, Derek tried the knob before ringing the bell, and then we waited. After a moment, there were footsteps inside, and then the door opened.

"Derek." Dr. Ben stood on the threshold knotting his tie. "And . . . Melissa?" His eyebrows shot up, and he looked around. I think he may have been just a little worried, which was nice of him. There was definite relief on his face when he spotted me. "Avery. There you are. What's going on, Son?"

"There's been an accident," Derek said, guiding Melissa through the door and into the front hall, and from there into the parlor on the left. He put her down on the same yellow brocade-upholstered sofa I'd sat on last summer when Dr. Ben had examined my leg. He had called Derek "Son" then, too, my first indication of the relationship between them.

"What sort of accident?" Dr. Ben watched Melissa, who sat as docile as a child, staring straight ahead, violet eyes unfocused.

"What looks like a break-in at the house on Cabot Street."

Dr. Ben knew all about the house on Cabot Street, of course; we hadn't talked about much else for the past couple of weeks.

"Looks like?" he repeated.

Derek shrugged. "I left the key in a planter on the porch last night. One of the crew said he might get there early to start setting up for the shoot."

"And when you got there this morning?"

"The key was gone, the door was open, and Tony Micelli was inside. Dead."

That was succinct and to the point. Maybe a little too succinct. I glanced at Melissa.

Dr. Ben nodded. "Cora's in the kitchen. Why don't you two go say hi and get some breakfast while I talk to Melissa." He turned to his former daughter-in-law. Derek looked like he might be thinking about protesting, but then he shrugged and went.

Cora, of course, had not heard anything about what had happened, and we had to go through the story again for her, sitting around the kitchen table in the Ellises' comfortable kitchen addition. "Tony Micelli?" she exclaimed when Derek had finished the sordid tale. "Who'd want to kill Tony Micelli?"

"I can't imagine it was premeditated," Derek answered, hands wrapped around a mug of coffee. "He probably just drove by on his way home from dropping Nina at the B and B last night and saw the door standing open or something. Maybe he thought I was there and he wanted to talk to me."

"Why would he want to talk to you?"

"Could be anything," Derek said. "It was his house, and I was working on it. Or he was engaged to Melissa, and I used to be married to her, so he wanted the inside scoop."

"Either that, or your blessing."

"He had it," Derek said and took a sip of coffee.

Cora looked from one to the other of us. "So you think it was random? Someone broke in to steal your tools, and Tony happened to be there and walked in on them, and they killed him? That's rather coincidental, isn't it?"

It was. Especially that it should happen on the same night that Derek had told the whole crew about houses under construction being magnets for thieves.

He seemed to disagree, however. "What else could it be? I mean, who'd want to kill Tony Micelli?"

"He *was* a reporter," I said. "Maybe he'd discovered something about someone."

"And he arranged to meet them in our fixer-upper? Why?"

"No idea. But it doesn't make sense to kill someone over a few tools, either."

Cora nodded in agreement. "How much did the things cost that you left in the house?"

Derek looked pensive. "Not much, now that you mention it. I hadn't brought over the tile saw yet, or any of the other expensive stuff, so it was just some hammers and chisels, an electric screwdriver that Avery used to take the cabinet doors off—it didn't cost more than twenty bucks brand-new—a crowbar, and the manual screwdriver, of course. . . ."

Of course. "Doesn't seem enough to murder someone over, does it?"

"No," Derek admitted, "but whoever broke in may not have realized that. Not until it was too late. Teenagers, maybe, trying to make a quick buck, never intending to hurt anyone. But when Tony walked in on them, they panicked. Maybe he grabbed hold of whoever had the screwdriver in his hand, and the kid lashed out, not even intending to stab him but just to buy enough time to get away."

"That would explain the first stab wound," I said, "but not the other half dozen."

"So maybe he accidentally got Tony in the chest, and Tony fell, and then they all freaked out and decided they'd better make sure he was really dead, and so they stabbed him a few more times for good measure."

"Maybe. But do you really think they'd be able to think clearly enough after something like that to take the murder weapon with them? Not to mention the other tools? Wouldn't they just drop everything and run?"

"Maybe they were afraid their fingerprints would be on the screwdriver," Derek said.

"If they broke in without wearing gloves, their fingerprints would be on everything else, too. Including the door-knobs and any other surfaces they touched."

Derek didn't answer. I added, "They took the time to gather the rest of the tools and bring them along. And that doesn't sound like panic. That sounds calculated to me."

"Do you think someone planned to kill Tony Micelli, then, Avery?" Cora asked in her soft voice. She looks decep-tively sweet and simple, with her round face and fluffy brown hair and soft blue eyes, but she's not stupid at all.

I shook my head. "Not necessarily. It could still be like Derek said: Someone broke in to steal our tools, and Tony caught them in the act. But I don't think they were pan-icked teenagers. They took the time to remove not only the murder weapon but all our tools afterward. So they weren't too freaked out about stabbing Tony to lose sight of why they were there in the first place."

"Someone who really needed the fifty bucks those tools would fetch at a pawnshop, then?" Derek said, eyebrows raised in mingled disbelief and incredulity.

I grimaced. "That doesn't make much sense, either, does it?"

"Not really, no. If they were old enough and coolheaded enough to stab Tony and remove the evidence, they'd be mature enough to realize that the profit wasn't worth the crime."

"You don't suppose . . ." But I stopped and shook my head. "No, surely not."

"What?"

I would have continued, but we could hear Dr. Ben's foot-steps in the hallway. After a few seconds, he came into the kitchen. Instead of sitting down at the table, he went around the island and pulled another mug out of the cabinet.

"Everything OK?" Derek asked when his father didn't immediately speak.

Dr. Ben nodded. "She'll be all right. I offered her a

prescription for something to help her sleep, but she said she already has something at home."

"If you want her to sleep, I don't think hopping her up on a stimulant is the way to go."

"I know that," Dr. Ben said. "I'm making tea. With lots of sugar for the shock."

He put the mug of water in the microwave and set the timer. The appliance whirred, and Dr. Ben leaned against the counter, watching the mug spin through the door.

"So, um . . ." I glanced at Derek before continuing. "She really is upset, right? She's not just faking?"

Derek and Cora both looked at me but neither spoke.

"Faking?" Dr. Ben repeated. "What makes you ask that?"

"Wayne said that when someone is killed, the significant other is always the first person they look at. She's the significant other. His fiancée or girlfriend or whatever."

"Why would she want to kill him?" Cora asked. "Haven't they just gotten engaged?"

I shrugged apologetically. "Well . . . Tony did go to dinner with Nina last night. Maybe Melissa objected."

"Enough to stab him several times with a screwdriver?" Derek said. "Surely that's overkill."

He flinched when he realized what he'd said. "I mean . . ."

"I know what you mean. And she probably didn't. It just struck me, is all. That she stopped by the house this morning because she knew the police would find her fingerprints and hair all over the kitchen, and she wanted to explain it away."

Nobody spoke for another few seconds. The microwave stopped running and the buzzer rang into the silence. Dr. Ben opened the door, grabbed the mug of hot water, and put it on the counter before hunting up a tea bag and dropping it in to steep. While it did, he assembled milk and sugar.

"I'll take this to her. You can drive her home in a few minutes."

He wandered out, holding the mug.

"You're not serious?" Derek said, turning to me.

I shrugged, avoiding his eyes. I wanted to tell him I wasn't, because I could see that the fact that I might be upset him, but I couldn't bring myself to say the words. Sure, I was probably wrong. I knew I was biased. I don't like Melissa. But the possibility should at least be noted. When someone's killed, the significant other is always a suspect. Melissa had no business at the house this morning. And if Tony had gone to dinner with another woman last night . . .

"You've got to be kidding!" Derek kept his voice low to make sure Melissa couldn't hear him, but his eyes were blazing blue fire. "You think Melissa killed Tony!"

"I didn't say that. I just think we need to consider the possibility. She does have a bit of a temper, doesn't she?"

Derek's face shuttered. "Who told you that?"

"Kate," I said. "Last summer. Before I met you. That day I got back to Waterfield from New York and discovered all of Aunt Inga's china broken on the kitchen floor. Wayne wanted the names of anyone I knew in town who might want to upset me, and she was one of the few people I'd met. Kate said it wouldn't have been the first time Melissa threw flatware around."

He didn't answer, and I added, "Are you saying Kate's wrong? That Melissa doesn't have a bad temper?"

"She has a short fuse," Cora said. Derek sent his stepmother a look across the table, but he didn't protest. "And she does get jealous. She never seemed to mind you hanging out with Jill—"

Jill Cortino nee Gers was Derek's high school sweetheart. They're still good friends, and Jill's husband, Peter, certainly doesn't seem to mind their continuing relationship.

"—but I remember when you were working with Kate McGillicutty on renovating the bed and breakfast. Melissa wasn't happy at all."

"She didn't stab me with a screwdriver, though," Derek said.

"But weren't things already unraveling by then? In your marriage?" Kate had been in town for seven years, and Derek and Melissa had been divorced for at least six.

He shrugged. "I suppose they were. As soon as I decided I didn't want to keep being a doctor, she started to look for a way out. So I guess it wasn't like she really cared what I did at that point."

"She never did," Cora said. "She was just jealous because you belonged to her and she didn't want anyone to think she couldn't keep you. If anyone was going to leave the relationship, it would be her."

"And she did," Derek said. "As soon as she had Ray firmly under her thumb." He shook his head. "Why are we talking about this? She never stabbed me; I don't think she'd have stabbed Tony."

"You never gave her a real reason to think you'd cheat," I pointed out. "You're not the type. But maybe Tony was. Maybe he and Nina were involved when they were younger, and now that he'd seen her again, he was planning to dump Melissa. If she can't handle rejection . . ."

"She didn't kill anyone!" He winced at the loudness of his own voice, and moderated his tone. "I was married to her for five years and dated her for a couple years before that. Don't you think I'd know if she's capable of murder?"

"I'm sure you would," I said, although I couldn't help involuntarily glancing at Cora. She was looking back at me, and I could tell that she shared my view. I'd definitely have to run this idea past Wayne, but it would have to be sometime when Derek wasn't around to contribute his two cents worth of opinion.

. . .

When my distant cousin Ray Stenham went to jail, Melissa sold their shared McMansion for a lot of money. She put half toward Ray's legal fees and used the other half to buy herself a loft on Main Street in downtown Waterfield. It was half a block from her office at Waterfield Realty, and right in the middle of the commercial and tourist district. Unfortunately, that meant that it was also directly across the street from Derek's loft above the hardware store. For the first couple of months after she bought it, she kept him on almost permanent retainer for things like leaking faucets and peeling paint and burned-out lightbulbs. For a few weeks at a time, it seemed like he spent almost as much time in her apartment as he did in my house. Derek swore I didn't have anything to worry about, that she wouldn't want him back even if he were willing to take another chance on her and he wasn't, and I believed him . . . but I didn't like it.

At any rate, he was familiar with Melissa's place. There was no hesitation at all when he walked her through the living room—painted in Melissa's trademark cream, with a cocoa-colored sofa and cool blue chair on a geometric brown rug—and into the only bedroom.

I trailed behind, looking right and left. She had invited me up before—heck, *Derek* had invited me up before to stand by and hand him his tools and at the same time see for myself that nothing was going on—but I'd declined, telling myself that I trusted him. Ergo, this was my first time inside.

The decor was what I'd have expected, knowing Melissa. Tasteful, elegant, expensive. Not much personality. The color choices were the same ones Melissa favored in her clothing. The kitchen was updated with mocha cabinets, stainless steel appliances, and granite. The artwork seemed to have been chosen to coordinate, whether or not Melissa had any particular affinity for it. There were no photographs anywhere, and no clutter. Everything looked perfect, like a photo spread in a home-and-garden magazine, right down to the two wineglasses and expensive bottle of Bordeaux grouped on the kitchen island. Idly, I wondered if she'd kept her and Derek's apartment looking like this when they were married, too, and how my casually untidy boyfriend had felt about that.

It wasn't until I wandered closer that I noticed that the atmospheric grouping of wine and glasses wasn't intended for show. The glasses were used—with Melissa's telltale lipstick marks on one—and the wine bottle was open and empty. Incidentally, it was Melissa's favorite Bordeaux, and coincidentally, the only wine she'd ever succeeded in getting Derek to drink. The one he'd told me about. Not that I was reading anything into that, of course.

It did cross my mind to wonder who she'd been drinking with, however. Given the pristine state of the loft, Melissa clearly wasn't in the habit of leaving dirty dishes sitting around, so the glasses had to be from last night or they'd already be washed and in the dish drainer. And if Tony had been having dinner with Nina, who had been here with Melissa? There were no lipstick marks on the second glass, so probably not another woman.

I had a quick look around, but there were no other clues. No Turkish cigarette butts in the ashtray—no ashtray, for that matter—no convenient package of matches bearing the logo of a hotel in Portland, and also no monogrammed handkerchief accidentally dropped under the coffee table. A man's jacket did hang in the coat closet just inside the front door, but it looked like something Tony would wear. Smelled like him, too.

When I got to the bedroom, Derek had finished tucking Melissa into bed. Her clothes were still on, but he had unstrapped her sandals and slid them off. They were lying on their sides on the floor next to the bed. I picked them up and set them upright in a corner, out of harm's way. They were Jimmy Choos, and, as such, deserved respect. Then I watched as Derek walked to the bathroom and came back with a glass of water.

"Here you go. I'll leave it here, along with the pills." He put the glass and two small white capsules on the night table.

Melissa nodded. She looked pitiful, like Greta Garbo on her deathbed in *Camille*. I felt guilty thinking it, but something seemed off. As if it were show rather than real emotion.

"Is she all right?" I whispered.

Derek glanced at me. "Fine. She just needs rest."

"Let's go, then. I want to talk to Wayne."

"Sure," Derek said. "See you, Melissa. Try to get some sleep."

Melissa nodded, looking wilted. But I could feel her eyes drilling into my back as I towed Derek toward the door.

—7—

"What was that about?" Derek asked when we were in the truck and on our way back to Cabot Street.

I glanced at him. "What?"

"Dragging me out of there. You're not upset, are you?"

"With you? Of course not." Derek's compassion is a wonderful quality, and one I really appreciate—when he's taking care of me.

I must not have sounded convincing enough, because Derek took his eyes off the road for a few seconds to look at me. "Doctors can't always choose who they treat, Tink. They can't pick only the fun cases, or the ones that don't make their girlfriends feel uncomfortable. I know I'm not a doctor anymore, but it's the way I was brought up. When someone needs my help, no matter who they are, I have to do what I can. Just like Dad."

"I'm glad to hear it," I said. "Listen, you know I'll never have warm feelings toward her, but I hope you know I didn't want this. No matter who she is. Losing a fiancé or a husband or a boyfriend isn't something I'd wish on my own worst enemy." Especially under circumstances like these. Accident or natural death is bad enough; brutal, bloody murder a whole lot worse.

"I know that, Avery," Derek said, reaching out with his free hand to take mine, twining our fingers together. "You're all talk. If Melissa really was in trouble, you'd be the first in line to help."

I wasn't so sure about that. But in any case—

"Hopefully it won't come to that," I said, thinking that the trouble Melissa was likely facing was being charged with her fiancé's murder.

"It won't," Derek answered.

• • •

By the time we made it to Cabot Street, Wayne and the television crew were long gone, and so was Tony's car.

"Peter Cortino came and picked it up," Brandon Thomas explained. Wayne's youngest and most gung-ho deputy, he's tall, blond, and strapping, with blue eyes and an easy smile, along with a rabid interest in anything forensic. If the Waterfield PD could afford to employ a full-time forensic tech, Brandon would be in heaven. As it is, he handles all the evidence and the crime scene investigations, but during the downtime, when nothing too exciting is going on, he's out on patrol like everyone else. I'd gotten to know him quite well during the time I'd lived in Waterfield, since he'd had more than his fair share of crime scenes to investigate in the past year, many of them in or around houses Derek and I were renovating.

"Anything else happen?" Derek wanted to know, looking around. There were smudges of fingerprint powder everywhere, where Brandon had checked windowsills and door frames and knobs for anything useful. I'd probably be the one who had to clean that up tomorrow or the next day, when Brandon was done and we were back at work. I'd cleaned fingerprint powder out of several of our houses in the past, so I had it down to a science by now.

Brandon shook his head. "Nothing. Wayne took the TV crew back to the B and B to talk to them. I haven't heard from him, so I guess the interviews are still going on. And there's nothing exciting here."

"No fingerprints?"

"Plenty of fingerprints. With as many people as have been through here, I'm not surprised. You two, the crew, Kate and Shannon, Tony and Melissa, and the people who used to live here . . . No way to tell whether any are unaccounted for yet."

Of course not. That'd have to wait until he got back to the police station and started processing and matching what he'd found.

"Sounds like you've got a busy day ahead of you," I said. Brandon nodded but then grinned, a little sheepishly.

"I have fun doing this. Probably shouldn't say that when someone's dead, but I like doing this stuff."

"Is there anything we can do to help?"

Brandon shook his head. "I should be done here in another hour or two. Don't think you'll get the house back until tomorrow, though. Sorry."

"We were prepared for that," I said. "It isn't the first time this has happened."

"The crew can't do any filming anyway," Derek added, hands in his pockets, "so even if we could work here, it wouldn't do any good. We can find something to do elsewhere until the morning."

"By tomorrow, Wayne'll probably be ready to release the crime scene. There's not much here." Brandon looked around with a shrug.

"No sign of forced entry?" I marveled, silently, at the life I'd led in the past year that had taught me to use expressions like that.

Brandon shook his head. "Whoever it was had a key."

Derek muttered something, probably about his own stupidity in leaving the key on the porch where anyone could find it.

"It could have been Tony who unlocked the place," I reminded him. "He probably had a key of his own."

"Did you find it on him?" Derek wanted to know. Brandon shook his head.

"Well, even if the killer used the key you hid on the porch to open the door, you couldn't have known that," I said. "You were just trying to be nice."

Brandon looked nonplussed. "What's this?"

I explained about Ted and the key in the planter.

"And it was his idea to leave the key outside? Show me where." He headed for the door.

"I don't know that I'd call it his idea, exactly. . . ." I threw after Brandon's departing back.

"He asked us to leave the place open," Derek said, following, "so he could come in early and set up. But I didn't want to. And it didn't make sense to have another key made, since we all planned to spend pretty much every waking moment here for the next week. Besides, I don't like a lot of keys floating around. Especially since it isn't our house."

"So this guy Ted suggested that you could leave the key outside?" Brandon stopped on the porch and looked around. "Where?"

"Right there." Derek pointed. "Corner of the planter. And I'm not sure it was his suggestion. I think it was my call where to put the key."

Brandon nodded, but he looked pensive. "I don't guess you noticed anything going on between this guy Ted and Tony Micelli?"

Derek and I exchanged another look. "Nothing out of the ordinary," I said. "The only person who admitted to knowing Tony from before was Nina Andrews. Ted didn't look like he cared for him a whole lot, but that could have been because Nina didn't seem happy to see him. At least not at first."

"That changed?"

"I expect it must have. She went to dinner with him last night. Or she was supposed to."

"Huh," Brandon said.

"They were planning to go to the Waymouth Tavern. I guess someone will check?"

"I will," Brandon said, coming back to reality, "when I'm done with everything else I have to do. And when they open this afternoon."

Derek looked around. The sun was shining, small white clouds were chasing each other across the blue bowl of the sky like pieces of cotton wool, and I could hear the sound of a bumblebee nearby. "What about the neighbors? Have you spoken to them? Did anyone see anything last night?"

"Just the old lady next door," Brandon said. "She didn't hear or see a thing. What can you tell me about the rest?"

Derek shook his head. "Not a lot. We haven't spent that much time here. Sounds like you've already met Miss Stevens. I know I've seen little children a couple houses down, playing in the yard. There's a family with teenagers in the blue house across the street. The father drives a truck and the mother is home with the kids for the summer.

"She works at the high school library during the school year," I contributed. "Her name is Donna. She introduced herself to me one day last week to ask what was going on. Tony hadn't told her he was thinking of putting the house on the market, so she was a little surprised. Then again, she said he's pretty much never around, so it wasn't like he'd have occasion to tell her anything."

Brandon nodded. "I'll go door to door in a little bit."

"Any word on my tools?" Derek wanted to know.

"Not that I've heard. Ramona is contacting pawnshops. It's probably too early to find them—whoever grabbed them last night may not have had time to do anything with them yet—but since they were marked, we can put the store owners on alert, just in case they do come in."

"Makes sense," Derek agreed. "Is there anything we can do for you?"

Brandon shook his head. "I'm just gonna finish up here, take the stuff down to the station, go over Tony's car—I doubt there's anything of interest there—and then I'll run out to the Waymouth Tavern."

"We'll see you later," Derek said, putting an arm around my shoulder.

"I know where to find you," Brandon answered, which—frankly—sounded just a little bit ominous.

．　．　．

The Waterfield Inn isn't far from Cabot Street, so it was just a few minutes before we pulled to a stop in the driveway. The white TV van was there, and so was Wayne's squad car. Kate's station wagon, too. Plus a small, blue Honda with Maine license plates.

"Looks like Josh is visiting," I remarked when Derek came around the truck to lift me down from the seat. It isn't like I can't get out on my own, but I enjoy the help, and he seems to enjoy giving it—at least most of the time—so I wasn't about to complain.

He nodded, sparing the Honda a glance while he slipped his hands around my waist and lifted me down. "Guess he's keeping Shannon company. Or maybe he's doing something for his dad. Checking someone's laptop or something."

Josh is by way of being a computer genius, or at least a very good student of computer technology. Since the Waterfield PD is so small and doesn't have a technology department any more than it has a forensics department for Brandon Thomas to head up, Josh sometimes pitches in when his dad needs someone's computer looked at or certain databases searched. Like a lot of people of his generation, Wayne didn't grow up surrounded by computers, and as a result, he doesn't feel terribly comfortable around them.

Josh, on the other hand, is practically hardwired into his PC. Although helping his dad wasn't what he was doing today. When we walked into the kitchen, he was sitting at the table sharing a cup of coffee and a plate of cookies with—I blinked—Fae.

True, Shannon was there, too, but the conversation flowed mostly between Josh, on one side of the table, and Fae opposite, while Shannon sat mutely off to the side, listening. She looked perfectly calm, with a tiny smile curving her lips, but her eyes were intent as they looked from Josh to Fae and back.

Josh was talking animatedly, hands waving in the air, reaching to push his glasses up his nose every few seconds. He was grinning, and the brown eyes behind the lenses were sparkling with excitement. He and Fae had obviously found common ground, or maybe he'd just decided he'd waited long enough for Shannon to sit up and take notice, and now it was time to move on.

Fae seemed equally fascinated, if more subdued. She sat with her chin in her hand and her eyes fastened on Josh's face, unblinking. Every once in a while, she'd smile and nod, or contribute a word or two to push him off on a new tangent.

All three of them turned when we pushed through the kitchen door.

"Oh," Josh said after a second, "hi." He blushed. "I came by to see if I could give Shannon a ride over to the house, since I was supposed to start helping you guys today, but when I got here, Kate told me what had happened."

"Where is she?" Derek looked around the obviously empty kitchen.

"Upstairs," Shannon said. "In the suite. Nina's a little upset."

Fae grimaced, and I got the impression that calling Nina a *little* upset might have been understating the point considerably.

Derek headed for the coffeemaker. He opened the cabinet

above the counter, got out two mugs, filled them, and added cream and sugar before handing one to me. Fae watched him make himself at home.

"Did anything else happen?" I asked, taking my coffee with a smile. "To make Nina upset, I mean?"

Fae shrugged. "No idea. When we got here, Chief Rasmussen made us all go into our rooms and wait. He said he'd talk to us one by one. After he finished with Nina, he came downstairs to ask Kate to make some hot tea with lots of sugar and take it up to her."

"I see." Surprising that Fae wasn't upstairs with her. Granted, being a nursemaid to Nina's nervous breakdowns may not have been part of Fae's job description, but she was supposed to make life easier for her boss, wasn't she?

"She said she was fine," Fae said, reading my mind. "I went up there with Kate and asked if there was anything Nina needed me to do. She said no, that I should take care of myself instead. And Chief Rasmussen told us to stay by ourselves until he'd spoken to us individually."

Derek pushed off from the refrigerator. "I'll go up. See if there's anything Kate needs. Or Wayne."

His eyes crossed mine briefly as he headed for the door.

"Did Nina say anything?" I wanted to know. "About last night? Going to dinner with Tony? Anything?"

Fae shrugged. "No idea. I wasn't there."

"Right." I glanced at the door. Put down my cup of coffee. "Excuse me. I'll just . . ."

"See you later, Avery," Josh said, his attention already completely focused on Fae again. "So, Fae, if you're not working tonight, maybe you'd like to come down to Guido's for a couple hours? With me? Have some pizza? Meet some people?"

He had his back to me, so I couldn't see the expression on his face, but I could see Fae's. It looked like she wanted to say yes, but I caught the sideways glance at Shannon out of the corner of her eye. "I'm not sure . . ."

Josh must have caught it, too. "Shannon doesn't care," he said. "Right, Shan?"

We all turned to Shannon. It took her a second to find her voice. "Oh, sure." She smiled, but it lacked her usual brilliance. I'm not sure Fae realized it, but I did. I'm sure Josh would have, too, had he bothered to look at her. He didn't.

"See?" he told Fae. "Shannon doesn't care. So whaddaya say?"

Fae smiled, and if Shannon's smile lacked brilliance, Fae's didn't. "I'd love to go out with you. Thanks."

"My pleasure," Josh said, and sounded like he meant it. I kept my eyes on Shannon, who looked up and met my gaze for a second before looking away again. The expression on her face was that of a little girl who has just realized there is no Santa Claus. I felt horrible as I slipped through the butler door and out into the dining room.

—8—

I found Kate and Wayne on the top-floor landing, conversing in low voices. They heard me coming up the stairs, of course, and stopped talking, so I had no idea what the conversation had been about.

"Derek's inside," Kate said, gesturing toward the closed door. "He's checking to make sure Nina doesn't need to go see Dr. Ben. This has been hard on everyone."

I nodded. "Interesting exchange downstairs just now."

"What do you mean?"

"Josh and Shannon and Fae are in the kitchen. He just asked her out."

"Josh asked Fae out?" Wayne said. "With Shannon there?"

"How did that go?" Kate wanted to know, a wrinkle between her brows. Like everyone else, they're obviously well aware that his son is hung up on her daughter.

"Depends. Fae said yes, so I imagine Josh is happy. Fae probably is, too. Shannon . . . maybe not so much."

"And you base that on . . . ?"

"He asked her if she minded. Right in front of Fae. Since Fae had obviously noticed that something was going on, you know? And there wasn't anything Shannon could say, really, except no. I don't think she was happy about it, though."

"It's her own fault," Wayne said bluntly. "He's been pining after her for years. I guess she's probably gotten used to it, but that doesn't mean he isn't gonna move on eventually, if she never gives him any encouragement."

Kate nodded, although she looked worried. "I'll go see what's going on." She headed down the stairs.

"How's Nina?" I asked Wayne before he could follow.

He turned back to me after watching Kate's bright coppery curls disappear from view. "Shook up. Upset. Nervous, I guess."

I lowered my voice. "D'you think she did it?"

Wayne lowered his, as well. "Killed him? She says she didn't."

"But that's what she'd say anyway, isn't it?"

Wayne shrugged.

I tried a different tack. "Did they really go to dinner last night?"

"Seems so. Brandon's heading out to the Tavern when they open to see if anyone noticed anything of interest. According to Nina, she and Tony ate, they talked, and he had her back here by ten thirty."

"Did anyone see her come in?"

Wayne shook his head. "Kate and I were already in the carriage house by then. Shannon locks up at eleven; anyone who's out after that lets themselves in with a key."

"Shannon and Fae were watching movies together last night, weren't they? So if Nina got home by ten thirty . . . ?"

Wayne looked a little frustrated. "They should have heard her come in, but Shannon says she didn't. Nina says she entered through the front door. She heard the sound of the TV from Shannon's room, but no one saw her come in, and she saw no one."

"That's unfortunate."

Wayne shrugged. "I'm not sure it matters, Avery. At least not until we can figure out exactly when Tony died. Derek guesstimated sometime between ten and two, but it was just a guess. For all we know, Nina killed him at nine forty-five and walked back to the B and B from Cabot Street. It wouldn't take more than ten minutes."

"Maybe fifteen, if she was wearing heels. If she did, someone should have seen her. One of the neighbors. Someone walking their dog. Someone jogging. Somewhere along the way."

"And we'll be checking for that, believe me." He folded his arms across his chest and looked down on me. Way down, since he's more than a foot taller than I am. "Any particular reason you want her to be guilty?"

I shook my head. "It just seems like a huge coincidence that the crew comes here to Waterfield, and Nina knows Tony from before, and then he ends up dead after taking her to dinner. But I don't want her to be guilty. I like her. As well as I can, after knowing her for less than a day."

Wayne nodded. "I'm gonna want to hear your impressions of the crew. Some other time. Right now, I have to talk to the rest of them."

"Hold on just a second." I told him about going to Melissa's loft and seeing the two wineglasses in the kitchen. "Maybe Tony stopped by after he dropped Nina off. I mean, if Melissa's engaged to Tony, it's not likely that she should be sharing a late-night glass of wine with anyone else, is it?"

"Could be a girlfriend," Wayne said, "if she has any. Or maybe she just couldn't find the first glass and poured herself another."

"I suppose." It was possible. At least the second suggestion. As far as the first, I had a hard time believing it. Melissa was the kind of woman that other women love to hate, and if she had any close girlfriends, I couldn't think who they were.

"I'll look into it," Wayne said. "Later. Right now, I gotta talk to the rest of the crew."

"I'll wait here for Derek to come out. Or maybe I'll go inside and see how Nina's doing." I glanced at the door.

"Go ahead. She keeps saying she's fine, but she doesn't look it. Maybe there's something you can do. I'll be down on the second floor talking to the men." He headed down the stairs. I tapped on the door and turned the knob without waiting for an answer.

The Waterfield Inn used to belong to a woman by the name of Helen Ritter. When she lost her husband back in the 1960s or '70s, she'd turned the three-story Queen Anne mansion into a triplex, the better to keep a roof over her head and her bills paid. When Kate came to town and bought the place, she hired Derek to turn it back into a single family home, and now the entire third-floor apartment was one big suite. The last time I'd been up here was around seven months ago, when my mom and Noel had been in town. It hadn't changed since then, except for the view and all of Nina's things. Back in December, the view through the windows had been shades of gray—bare tree branches against the snow, low-hanging clouds, the steel gray of the Atlantic in the distance—while now the trees were green, the sky was blue, and the ocean was blinking in the sunlight. Nina's junk was everywhere: discarded clothes littering the floor, papers all over the small desk in the alcove next to an open but dark laptop, and a half-empty bottle of scotch and a glass on the table by the sofa. The pair of high-heeled shoes Nina had on when we first met her yesterday morning were lying under the table, and what looked like a dress was draped across the arm of the sofa. Maybe it was the dress she'd worn for dinner yesterday. A saucer with a mound of ashes in it sat on the table next to a disposable lighter, and I wondered if Kate knew that Nina was sneaking cigarettes in her nonsmoking establishment.

Looking at the pile in the saucer, it was amazing that

she could have accumulated that much ash in just the day and a half she'd been here. She'd have had to have been chain smoking the entire time she was in her room. Funny that I hadn't seen her smoke a single cigarette all day yesterday. I'd have thought the acrid scent of smoke would have been hanging in the air, too, but it wasn't.

I looked around but saw nothing else of interest in the sitting room, so I made my way to the door to the bedroom.

Nina was on the bed, propped up against a mound of pillows, clutching a tissue in her hand, her eyes red and puffy from crying. The Kleenex box was next to her on the nightstand, and crumpled tissues littered the bed. Derek stood at parade rest, legs apart and arms folded across his chest. When I walked in, they both turned to me.

"I just wanted to see how you were doing." I smiled.

Nina cleared her throat. "I'm all right."

"I'm sorry for your loss." She was obviously distraught, enough to barrel through a box of tissues so far.

Nina waved my condolence away. "I don't know why this is hitting me so hard," she confessed in a voice that was husky from tears. "I hadn't even seen Tony for twenty years. But after what happened . . ."

She broke off.

"Something happened yesterday?"

But Nina shook her head. "Nothing happened yesterday. We just . . . didn't part on the best of terms twenty years ago. And now . . ." She shrugged, sort of helplessly. It was weird to see the capable, put-together, professional woman we'd met yesterday look so lost.

"I'm sorry," I said again, since there really wasn't anything else to say. Sure, I wanted to push her, to try to figure out why she and Tony had parted on bad terms more than twenty years ago, but it wasn't any of my business, and she probably wouldn't answer me anyway. "Um . . . is there anything we can do for you? Someone we can call? Do you want me to ask Fae to—"

Nina shook her head. "No. I just . . . I want to be alone."

It seemed to be a day for channeling Garbo. I glanced at Derek. He made an almost imperceptible shrug before addressing himself to Nina. "Kate's downstairs if you need anything. And you've got my number. I'll be happy to ask my dad to stop by if you think you might want . . ."

But Nina shook her head again. "It isn't that I don't appreciate it. But I'll be fine. I just need some time by myself."

"Sure." Derek started moving toward the door. "Avery?"

"Coming." I glanced again at Nina, feeling like I should say something more. The best I could come up with was a reiteration of, "I'm sorry for your loss."

She nodded, and I could see tears gathering in her eyes again as I left the room behind Derek.

He closed the door to the suite with a soft but definite click, and turned to me. We exchanged a look but no words until we were halfway down the stairs and away from the door. Then—

"What did you tell Wayne about Melissa?" Derek asked, glancing over his shoulder at me.

"Me?" I was two steps behind, so we were almost at eye level. I actually had him beat by a few inches, and those beautiful sky blue eyes looked directly into mine when he stopped and turned. I saw a hint of worry in their depths. "How do you know I talked to him about Melissa?"

"Heard you through the door."

"Why did you ask, if you could hear us?"

"I could hear you," Derek said, "but I couldn't hear every word."

"Oh. Well, I just told him that when we were there, I noticed two wineglasses in the kitchen. Two used glasses, I guess from last night. With an empty bottle of wine. Bordeaux. The one you said was her favorite."

"So?" Derek said, but I noticed he didn't meet my eyes.

"So it looked like she had someone over last night. And

if she was engaged to Tony, it doesn't seem likely it would be another man, right? So maybe Tony stopped by after he dropped Nina off. And maybe one thing led to another, and . . ."

"And Melissa stabbed him six times with the corkscrew and then he dragged himself down the stairs and into his car and drove himself over to the house on Cabot Street because he mistook it for the hospital?"

"There's no need to be snide," I said.

Derek looked at me for a second before he blew out his breath. "I'm sorry, Tink. You're right. Listen, I'm gonna wait up here and have a word with Wayne when he comes out, OK? Why don't you go back down to the kitchen and see what's going on? Keep Kate and Shannon company."

"Sure," I said. Although I couldn't help feeling a little as if I'd gotten the brush-off as I made my way down the stairs to the first floor.

· · ·

By the time I got to the kitchen, Fae had gone to her room. Maybe she had noticed the tension that hung heavy in the kitchen and thought it better to excuse herself. The atmosphere was thick enough to cut with a Skilsaw.

However, no one was talking about it. Kate and Shannon were deep in a conversation about upcoming reservations for the B&B, while Josh was just staring into space, looking moony. I sat down across from him in Fae's former seat.

"How's it going?"

His eyes focused, and he grinned. "Great."

"I'm sorry we don't have any work for you today."

"That's all right. I can find things to keep me busy."

No doubt.

"Did Fae say anything about going out last night? Or anything she might have been doing?"

"She was with me," Shannon said, from the other end of

the table. "We watched a couple of movies and then went to bed. At least I did. Around eleven thirty."

"Would you have heard it if she left? Or came back?"

"Not necessarily," Shannon admitted, with a sheepish look at her mother. "We had a couple of glasses of wine each, and a lot of pizza, and I was tired. Housekeeping is hard work, and Mom kept me hopping most of the day yesterday. I locked the back door, and then I dropped right off to sleep when I went to bed. If someone had made a ruckus, I'm sure I would have woken up, but if they were quiet—and they probably would have been, since they all knew I was down there—I can't be sure I would have heard them. Especially if they left by the front door."

I nodded. "And you keep spare keys, right? Just in case someone has to leave or come home late?"

Kate nodded. "Nina asked for one when she left. She didn't know when she'd be back, and if it was after eleven, she didn't want to have to wake anyone up."

"Except she came in earlier—around ten thirty. What happened to the key?"

Kate and Shannon exchanged a look. "She said she left it on the console in the foyer."

"Was it there this morning?"

"I didn't look," Shannon said. "What are you thinking, Avery?"

I shrugged apologetically. "If Nina came home at ten thirty and left the key on the console in the foyer, anyone could have taken it and gone back out. Right?"

"You're not thinking that Fae . . ." Josh began, already affronted on her behalf, even though he hadn't so much as taken her on a date yet.

"I'm not thinking anything," I said. "I'm just checking. Did you really not hear Nina come home last night, Shannon? If it was around ten thirty, you were still up."

Shannon shook her head. "I didn't. Fae and I were in my

room with the TV going. And there are two or three doors, at least, between my room and the front hall."

Right. So Nina could be telling the truth, and she really had come home at ten thirty and gone up to her room without anyone seeing her. Or she could be lying to try to establish an alibi, because she'd killed Tony at ten thirty or eleven.

From out in the front hall, I heard a slithering sound, and then a sort of rattling, metallic slap.

"Mail slot," Kate said at my questioning glance.

"I'll go." Shannon jumped up and headed out through the swinging butler door. Josh watched her go, but distractedly, like he wasn't really paying attention. More like it was his habit to watch Shannon, but right at the moment, his thoughts were occupied elsewhere and he wasn't really aware of what—or who—he was looking at.

"So you and Fae are going to Guido's tonight," I said into the silence.

Josh turned back to me from the still-moving door. "That's right." *And what's it to you?* was implied but remained unsaid. Josh isn't rude, at least not directly.

"She seems nice," Kate said peacefully; the perfect stepmother. "Not that I know her well, but from what I've seen."

Josh nodded, and I swear his eyes lit up. But before he could say anything, Shannon was back, with a small stack of mail in her hand, as well as a key. "Here. It was on the console, just like she said."

She dropped it on the table. Stopping between Kate and Josh, she proceeded to sort through the cards, envelopes, and circulars that had arrived, muttering under her breath as she put everything into piles. "Bill, bill, deposit check— look, Mom; the Fergusons finally got it together—*B&B Today* magazine, junk mail, more junk mail, a postcard from Paige . . ."

"Where's Paige?" I asked, reaching for it. Josh, who had been doing the same thing, pulled his hand back.

Paige Thompson is Shannon's best friend, or maybe she's Josh's best friend, or if the two of them are best friends, then maybe Paige is the third wheel. Whatever. She's a nice girl, as small and slight and fair and unobtrusive as Shannon is tall, dark, and dynamic, and I was chagrined to realize that until now, I hadn't even realized that I hadn't seen her for weeks.

The postcard had a photograph of a funicular on the front, with a Victorian building with a little cupola on top, all of it painted sort of lipstick red with teal accents. A curved sign on the side wall of the building said 1870 and Monongahela Incline.

"Pittsburgh," Josh said, at the same time as Shannon explained, "She's gone home with Ricky. To meet his family."

Ricky and Paige had developed their relationship with the slow deliberation of two turtles, but it seemed like they were getting serious if she'd been invited home to meet the family.

Shannon nodded when I said as much. "They took forever to admit they even liked each other, but now they're talking marriage."

"Wow. Already?"

"I always figured Paige would marry young. She's the type who wants to be settled with a husband and a bunch of kids."

"What about you?" I asked, handing the postcard off to Josh after skimming the message on the back:

Having a great time. Ricky's family's wonderful. Miss you. Tell Josh and your mom hi for me. xoxo

"I'm not in a hurry," Shannon answered, without looking at me. "The world's full of men." She turned to her mother. "Look, here's another letter for Nina Andrews."

She held out a small ecru-colored envelope with Nina's name and "c/o Waterfield Inn" on the front. The name and address were typed in faded, old-fashioned letters, the kind you get from an ancient manual typewriter when the ribbon is almost completely dried up and the keys hit at different strengths and don't go in straight lines. It looked like a clue out of on an old-fashioned legal thriller, starring Perry Mason or Hercule Poirot.

"Did you say 'another'?" I inquired.

Kate nodded. "There was one yesterday, as well. Looked the same as this one. I gave it to her when the crew got home yesterday evening. Before she went upstairs to get ready for her date with Tony."

"Strange that she should be getting personal mail here in Waterfield. Especially more than once. What's the postmark say? Is it local?"

Kate peered at it and shook her head. "Looks like it says Missouri."

"Nina said her first job was in the Midwest. Where she and Tony worked together. Maybe it was in Missouri."

"I wouldn't know," Kate said. She got to her feet. "I'll take it up to her."

"Maybe it's from someone they both knew back then, who knew that Tony lived here, and who was letting Nina know she might run into him," Shannon suggested.

"Maybe." I turned on my chair to watch Kate walk toward the door. "Did she say anything about the one you gave her yesterday?"

Kate shook her head.

"Did she open it while you were there?"

But Kate said Nina hadn't. "I'm sure it's just a friendly note from someone she knows, Avery. Nothing to do with anything."

"Right." I bit my bottom lip.

"Why are you so interested?" Shannon wanted to know. I turned to her. "No reason. It just seems like an interesting coincidence. Nina comes to Waterfield, she knows Tony from the Midwest, someone from Missouri is writing letters to her, and now Tony's dead."

"I'm sure a coincidence is all it is," Kate said, and ducked out the door.

Perhaps. But suddenly that pile of ashes on the saucer in the sitting room of the suite was taking on a whole 'nother meaning. Maybe Nina hadn't been smoking, after all. Maybe she'd been burning correspondence.

—9—

When Kate came back downstairs, she was minus the letter but followed by Derek.

"Ready to go, Avery?" he wanted to know.

"Sure," I said, without pointing out that he was the one who had wanted to hang back to talk to Wayne. "We'll see you later, guys. Let me know if anything happens."

Kate said she would, and Derek and I headed back out into the heat of the day. He was acting sort of weird, I thought—alternately brusque and quiet—and it made me uneasy. In the year I'd known him, I'd learned that he's usually even-keeled, hardly ever moody. The fact that he was now was worrisome. Although between Tony's death and the fact that we were, once again, involved on the periphery of a murder investigation and had to postpone our project, he had reason to be, I suppose. This seemed to be more than that, though, and I wasn't quite sure how to handle it.

By this time it was close to lunch, and in an effort to

cheer him up, I suggested we head downtown to the little hole-in-the-wall deli that has the best lobster rolls in down east Maine. Derek does get cranky when he doesn't eat regularly, and I thought that might be part of the problem. There wasn't anything I could do about the dead body or the fact that we couldn't get into our house to work, but I could make sure he got fed, and maybe I could also find something to do that would keep his hands busy for the next few hours, at least.

"They haven't told us we have to stop work yet," I said when we were seated on orange plastic chairs at one of the rickety tables in the deli. "I know we can't go inside the house and mess up Brandon's crime scene, but maybe he wouldn't mind if we worked outside in the yard. We could drive out to the nursery and load up the back of the truck with plants and flowers, and ask Cora and Beatrice to help us plant them."

Derek took a pensive bite of lobster roll. "I don't know, Tink. I mean, Tony's dead. We can't just carry on like nothing's happened."

"Of course not. But he wanted us to renovate the house. He signed a contract, both with us and with the television company. And Melissa is all set to put the house on the market next week. I don't think he'd change his mind just because he's dead. Do you?"

"Not sure I knew him well enough to determine that," Derek said. "At this point I guess it would depend on what his heir wanted."

"Who's that?"

"No idea. There's no family that I know of. Might be Melissa."

If so, at least I was sure we'd get the go-ahead to continue. And get reimbursed for the money we'd spend so far, too.

"Well, while we wait to find out, do you think we could start on the landscaping? I know it isn't what we planned to do today," I added, since we'd worked out a schedule for what needed to be done by the hour, if not the minute, "but when people die, the rest of us have to be a little flexible. And if we do end up going forward with the renovations, I'd hate to lose the whole day."

Derek nodded and swallowed before he said, "We were planning to do the landscaping on . . . what . . . Thursday?"

"While we waited for the paint and the second coat of polyurethane to dry. We were going to paint all day Tuesday and Wednesday, with Kate and Shannon and Josh and anyone else who were willing to lend a hand, and then you were going to do the first coat of poly on Wednesday night before we left. When we got to the house on Thursday morning, you were going to do the second coat, and then we were going to work outside all day on Thursday to let it dry. And then finish up all the piddly details on Friday."

Derek nodded. "You keep saying Wednesday, and on Wednesday we were going to do this, that, and the other, but I'm not sure you realize that Wednesday's tomorrow."

I choked on the bite of lobster roll I'd just taken. "It is? Oh, my God. Maybe it would be better if we just gave up. There's no way we can get everything done in time!"

For a few hours, I'd actually managed to forget that we had a house to flip in three and a half days, but now the thought was back and with a vengeance.

"I think we can," Derek said, "but we have to work smarter. And you're right, we can't sit around today and do nothing, even if we can't get into the house. When we leave here, we'll stop by the hardware store and pick up a power washer. I'll take that over to the house and get started on the roof. Meanwhile, you take Cora and go to the nursery and start picking out flowers. Cora'll tell you what to buy. By the time you get back, I'll be finished with the power washing, and the ground will be nice and wet and easy to dig. Then we'll begin planting."

He started taking bigger bites of his lobster roll now that

he had a plan and a purpose again. "Hurry up, OK? We don't have any time to waste."

I resisted the temptation to salute and just nodded. My mouth was too full to speak.

. . .

Thirty minutes later, I was on my way to the Waterfield Nursery with Cora. We'd called Wayne, who had told us that he had no idea whether we'd be able to finish the renovations or not—that would be up to Tony's heir—but that if we wanted to plant flowers today, he wasn't going to stop us. Brandon had already gone over the porch and yard for clues, and we were welcome to go ahead, as long as we realized we might be doing it all for nothing. Derek had rented his power washer, and when I left, he was walking around on the roof of the cottage letting it rip. I'd gotten somewhat inured to this stunt by now, having watched him wander around the roof of the two-and-a-half story Colonial on Rowanberry Island for a few days this spring. This small cottage was nothing in comparison. He'd probably break a few bones if he fell off, but chances were he wouldn't break his neck.

So I left him there and went to pick up Cora. And now the two of us were headed north out of town, to the nursery. Beatrice had been in the middle of something when I called, so she'd finish what she was doing first before meeting us at the house, and then all four of us would get busy planting.

Cora helped me choose flowers and shrubs that would look good in the yard on Cabot Street, and then we loaded the pickup bed full and headed back. Derek had finished his power washing by the time we got there, and Beatrice was waiting, and then all four of us got down on our hands and knees and got busy digging holes and planting. We kept at it until every single flower or shrub was in the ground and the sun was thinking of sliding behind the horizon.

The conversation while we worked turned to Tony and

the murder right off the bat, of course, with Beatrice wanting to know what had happened and me doing my best to
answer her questions. Like me, her first thought had been
the fact that Melissa was Tony's fiancée, and as such, she
was the logical suspect. Eventually, though, we all agreed
that she probably really hadn't killed Tony. As Derek had
once said, when I'd tried to pin another murder—or maybe
it was a kidnapping—on Melissa: She wasn't the type to
risk doing anything truly illegal. Too fond of her skin to
take the chance of anything happening to it.

"She does have a short fuse," Cora said.

"There's a big difference between breaking china and
stabbing someone with a screwdriver," Derek answered,
not even looking up from the flowerbed he was working on.

No arguing with that. And we couldn't anyway, because
just then Donna from across the street showed up to say
hello and find out about what had been going on today.

"Oh, wow," she said when we explained that Tony was
dead, "who'd do something like that?"

"We thought maybe teenagers. You know, for the tools.
They're missing."

"Teenagers?" She glanced across the street, involuntarily. "You're not accusing *my* teenagers, are you? Because
they wouldn't do that."

Cora hastened to reassure her. "Of course not. I'm sure
your kids are wonderful. How many do you have?"

Donna said she had two, both boys. Johnny was four-
teen and Matthew sixteen. "But they're not murderers. And
they wouldn't steal anything. When did you say he was
killed?"

We looked at each other. "I have no idea, really," I said.
"I know that Nina said she came back from dinner around
ten thirty. If Tony came straight here from the Waterfield
Inn, I guess it couldn't have been too long after that."

"But you don't know that he came straight here," Derek
pointed out. "He could have gone somewhere else first."

I nodded. Like Melissa's loft to share that bottle of wine with her. Although if he'd been drinking wine with his fiancée, in her apartment, why hadn't he just spent the night there? Why come here at all?

"You didn't happen to look out the window last night and see anything, did you, Donna? Like when Tony's car arrived?"

But Donna shook her head. She was a tall, angular woman with short, brown hair, and it flapped around her ears when she moved her head. "We stayed in the backyard last night. On the deck. The weather was nice, and the boys each had a couple of friends over, so there were eight or ten of us altogether."

"Any chance anyone else might have seen anything? When did the kids who were visiting go home?"

It had been after eleven, Donna admitted. With the sun still in the sky well into the evening, and the weather nice and warm, and no school in the morning so everyone could sleep in, there hadn't seemed any rush in getting the other kids home. "They left together. Everyone lives within a couple of blocks, anyway. Matthew walked with them. His girlfriend was there, and he wanted to make sure she got home all right. Waterfield's a safe town, but then once in a while something like this happens." She shook her head.

"The police will probably want to talk to your family," I said. "Especially Matthew, if he was out here on the street late."

Donna looked a little alarmed, and I added, quickly, "Just in case he might have noticed someone. Or something. Or at least whether Tony's car was here. You never know what might be helpful."

"Right," Donna said, but she still looked a little apprehensive when she excused herself to hustle back across the street.

By tacit understanding, we all waited to speak until she was back inside her own garden gate. Then Derek opened his mouth. "So there really was a group of teenagers wandering around last night."

"Fourteen- to sixteen-year-olds. I don't think that's what Wayne had in mind, do you? Would they even know what a pawnshop is? Or realize that tools can be worth money?"

"They're not stupid," Derek said. "And these are small-town kids. Not like the ones you grew up with down there in Noo Yawk." He pronounced the two syllables in the most obnoxious drawl he could manage. "They'll know that tools are worth money. Kids from around here are used to tools."

"Fine. Although Donna seems like a nice lady. I doubt she'd have brought up hoodlums. And if they're the kind of kids who hang out in their parents' backyard on a summer night, they can't be that bad. They or their friends."

Derek shrugged. "We'll find out. I'm gonna call Wayne, let him know." He wiped his hand against his jeans before digging in his pocket for his phone. Cora straightened and arched her back.

"I think I'm about done in for the day. What about you, Bea?"

"I could leave," Beatrice said, rotating her head to work out the kinks. She's as tall and rail-thin as her mother is short and plump, but they have the same soft, brown hair—Cora's is short, Beatrice's long and straight—and the same blue eyes. "I'll drive you home."

"I'd appreciate that." Cora turned to me. "You and Derek are welcome to come over for supper later, Avery. I'm sure you'll want to clean up first. And it'll be basic; I won't have much time to put anything fancy together."

"That's all right," I answered. "We'd be happy . . . No?"

Derek shook his head, still on the phone with Wayne. I turned back to Cora, apologetically. "Guess not. Something must be going on."

"Some other time," Cora said easily. "You know you're always welcome. C'mon, Beatrice."

The two of them headed toward the gate and the car parked beyond. I waited for Derek to get off the phone. "What's up?"

"Wayne's gonna look into Donna's kids. He wants us to have dinner at Guido's Pizzeria."

I blinked. "Is he meeting us there?"

Derek shook his head. "Josh is taking Fae Cameron there. And now Adam has asked Shannon to go, too. Wayne wants someone there to keep an eye on things."

He must not trust Adam. Or maybe he was afraid Adam and Josh would come to blows over one of the girls. I shook my head, smiling. "I should have known Shannon would figure out a way to get there."

"She might not care," Derek said.

"You didn't see her this morning. She looked upset. I guess she finally realized that Josh isn't gonna wait for her forever. Might be just what she needs to get her act together."

"But if he's interested in Fae . . ."

"Fae lives in California. She'll be leaving in a few days. Even if he's interested now, it'll end soon enough." And then he'd go back to pining for Shannon. Maybe.

"I guess we'll see tonight," Derek said.

I nodded. Guess we would.

—10—

Guido's is located in a little cinderblock building on the outskirts of town, down near Barnham College. During the school year, it's always filled to the rafters with college students. In the summer, things are a little less crazy. Waterfield, like all of down east Maine, gets its fair share of tourists, not to mention summer people: the snowbirds who winter in Florida and come back north for the mild season. But Guido's is off the beaten track, and unless you know it's there, you might be excused for thinking it's a strip joint because of a neon sign in the window that blinks "HOT-HOT-HOT."

It isn't. It's a pizza parlor, and it's become something of a favorite haunt of Derek's and mine. The food is good, but more than that, we always seem to learn something interesting when we stop by. I hoped tonight would be no exception.

Things were considerably calmer today than the last time I'd been here. Then, we'd had to use our elbows to get across the floor, and Barnham students had all but swung from the rafters like chimpanzees. Tonight was still busy, but the audio level was manageable, and we had no problem finding an empty booth. Like always, the tabletop was covered by a checkered plastic cloth and sported a candle in an empty Chianti bottle. The waitress was also an old acquaintance: Candy, a gum-chewing blonde with a ponytail and a pink cropped shirt, which completely failed to meet the top of her low-riding jeans. As usual, she all but ignored me, preferring instead to address herself exclusively to Derek. Starting with a melting smile. "Hi, again!"

Derek smiled back. "Hi, Candy. A beer and a Diet Coke, OK?"

"Sure thing, handsome." Candy swung on her heel and sashayed away, posterior swinging. Derek turned to me and grinned when he saw my sour expression.

"Don't say it, Tink"

"What's to say? You're irresistible."

"Glad to hear it." He reached across the table and took my hand, linking our fingers together. For a second, I allowed myself to fall into those blue, blue eyes, and then he opened his mouth again. "So what kind of pizza do you want?"

"Such a romantic," I said, but I didn't take my hand back. His was warm and hard and felt good. "Whatever you want. I'm not picky."

"Something else I like about you." He let go of my hand to lean back on the chair. "So Josh asked Fae out?"

"While Shannon was sitting on the other side of the table. He even asked her if she minded. What could she say but no? I don't think she was happy, though."

"I imagine not," Derek said. "Was he doing it to try to get her riled up, do you think?"

"I wish. But no, I think he did it because he actually likes Fae. Did Shannon agree to go out with Adam to get back at Josh?"

"I'm sure she did," Derek said. "Or because she wanted to keep an eye on them. What other reason would a girl have for going out with someone like Adam?"

"I can't imagine." I grinned.

After a minute, Candy came back and put our drinks on the table. Derek ordered shellfish pizza with shrimp, mussels, crabmeat, and mushrooms, and Candy took herself off a second time while Derek downed half his beer in one gulp.

"Crazy day, huh?" I said sympathetically.

He looked at me across the table. "It's just two days since we toasted to a successful week with no dead bodies. I can't believe Tony's dead."

I had a hard time believing it myself, and not in the way he meant. Why would anyone bother to kill Tony Micelli? He wasn't the most personable guy in the world—a little too slick and self-absorbed for my taste, and way too concerned with ratings—but that's hardly reason enough to kill someone. Is it?

"What are the usual reasons why someone commits murder?" I asked across the table.

Derek contemplated me in silence for a second before he said, "You're not gonna interfere in Wayne's investigation again, are you, Avery?"

"Of course not," I said. "I never interfere. Especially this week, since we have way too much to do. Although we can talk about it, can't we? And if we happen to come up with something interesting—entirely by accident, of course—then we'll have to let Wayne know about it."

"Of course." Derek didn't bother to suppress his amusement. "To answer your question, I think the most common reasons for murder fall into four or five categories. At least they do in books and movies. There's insanity. I don't think we have to worry about that one. If there were any homicidal maniacs wandering around Waterfield, I think we'd have seen signs of it. Beyond Tony, I mean."

"Let's hope so. Greed is another reason, right? Someone benefitting financially."

Derek nodded. "Tony was probably fairly well off. He had a good job, and he owned property. And besides, I doubt Melissa would give him the time of day if he didn't have money."

"But they weren't married, so she won't inherit."

"Not unless Tony wrote a will. I have no idea who'd inherit. He's never been married that I know of. His parents are dead, and I think he was an only child. He's . . . he *was* six or seven years older than me, so we didn't know each other well growing up, and back then—thirty years ago, when I was little and Tony was a teenager—Cabot Street was on the 'bad' side of the Village."

"There was a bad side of Waterfield Village?" Hard to imagine, the way things were today.

Derek nodded. "The 'good' part of the Village was the area north and east of town, where the Victorian houses are. Kate's B and B, your aunt's house, my dad's. But once you got past the church and the cemetery, everything on that side was a little less desirable. Those houses were smaller and built later, and that was where the 'common' people lived. The doctors and lawyers, and the folks from the old families, like your Aunt Inga and Helen Ritter, they all lived on the 'good' side of the Village."

"Weird."

Derek shrugged. "A lot of the change is Melissa's doing, to be honest. She's done more than anyone to make every part of Waterfield a desirable place to live. People from Portland move up here and commute to work because they want to raise their kids in a small town by the ocean. So prices have gone up, and the 'bad' side of the Village has become just as good as the 'good' side."

"Remind me to thank her later," I said, not entirely truthfully, since we were all annoyed with the new developments and the urbanization of our small town, even those of us who were profiting by the out-of-towners. "So someone might have killed Tony for his money, but we don't know who. I'm sure Wayne will be looking into that. What other reasons are there to commit murder?"

"Revenge?" Derek suggested.

"Like, if Tony did something to someone? Accidentally killed them, or bankrupted them, or caused someone's divorce, or got someone thrown in jail?"

"Something like that. He was a reporter; he might have stumbled over some tidbit of information that someone wanted to keep hidden. And then that someone killed him to shut him up. That'd be considered fear, right? Fear of exposure?"

"Sounds like it. But surely there's not that many people in Waterfield with things to hide."

Derek stared at me. "You're not serious, are you? Doesn't everyone have something to hide?"

"Well, sure. But in a small place like this, it's not usually things that are worth murder, is it?"

"I would think that depends," Derek said. "I mean, something that you'd be desperate to hide may not be that big a deal to someone else. Or vice versa."

"True." I cocked my head and looked at him. "What would make you commit murder?"

He looked surprised. "Me personally? I'm not sure anything would. That whole 'do no harm' thing, you know. Although . . . if someone hurt Dad, or Cora, or you . . ."

"Revenge, then. No other reason? You wouldn't kill for money or to stop someone from telling the world that you still eat Frosted Flakes for breakfast, or because they threatened to leave you for someone else?"

He looked vaguely insulted. "Of course not. If money was important to me, I wouldn't have left the medical practice, and why would I care what people think about my breakfast habits? As for someone leaving me for someone else . . . I didn't mind when Melissa left. Although if this is your way of telling me that you've decided to go back to New York and Phil . . ."

I shuddered. Philippe Aubert, aka Phil Albertson, was the boyfriend I'd had before I met Derek. And he was exactly what he sounds like: a fake Frenchman with a little ponytail, tight leather pants, and flowing poet shirts he kept unbuttoned to show off his nicely browned—in a tanning booth—chest. There was no comparison to Derek. None. And also no way in hell I'd ever have anything to do with Philippe again. "Not on your life."

"Good to know. Here's the pizza." He moved his empty beer bottle out of the way so Candy could put the pie on the table. "I'll take another of these, please, when you have a minute."

Candy nodded and dimpled and wiggled off with the bottle, without asking me if I needed a refill.

For a few minutes, everything was quiet while we both ate. It had been a long day, and I've noticed that yard work tends to boost the appetite. After devouring two slices of pizza practically whole, Derek sat back to take a break and look at me.

"So what about you? Any reason you would commit murder?"

I lowered the slice of pizza I'd been nibbling the edge of, and thought about it. "None I can imagine right now. I've never considered killing for money. Wouldn't know who to kill, for one thing, and besides, I can always go out and get a job. No one's ever done anything to me that I felt like I needed to get revenge for. I don't have any deep, dark secrets I'd kill to keep. And although I love you, I wouldn't kill for you, or in order to keep you. The only person I've ever felt like killing, at least recently, is Melissa, and I don't think I was serious."

"You don't, huh?" He grinned. "So is that all of them? The reasons? What's left?"

I shook my head and picked up the pizza again. "No

idea. But someone killed Tony, and there had to be something behind it."

Derek reached for another slice. "Maybe it really was teenagers. Just random. Wrong place at the wrong time."

"I guess we'll find out. Wayne will talk to Donna's kids this evening or tomorrow, I'm sure. If he hasn't already. They'll be able to tell him whether Tony's car was outside the house at eleven thirty."

"True." He glanced toward the door. "There they are."

"Who? Oh, yeah." There they were. Josh and Fae. Just arriving. He was holding the door for her, just as a gentleman should.

She had dressed up for the occasion, left the ubiquitous jeans at home and pulled on what looked like part of a Catholic school-girl uniform, slightly X-rated. The skirt barely covered the essentials, and she'd paired it with fishnet stockings and combat boots, along with a black cropped top that left her stomach bare. A red stone glittered in her navel and matched the bloodred, sparkly Gothic script across her chest: Bite Me. Her lips were equally red, and she'd left her hair down in a long, jet-black tangle, with a floppy, red flower stuck behind one ear. She should have looked a combination of scary and ridiculous, but somehow she made the ensemble work, and even managed to look somewhat cute in spite of it. Josh was clearly smitten; he kept looking down at her and smiling, as if he couldn't quite believe his good luck.

They found a small booth on the opposite wall and settled in. Josh didn't even glance our way, he was so busy looking at Fae. She was busy looking around, and getting stared at in return. The whole Goth-look isn't big in Waterfield, and it was possible that a few of the locals had never seen anyone who looked like this before. Or maybe they were staring just because she was a stranger, and because most of them knew Josh and they were interested to see him with someone who wasn't Shannon or Paige. Candy certainly goggled when she undulated over to take their order, but then Candy was as diametrically opposed to Fae as it's possible to be, with her blond cheerleader ponytail and her faded jeans and petal pink T-shirt.

I grinned.

"What?" Derek asked.

"It's just fun to watch how people react to her. She looks so different from everyone here."

Derek glanced at her and then around the room before looking back at me. "People looked at you that way too last year, you know."

"They did?" I glanced around, too. No one was staring at me now. "Why? I don't look like that."

The Goth-thing has never been for me. I like color too much to go all black. Like the lime green and hot pink and orange tunic I'd slipped into, with a pair of cropped pants, for dinner. My own design, of course, with black piping and a border of black stick people along the hem.

"You look different, though," Derek said. "From most of the locals. At first, they weren't quite sure what to make of you."

Huh. "And now?"

He smiled. "They've gotten used to you. And they've realized you're not gonna break my heart by going back to New York and leaving me."

"No," I said, "I'm not gonna do that." He was stuck with me for however long he was willing to keep me around. It had taken me the best part of a year to get to this place, mentally, but I was committed to Waterfield now. And to Derek. I'd survived the winter, and although I hadn't enjoyed it much, I knew I could survive it again. The time of turning back on my decision had passed.

Over at the other table, Candy had left and Josh and Fae were staring deeply into one another's eyes while they waited for their drinks to arrive. They looked like they were having a good time together, just like when I'd watched them in Kate's kitchen this morning. Josh was talking animatedly, using his hands, and Fae was listening with a smile on her face, clearly hanging on every word. I was happy for Josh; he'd waited patiently for Shannon for long years, and it was nice that he'd finally found someone who appreciated him, even if she was only in Waterfield for a few days. Although the look on Shannon's face earlier . . .

"Speaking of Shannon—"

"We weren't," Derek said.

"I know we weren't. But there she is."

Coming through the front door right now. The door that was held for her by Adam Ramsey, who gave her backside a look that was just as much lecherous as admiring as she moved past him with a smile and a swing in her hips. Ted, who walked in behind her, shot Adam a dirty look, and Wilson, bringing up the rear, went one step further and uttered a few words that I couldn't hear, but which managed to wipe the grin and most of the drool off Adam's chin.

"Bastard," Derek said, scowling.

I smiled. "She'll be fine. Look how many men she's got protecting her. You, Wilson, Ted. If Adam gets too grabby, Josh might even leave Fae sitting there to come to the rescue, too. He and Shannon have been friends for too long for him to let Adam get away with anything."

"She doesn't actually look like she minds," Derek said, his voice and expression somewhere between incredulity and disgust. I turned my head again. The foursome had headed for the big, round booth in the back, the one that is usually occupied by Josh, Shannon, Paige, and Ricky. Shannon had scooted into the far corner—where, incidentally—she could see the entire room without turning around, including the table where Josh and Fae were sitting—and now she was smiling up at Adam, who was sliding in next to her. Derek and me, she hadn't even noticed.

Adam did look particularly glossy tonight, with his bouncy brown curls and dazzling white teeth. He was still wearing the tight jeans and the boots, and a sleeveless work-out shirt, one that exposed his arms all the way up to the shoulders and clung to every gym-rat muscle he had. Candy's eyes threatened to fall right out of her skull when she looked at him, and quite a few of the other young women in the room were staring openly, as well. And this time I don't think it was because the men were strangers in town.

Shannon may not have noticed us, but Wilson did, and gave us a friendly wave across the room. He'd also seen Fae and Josh and had stopped beside their table a moment for what looked like a friendly hello.

Derek chuckled. "Doing her level best to flaunt Adam in Josh's face, isn't she?"

"Shannon? Oh, yes. She didn't just reach into her closet blindly and pull out Josh's favorite shirt."

The top was white crochet with a deep, scalloped V-neck, and she looked stunning. Adam was back to drool-ing, practically dripping into her cleavage. Until Candy traipsed up to the table, anyway, and he was forced to divide his attention, and his questionable charm. Her chest was right at his eye level, and he took full advantage. Shannon took the opportunity to glance at Fae and Josh, and the corners of her mouth turned down.

The whole situation was sort of farcical, and if I hadn't felt so bad for her, I might have thought it was pretty funny. Clearly, though, she was unhappy. Whether because she was losing her best friend, or whether because she'd real-ized she was actually in love with Josh remained to be seen, but either way, I felt bad for her.

Adam finished ogling Candy's assets, and immediately Shannon was all smiles again. I turned to Derek. "This is almost painful to watch."

"We can leave," Derek said.

"Not on your life. At least not yet. And you promised Wayne we'd look out for her."

"Between Wilson and Ted," Derek said, "I think she's amply protected."

Maybe so. "I want to talk to them before we go."

"Them who?"

"Wilson and Ted and Adam. I know where Nina was last night, or where she said she was. Same for Fae. But I have no idea what the men did after they went back to the B and B."

"You think one of them killed Tony? Why would they?"

"I have no idea," I admitted, "but someone did. And it makes sense that it was someone on the crew. Tony was just fine until they got here."

"Unless someone here in Waterfield wanted him dead and thought the crew showing up would throw a few new suspects into the mix."

"That'd only work if there was a connection between Tony and some of the crew, and how could anyone know that Nina and Tony used to be colleagues?" I shrugged. "Either way, I'd like to hear what they have to say for themselves. Besides, it's just polite to stop by and say hello."

"Of course," Derek said, reaching for the check that Candy had left along with the pizza earlier. "I'll take care of this. You head on over there."

He went in his direction and I went in mine.

Adam wasn't above giving me an ogling, too, when I stopped beside the table. Aside from that, everyone else was nice. Shannon greeted me with a dazzling smile. "Hi, Avery. Fancy meeting you here!"

"I know. Quite a coincidence. Must be a full moon or something, if all of us got a craving for pizza on the same night."

Wilson grinned. "Not hardly. We came to keep an eye on Fae. Shannon swore up and down that this kid she's with is safe, but we thought it couldn't hurt to let him know we've got her back."

So that's what he'd been doing when he stopped by their table earlier. Being fatherly.

"Oh, Josh is absolutely safe," I said. "His dad's the chief of police. He's Kate's stepson. And he's a super-nice guy. She couldn't be in better hands."

Shannon's face curdled, and I bit my tongue a sentence too late. "Where's Derek?" she asked, looking around. "You wanna join us?"

I shook my head. "We're actually on our way out. It's been a long day. Since we couldn't get into the house to do any work, we switched the schedule around and worked on landscaping instead. The place looks good. At least on the outside."

"I'll swing by in the morning and shoot a few frames," Wilson said. "Maybe have you mime planting a few flowers for the camera."

I nodded. "Any word from Wayne on whether we'll be able to get back inside tomorrow? I don't know how we'll be able to finish the work if we lose another day."

They all looked at one another. Shannon shook her head. "He didn't say anything to me. Then again, he's been busy talking to other people all day. Mom's hardly seen him at all."

I couldn't ask for a better segue. I slipped into the booth next to Adam and glanced around the table, lowering my voice. "I don't suppose Wayne said anything to you about . . . you know . . . anything? Tony? The case? Whether we'll be able to go back to work tomorrow?"

"You looked like you were friendly with him," Wilson said. "Isn't it more likely that he'd tell you?"

"I've hardly seen him at all today. Since you guys spoke to him, I thought maybe he'd let something slip." I waited.

"Not in my interview," Ted said. "He just asked if I'd ever met Tony before yesterday and whether I'd seen him after we went our separate ways in the afternoon."

He didn't continue, and eventually I had to ask. "And had you?"

"I saw him when he came to pick up Nina for dinner. Not after that."

"I did, too," Adam piped up. "And Nina looked hot last night, too."

All three of the others looked at him. Adam added, quickly, "For someone older, I mean."

It didn't help.

"Nina's forty-two," Wilson said. "That's not exactly at death's door. My wife's in her fifties, and she's still a knock-out. You wanna see a picture?" He fumbled for his wallet while Ted just stared at Adam, his disgust and distaste evident without his having to say a word.

The picture of Wilson's wife showed a stunning Raquel Welch lookalike, with lots of curly, shoulder-length brown hair and mile-long legs and what was either a dark tan or a Mediterranean complexion. "Veronica," Wilson explained with a fond look at the photo. "She's a grandmother four times now and still looks as good as when I met her."

"She's gorgeous." I passed the picture to Adam, who whistled.

"You lucky dog, Will."

"She has children older than you," Wilson said as Adam passed the picture to Shannon.

"Did anyone else see Tony last night?" I looked around the table. "Maybe when he dropped Nina off?"

But they all shook their heads. "Ted and I went out," Wilson said, taking his photograph and tucking it lovingly back into his wallet. "Took the van to Portland. We didn't get back until late."

"We don't get much of a chance to look around when we visit places," Ted added. "I thought it'd be nice to check it out, since we had the night off."

I nodded. "I don't suppose you happened to drive by the house on your way back?"

"The house we're filming?" Wilson shook his head. "Why?"

"Just trying to figure out when Tony got there. There really was a group of teenagers walking around Cabot Street last night, and I thought . . ." I looked up when a hand landed on my shoulder. "All done?"

Derek nodded.

"Wait a second," Adam said. "What about his girl-friend? That hot blonde he was with yesterday? I thought she killed him."

"My ex-wife," Derek said, at the same time as I asked, "Where did you get that idea?"

"I thought the police arrested her," Adam said.

We were all staring at him now, Wilson and Ted, too. "Where'd you hear that?" Wilson wanted to know.

Adam turned to him. After a second, he said, "Can't remember. But I'm pretty sure they did."

"No kidding." Wilson turned to Derek and me. "You know anything about that?"

I glanced at Derek. He shook his head. "We need to go."

"I guess we'd better. Nice to see you. Enjoy your pizza." I had to toss the last sentence over my shoulder as Derek dragged me out of the restaurant. He wouldn't even let me stop at Fae and Josh's table; I had to content myself with waving to them on the way past.

11

"Where are we going?" I asked when we were in the truck driving hell for leather back toward town, taking corners on two wheels. Derek shot me a look before turning his attention back to the road, and the look pretty much said it all.

"Well, I'm sorry," I added defensively, "but what are you planning to do? Storm into Wayne's house and yank him out of bed to tell him your ex-wife couldn't have murdered anyone?"

"It's only nine thirty," Derek answered, concentrating on the road, "so I doubt he's in bed. He may not even be home. He has a murder to solve, and you know what they say: The first twenty-four hours are crucial."

"I thought that was kidnappings," I said.

"Whatever."

He floored the gas pedal and the truck shot up the hill alongside the Stenhams' construction site, Devon Highlands, that had been lying barren since my cousins went off to jail six months ago. I'd once driven off the road right here, after someone had tampered with the brake lines on Derek's truck.

"And if he is," I said now, meaning Wayne, "I suppose you'll wake him?"

Derek glanced over at me again, a flash of blue eyes. "Do *you* think Melissa killed Tony?"

I hesitated. "Not really, I guess. Although I'm not as convinced of her innocence as you seem to be."

"She didn't. Trust me."

"But how can you know that? Unless you . . ." I stopped. Dead, if you'll pardon the pun, as a horrible suspicion stole over me.

Derek didn't look at me to see what was wrong. Instead he kept staring fixedly at the road, a flush creeping into his cheeks.

And granted, at fifty-five miles per hour, it was just as well that he was watching where we were going . . . but my intuition still told me that something was going on.

"Derek?" I said.

He glanced at me. And I have to admit it, he looked sheepish, maybe even a little guilty.

"What do you know that I don't?"

He took a breath. And let it out in a rush. "I spent part of the night at Melissa's last night."

I blinked. I'd heard the words, but they didn't make sense to me. "What?"

He squirmed. "Remember that bottle of wine and two glasses? Well, when I got home from your place last night, Melissa was still awake. And outside. In the parking lot."

"Your parking lot? Or her own?" If she'd been in her own, behind her building, he wouldn't have had occasion to see her. Unless he'd gone looking.

"Mine," Derek said. "The parking lot behind the hardware store. She was upset about Tony and Nina, and she asked me if I'd come up for a minute."

The numb feeling his words had caused started to fade,

and I was getting hot. And bothered. And not in a good way. My skin prickled and I had to fight to keep my voice steady. "And it didn't occur to you to say no?"

"She said she wanted to talk."

That didn't really answer my question, but now I had another. "Well, of course she wanted to talk. What else did you think she wanted?"

"Nothing," Derek said quickly. "Of course not. I didn't think she wanted anything else. She was upset and she wanted someone to talk to, and when she asked if I'd come up for a minute, to talk, I did."

"And?"

Another flash of blue came my way. "And nothing. We talked."

"About what?" hung on my lips, but I held it back. It was my turn to take a deep breath and try to settle my nerves before I started yelling and crying and accusing. After a minute, I managed an under-the-circumstances very restrained, "Do I need to worry?"

"What?" He looked over at me. "No! Hell, no!"

"You sure?"

"Yes, of course I'm sure! Avery . . . !"

But then he shook his head and turned his attention back to the road. And instead of continuing in the direction we were going, toward Kate's B&B and the carriage house, he turned the other way, up the hill toward Bayberry Lane and Aunt Inga's house. Once there, he squealed to a stop behind my car, close enough to the bumper that, for a second, I worried he might slam right into my beloved VW Beetle and reduce it to scraps of metal. He got out of the truck and closed his door with a slam. I opened mine, but I didn't have time to do anything but swing my legs out before he was on my side of the car. He grabbed me around the waist and lifted me down, then slammed my door, too, before lifting me again to toss me over his shoulder.

It wasn't the first time he'd done that. It had actually

happened quite a lot over the past year. The first time it had been because I'd twisted my ankle falling down the basement steps in the dark, and I'd been giving him a hard time about carrying me—the usual, proper and respectful way—and instead of putting up with my complaining, he'd tossed me over his shoulder and hauled me into the house like a sack of grain instead. After that, it had become sort of a thing with us. He did it as a joke, playing up the possessive caveman demeanor that some women enjoy and that I usually find endearing.

This time I didn't. There was nothing funny about this, and it was no joke. He was upset and angry, and so was I.

When he put me down on the porch to unlock the front door, I kicked him in the shin. Not hard, not because I really wanted to hurt him, but hard enough to make my point. "Stop it. I can walk."

He looked at me from the corner of his eye, focused on digging the key out of his pocket and inserting it in the lock. "I know you can. I just don't want you to walk the other way."

"Where am I gonna go?" I wanted to know, annoyed. "I live here!"

"Fine. I didn't want you to walk into the house and lock the door behind you." He twisted the key and opened the door.

"That wouldn't have stopped you," I said, pushing past him to get inside. "You have your own key."

"Yeah, but if you slammed the door in my face and told me to get lost, I'm not sure I would have dared use it."

He dropped the key chain back in his pocket and followed me into the house, closing and locking the front door behind us. From the dark on the stairs, two tiny circles of light regarded him unblinkingly. I flicked the light switch, and they translated themselves into Mischa's eyes. A second later, the kitten had launched himself through the air to attack the intruder. For once, I did nothing to try to intercept him. I was tempted to scratch Derek myself, and I appreciated Mischa doing it for me. If I could find a way to let him loose on Melissa, I would.

"Damn cat," Derek growled a second later, hopping on one foot and shaking the other to discourage the kitten, who was digging his claws into Derek's jeans and hanging on for dear life, growling, too. He sounded like an angry emery board.

I giggled. Derek shot me a dark look. "Get him off me, please."

"I don't really want to," I said. "I'm enjoying this."

"You would." He limped over to the stairs and sat down to start the removal himself. In spite of his obvious irritation, his hands were gentle as he unhooked Mischa's claws from the denim. The kitten kept up a yowling accompaniment of protest the whole time, but when Derek set him down on the floor with a final pat, Mischa did not turn around and attack again, he just wandered down the hallway toward the kitchen with his tail sticking straight up in the air. Clearly, he felt he had come out of the skirmish the champion.

My grin faded as Derek looked up at me, his eyes very blue in the brightly lit hallway. "I love you, Avery."

"I know you do," I said.

He shook his head. "I don't think so. If you knew, you wouldn't worry about me spending time with someone else."

Yeah, right. "Melissa's not just anyone. You used to be married to her."

"Used to be. Operative word there. We're not married anymore."

"I know that," I said.

"You sure? Because believe me, that's all the more reason not to want anything to do with her ever again." He shook his head, and that floppy lock of hair fell over his forehead. "We weren't happy together, Tink. Even in the beginning, when I was crazy about her, things were strained. You just put up with it because you don't know any better, and because . . ."

He trailed off. I nodded; I knew exactly what he was talking about. I'd put up with my own share of arguing, friction, and tension over the years, from one boyfriend or another. You do it because you hope things will get better, and because some of the time things are wonderful and you don't want to lose the part-time good stuff. And then you do it because you're afraid that if you let the person you've got get away, you'll never find another to love.

"I spent seven years of my life with Melissa," Derek said, leaning back on his elbows and looking straight ahead, into the past, his eyes unfocused. "Two years dating, and then five years of being married. It was all ups and downs, right from the beginning. I guess I didn't realize how different we were at first. I fell in love with the way she looked, and the way she seemed to like me so much, and it wasn't until later that I realized that she liked me because I was going to end up being a doctor, and I was going to give her the things she wanted. She wasn't born rich, you know."

"Really?" I'd assumed the expensive and elegant creature I knew had come from a long line of expensive and elegant women down there in Maryland or West Virginia. Old family, lots of money.

Derek shook his head. "When I met her, she was waiting tables to put herself through college."

"Melissa!"

"Sure. And it wasn't in a fancy restaurant, either. She was like Candy: ponytail and jeans, serving up coffee and eggs in an IHOP around the corner from the hospital."

"Wow," I said.

He smiled. "We started talking, and then we started dating, and then sleeping together, and by the time she started hinting about marriage, I was too far gone to even realize what a mistake that would be. I knew my mom and dad hadn't taken to her when I brought her up here to meet them, but I figured that was on them, and not because there was anything wrong with Melissa."

"What about her family?" I'd gotten interested in the conversation in spite of myself. And in spite of the fact that I was still upset with him, and with her. "Did you meet them? Before you got married?"

"Just once. She'd made sure she went to school hours away from them. They lived in a dingy tenement-type apartment in a coal mining town in West Virginia. And they were nice enough, but I felt a little like a show dog on display. I assumed they were just looking out for their daughter and were protective of her in case she'd hooked up with a jerk, but later . . ." He shook his head. "After I realized that Melissa wanted me because she wanted to be a doctor's wife, I guessed that they were really trying to figure out how much I'd be worth in a few years."

"That's crappy."

"To be fair to Melissa, she didn't have much contact with them. After we got married, they kept asking for handouts, and although she would help them with things like keeping the power and water on and medical bills and such, she didn't go overboard. At least not with my money. I don't know about Ray's."

I folded my arms across my chest and leaned my shoulder against the newel post. "Why are you telling me this?"

His eyes were the blue of cornflowers in the bright light from above. "Because I want you to understand why you don't have to worry about Melissa. When she packed up and moved out, it was like I could finally breathe again. I didn't have to justify why I didn't want to stay in medicine, or explain that I just wanted to do something that made me happy. All she saw was that I was ruining her perfect life. She didn't understand that it didn't feel perfect to me, and there wasn't anything I could say to make her understand, and every day was just one fight after the other. When she left, I felt like a weight had been lifted. There's nothing in the world that would make me go back to her."

I blinked. "You sure?"

"Positive. C'mere." He held out his arms. I hesitated for no more than a second before I moved into them. He pulled me down on his lap and buried his face in my hair, his voice muffled. "I love you, Tink. Why would I ever go back to Melissa when I've got you?"

"You loved her?" I suggested, a little distracted by his warm breath against my skin and the way his arms tightened around me.

"Past tense. I don't feel that way about her anymore. Not sure I ever did. Not the way I feel about you." He braced his legs and stood, still holding me. I held on as he turned and started up the stairs. And nothing more was said—at least not about Melissa and her marriage to Derek—for the rest of the night.

．　．　．

Our first move the next morning, after getting showered and dressed, was to head over to the Waterfield Inn. Wayne might be there, but if he wasn't, Kate would probably know whether we could go back to work on the house today. If we couldn't, we had to find something to do to keep the crew occupied if we had any hopes of getting enough footage for an episode of *Flipped Out!* in the can by Friday night. Maybe we could take Adam to the salvage yard while Wilson filmed us picking out a porch swing.

Shannon was sitting at the breakfast table when we got there, nursing a cup of coffee and looking like she'd spent a mostly sleepless night. And then I wondered whether I was imagining things, because she looked up when we came in and managed a very passable smile, as if nothing much was wrong. "Good morning."

"Hi," I said, taking a seat while Derek headed for the coffeepot. "Where's everyone?"

"Mom and Wayne are still at the carriage house, and no one else is down yet. Up, maybe, but not down. You guys are out and about early."

I glanced over at the lighted display on the stove. 6:58. I guess we were. "We went to bed early."

Shannon sent Derek a speculative look. "You left Guido's early, too. I thought I'd find you here when we got back, arguing with Wayne about why he can't keep Melissa in jail."

"Shit," Derek said, and when I turned to look at him, I saw that he had turned pale under the tan. He must have remembered last night and realized that while we'd been busy doing what we'd been doing, Melissa had been languishing in lockup. I wondered if he regretted his priorities.

But no, it didn't look that way. When he met my eyes, his expression was half sheepish, half rueful, with a grin tugging at the corners of his mouth. "Oops."

"That'll teach you not to get distracted." I was unable to hide my own smile. "I guess we should probably go look for Wayne, huh?"

"I'll go. You stay here and keep Shannon company." He headed for the back door.

"What was that all about?" Shannon wanted to know when the door had swung shut behind him.

I turned back to her. And decided that she'd find out anyway, so I might as well tell her. "Derek was with Melissa the night Tony died. I guess he has personal knowledge that she couldn't have done it."

Shannon's eyes widened. She has her father's eyes, big and dark, surrounded by long, thick lashes. Even without makeup, they're stunning. "He was with Melissa? Like . . . *with* her?"

I shook my head. "Of course not *with* her. Just with her. Apparently she wanted to talk."

"And you believe that?"

I blinked. "Of course I do. Why?"

"That's what Josh said he and Fae did," Shannon said darkly.

Ah. So her incredulousness had nothing to do with suspecting that Derek and/or Melissa were lying, but everything to do with being jealous of whatever Josh and Fae had been doing last night. I made sure my voice was sympathetic when I leaned my elbows on the table and settled in to talk. "What happened?"

"After you two left Guido's, you mean?" She shot me a quick look from under those thick lashes and focused her attention on the cloth napkin she was pleating and repleating on the table. "I put up with Adam breathing on me and sat and talked to him and Wilson and Ted for an hour. Those two are all right, but give Adam an inch, and he's all over you."

"I got that impression, too," I admitted, although of course he hadn't come within a foot of me. Derek had made sure Adam knew I was off-limits. Apparently Shannon hadn't been so lucky.

"Usually Josh makes sure nobody bothers me. But he was too busy with Fae to notice. And it was my own stupid fault, anyway. I encouraged him."

"Adam?"

She nodded.

"To make Josh jealous?"

She shrugged.

"He's waited a long time for you to notice him, you know."

"Notice?" Shannon said, her voice just a little shrill. "I'm not stupid, Avery. It's been impossible not to notice, yeah?"

Well, yeah. Josh's feelings had been rather obvious, and I'd often wondered why Shannon didn't say or do anything to acknowledge them.

"I guess you didn't want to mess up your friendship, right? Starting a relationship with your best friend can be awkward. I mean, what if it doesn't work out? You've lost your boyfriend *and* your best buddy."

Shannon nodded. "He's been making eyes at me for years now. And I love him, I really do. I could even see myself being with him. You know . . . *with* him?"

I nodded.

"But what if it doesn't last? I'm twenty. That's kind of young to choose someone to spend the rest of your life with. And when it ends . . ." She shook her head. "He's not gonna wanna stay my best friend after we break up, and I don't know what I'd do without him."

I didn't know what to say to that, so I just nodded and waited for her to continue.

"So maybe we're better off just being friends, you know? And not trying for anything more? At least I'd never lose him totally."

It made sense, as far as it went. And it was obvious she had it all figured out and didn't need any help from me.

She continued, "I just thought, if I never said anything, then after a while, he'd stop feeling the way he did, and we'd be just friends again. But then *she* showed up!"

"Fae."

Shannon nodded. "I guess I just never considered that if *I* didn't want him—you know, that way—then sooner or later he'd find someone who did. I guess I just thought that we'd keep going the way things were."

"With both of you single and best friends."

Shannon looked miserable. "The thing is, I liked her. We spent a couple of hours together the other night, watching movies, and she's nice. If I wanted Josh to be with anybody, I'd want him to be with someone like that. Someone who makes him happy. And someone I like."

"But you don't want him to be with anyone?"

She looked miserable. "I don't think I do. I think I want him to be with me. But he's happy. And I can't ruin that."

"No," I said, "I really don't think you can. But she's only here for a few more days. Surely they can't get too serious in that time."

What kind of attachment could they form in just five days, after all?

"You don't know Josh," Shannon said, not entirely accurately. I did know Josh, although obviously not as well as she did. "He makes his mind up quickly. The first time I met him, the first day of eighth grade, just after Mom and I had moved here from Boston, he took one look at me and decided we were going to be best friends, and that was it. There was nothing I could say or do about it."

"So if he's chosen to fall in love with Fae, then it's already a done deal? He's not stupid, Shannon. He knows she's leaving on Saturday. And that she lives on the other side of the country."

"You don't know him," Shannon said again, her voice wobbly.

I abandoned the argument. Apparently Josh wasn't the only one who, when he made up his mind, was unmovable. "So what happened last night? Anything?"

Shannon shrugged. "After you left, we all sat and ate pizza. Then they left, so we left, too. I thought Fae would be back here, but he must have taken her somewhere, because she didn't come home until late."

"And . . . ?"

"I didn't want to ask her." She hesitated a second, and then she added, her voice low, "Guess I was afraid of what she'd say."

I could understand that. "You said Josh said they'd been talking. . . ."

"I called him. He'd just dropped her off, so I knew he was still up." She looked up at me, her eyes miserable. "He didn't even come in. He always comes in, and he just dropped her off and went home!"

"Probably afraid of facing you," I said.

"Yeah, well, he didn't have to be! I was nice on the phone. I pretended I didn't care and that I just wanted to make sure he'd had a good time. He said he'd taken her up the coast and shown her the view of the islands and they'd *talked*."

"They probably did," I said.

"Well, of course they did! But what else did they do?"

"In Josh's Honda? Probably not much. It's tiny. And

he's, like, six-five. And it was a first date. He wouldn't seduce a girl on a first date, would he?"

"Of course he wouldn't," Shannon said, offended.

"Then I don't think you have anything to worry about. But you could ask Fae if you're worried. I think I hear her coming."

The murmur of voices out in the dining room had gotten louder, and a moment later, the swinging butler door opened, and Fae stepped through. Backward, facing the camera, which Wilson kept pointed at her face.

". . . and here we are," she said, in her best plummy television voice, gesturing with her hand, "back in Kate's kitchen at the Waterfield Inn to see whether we will in fact be going back to work today after the terrible events of yesterday."

They both passed through the door and into the kitchen, followed by Adam and Ted. Ted was his usual impassive self, but Adam was grinning as he watched Fae. There was a flash of unease in his eyes, though. Maybe he was worried that Nina would think Fae was doing such a good job that she'd replace Adam with her.

I didn't think he had anything to worry about. Fae, though glib in front of the camera, didn't look like the host of a DIY television show. A little too unrelatable to Middle America, maybe, with her pigtails and Goth-girl makeup and clothes. Not like the injured Stuart, with his sandy hair and freckles and corn-fed grin, or even Adam, with his glossy good looks and solid all-American charm. But Fae was clearly having fun, and so was Wilson, grinning as he aimed the camera at her.

"Here's our hostess with the mostest, Shannon McGillicutty, and half our renovating team, Avery Baker, sharing a cup of coffee." She nailed both names, unlike Adam. "Tell us, Avery, do you have any news about today?"

I had no idea whether the camera was in fact rolling or not, or whether they were just having some fun, but I smiled and talked to it anyway. "So far, no word. Derek's out in the carriage house talking to the chief of police. Once he gets back, I guess we'll find out."

"And that's a wrap," Wilson said, lowering the camera. "Good work, ladies. You better watch out, Adam, or she'll take your job." He grinned. Fae did, too. Adam smiled, but I thought it looked forced.

"You were actually filming?" I said.

Wilson turned to me after putting the camera down on the counter next to the eight-slot toaster. "Well, sure. It started out as just fun, but we use so much tape anyway, and film so much footage we never end up using, that when something's going on, I usually just keep things rolling. You never know what you might end up with and how it can be used."

"How long have you been doing this job?"

He passed a hand over his thinning hair. "I've been with *Flipped Out!* since the beginning. Four years now. But I've been a cameraman for over thirty years. Started out back in the days of black and white." He winked.

"Really?" Adam said.

Wilson shook his head. "No, not really. Black and white was a whole lot longer ago than thirty years. NBC made the first coast-to-coast color broadcast in 1954, with the Tournament of Roses parade."

Ted nodded. "By 1972, more than half the households in the country had a color TV set, and that was the year when 'in color' notices before programs ended."

"Wow." I looked from one to the other of them. "You two know a lot about this."

Ted shrugged. "You know your business, we know ours."

"So how long have you been working in television?"

Ted opened his mouth to answer, but before he could, the back door opened and hit the wall with a thud.

"I don't care what you think of it!" Wayne growled, striding in. "I've got her where I want her, and that's where she's gonna stay until I say otherwise!"

12

I cut my eyes to Derek, following on Wayne's heels. He looked unhappy. Obviously the "she" they were talking about was Melissa, who was still in jail and would stay there until Wayne was good and ready to let her out.

"You tried," I told Derek when he came to stand behind me.

He snorted, resting both hands on my shoulders. "You think that's gonna carry any weight when Melissa asks me why I let her spend the night in jail?"

"You're not married to her anymore," I reminded him, twisting my neck to look up into his face.

"I know that, Tink. But she's still gonna wanna know why I didn't just convince Wayne she didn't do it."

"It's not up to you to convince Wayne of anything. And anyway, you tried."

"Obviously not hard enough," Derek said, with a scowl at the chief of police. Wayne sent him a flat glare back.

"Watch it, or I'll run you in, too, for interference."

"You wouldn't dare," Derek said.

Personally, I didn't think so, either. But only because he had no reason to. Nobody in their right mind would think Derek had had anything to do with Tony's death, and dragging him to lockup would be a supremely stupid move. Wayne wasn't stupid. He proved it when he said, "You can have your house back. That should keep you out of my hair for today."

He had that right.

"C'mon." Derek took his hands off my shoulders and pulled the chair out with me on it. The legs scraped across the tiled floor.

"Just give me an hour to clean the kitchen and change the beds," Kate said, "and I'll be over."

"I'll call Josh," Shannon added, and then she looked at Fae. "Unless you want to?"

Fae shrugged. She was back into her jeans today, with a black shirt and matching nail polish. "You can if you want. I don't mind."

"Big of you," Shannon muttered, but under her breath. I don't think Fae heard, or if she did, she didn't comment.

I sent Wilson a look on my way past. "You guys will be coming, too, right?"

He nodded. "Just give us a few minutes to drag Nina out of her room, and we'll be there."

"See you." The back door closed behind me, and then Derek was hustling me toward the truck almost as fast as I could walk. I could tell he had momentarily forgotten about Melissa and her plight in the excitement of getting back to work, and I was determined not to remind him.

Pretty soon Tony's murder and Melissa's arrest were pushed into the back of my own mind, too, by more immediate concerns. I called Cora from the car, and she said she'd round up Beatrice and meet us over at the house. Derek got busy leveling and laying tile in the bathroom, and I cracked open the yellow paint cans and started painting the kitchen cabinets. Brandon, bless him, had dispatched someone to clean Tony's blood off the floor (and the fingerprint powder off all the surfaces), so not even that reminder was there. When Bea and Cora arrived, Derek put them to work in the bedrooms, cutting in along the ceiling and around the doors and windows.

Josh showed up a few minutes later, his eyelids at half-mast behind the glasses and a cardboard cup of steaming coffee in his hand. Derek popped his head out of the bathroom to look him over. "You have three minutes to finish that. Then I want you rolling paint in the bedrooms."

Josh arched his brows. "You know, you're not paying me for this. I'm doing it out of the goodness of my heart. So there's no need to boss me around."

Derek just shook his head and went back to tiling.

"Your new girlfriend is coming," I said.

Josh turned to me. "When?"

"Whenever they get their stuff together. With five of them, I guess it can take a little while. Nina still wasn't downstairs when we left the bed and breakfast."

Josh tilted his head. "You don't think anything's happened to her, do you?"

I blinked. "Why?"

He shrugged. "Oh, no reason. Murders usually come in twos, don't they? Or more? Someone dies, and then someone else dies."

"Cause and effect." Now that I thought back over my adventures over the past year, the first body had all too frequently been followed by another.

"And she did know Tony from before," Josh reminded me. "So she might be next in line."

"God." I pulled out my phone and called Kate. As soon as I heard her voice, I blurted out, "Is Nina dead?"

"I'm sorry," Kate said, "Avery? I don't think I heard you right. Did you just ask, 'Is Nina there?'"

"No, I asked if Nina was dead. D. E. A. D. Dead."

Kate sounded confused, which probably meant I didn't have to worry. "Why would you think she'd be dead?"

"Josh suggested it. I said I hadn't seen her this morning, and he said maybe she's dead. That murders usually come in twos."

"God," Kate said. "No, Nina's fine. She came downstairs a few minutes after you and Derek left. Said she hadn't slept well after what happened yesterday."

"Great. Thanks. You coming?"

She promised me she'd be there as soon as she had finished the chores, and I hung up and turned to Josh. "Nina's fine."

"I gathered." He lifted the coffee to his mouth and took a swallow.

"You freaked me out there for a minute."

He grinned. "I gathered that, too."

"So how did you know that she knew Tony? You weren't here when they met on Monday."

"Fae told me," Josh said.

"Really? You talked about that?"

"You're kidding, right? Everyone's talking about it."

"I just thought the two of you would be busy talking about yourselves. You know, getting to know each other. First date and all that."

"We did some of that, too," Josh said.

I thought for a second. "Nice girl?"

"She seems to be. You wouldn't think it to look at her, but she's actually kinda innocent, even a little bit naive. Grew up with her grandparents, and they kept her pretty sheltered." He took another sip of coffee.

After a second, he added, "I think she's a little hung up on that guy who used to host the show. Stuart?"

I nodded. "They were telling me about him. He had some kind of freak accident and ended up in the hospital."

"That's what she said. Apparently he was lucky it wasn't worse. Although she said he probably won't be back to the show again. I guess they're stuck with Adam."

"Or not," I said. When Josh looked surprised, I added, "You haven't seen him, but he's awful. Can't remember details to save his life. He kept calling Waterfield Waterford, and he called Derek Erik and me Ivory. . . . It must have taken an hour to film a two-minute segment of introductions on Monday."

"No kidding?" Josh grinned. "So he's stupid?"

"I don't know that I'd go that far, but he doesn't seem especially bright. Then again, drop-dead gorgeous looks and a brilliant mind very rarely go together." Most fabulously good-looking people tend to be terribly self-absorbed, which kills a lot of the charm.

"Shannon is gorgeous and smart," Josh said.

I glanced at him, but he didn't seem to have realized what he'd said. Maybe it was just reflex. "That's true. So what else did you and Fae talk about last night? Did she say anything else about Nina and Tony?"

"I don't think she knows anything else about Nina and Tony," Josh said, tossing back the dregs of his coffee and looking around for a place to put the empty cup. Since the counter was gone, preparatory to putting in a new one, he held on to it. "Just that they worked together a lifetime ago. Mostly we talked about computers."

"Fae knows about computers?"

He stared at me. "That's her major. She's just taking time off from college to do this gig during the summer."

"And she just happened to snag a summer job working in television? That's nice work if you can get it."

"No," Josh said, "I don't think it just happened. The camera guy is her uncle or something. Apparently, he set it up."

"Really?" They hadn't mentioned that. Of course, there was no reason why they would have. It was none of my business. But it explained Wilson's interest in her well-being, and the way he had stopped by their table at Guido's last night. Checking up on his niece and the guy she was having dinner with . . .

"It's been three minutes." Derek's voice floated to us from out of the bathroom. "You done with that coffee yet?"

Josh looked like he might want to say something, but he chose not to.

"Yes, Derek," I called back. "He's coming."

I turned to Josh. "You can have your pick: Cora is in one bedroom and Beatrice in the other. You're gonna have to paint both, so you can choose whether you feel like starting with blue or green."

Josh looked at me like I'd lost my mind. "Does it matter?"

"Not at all. Like I said, you'll end up painting both anyway. Have fun." I went back to my kitchen cabinets and my own yellow paint.

Silence descended again, only broken by the swish of paint brushes and rollers. All four of the others were on the other side of the house, where the two bedrooms flanked the one bath, while I was on my own over on this side. I could hear them chattering and caught an occasional snatch of conversation, but I was too far away to participate without yelling. Instead I enjoyed the sharp smell of fresh paint and the morning sun coming through the kitchen window while I concentrated on making smooth strokes across the wood.

Painting is the kind of mindless activity that makes it easy to think. And I had a few things to think about.

OK, so there was Derek and Melissa. Together, sharing a glass of wine. Late at night, after he'd left my house.

But I didn't want to think about that. And besides, I trusted him. So I forced myself to consider Tony instead, and the future instead of the past.

Josh had a point: Murders sometimes did come in twos. Maybe the murderer kills again, usually to silence someone who knows he—or she—killed the first time, and sometimes the second victim is the murderer of the first, and someone else has decided to take revenge. Sometimes the first death isn't even a murder, just some kind of accident that someone wants to hush up. If that happened here, who would the next target be?

OK, so here was Tony, right? Local boy done good. He'd probably moved around a bit in his younger days, but he was back here now and had been working for Portland's channel eight for a few years. Long enough to become one of their go-to guys. Long enough to get his face, many times life size, on the side of the station news van.

And then he'd died. Here in his childhood home. The same night he came face-to-face with Nina, who had known him twenty years ago. Nina, who hadn't seemed thrilled to see him at first, but who had come around and agreed to go to dinner with him.

Had someone used the crew as a distraction, knowing that the logical thing for Wayne to do was focus on the newcomers? Or had someone on the crew actually killed Tony? And if so, who?

The only person I could imagine might have had a reason would be Nina herself. The others hadn't mentioned meeting him before. Wilson was happily married, so it wasn't like he would have killed Tony to uphold Nina's honor. If it had been Fae, maybe. But Tony hadn't had anything to do with Fae. She'd been with Shannon when Nina and Tony went to dinner. And Ted . . .

Maybe Ted had a silent crush on Nina. And maybe he thought Nina and Tony were about to get together, and so he'd decided to do away with Tony. Although he and Wilson had been together in Portland, hadn't they?

And then there was Melissa. She was Tony's fiancée. If she hadn't killed him—and Derek seemed convinced she hadn't—was it possible that she was the next target? She knew him better than anyone. If something was going on—if Tony had dug up dirt on someone, for instance—Melissa was the most likely person to know who and what. They'd been together awhile, and dirt was something that Melissa might also enjoy. I wouldn't go so far as to accuse her of blackmail, nor Tony, for that matter, but she was the type of person who liked to know things about people.

Maybe Wayne had done her a favor by putting her in jail. If she knew something about Tony's killer, and that person was out to get her, jail might be the safest place for her.

That's as far as I got in my musings, and then the crew arrived at the house and took my mind off things. Nina did look rather the worse for wear, I noticed; she'd told Kate she hadn't slept well, and it was obvious in her heavy eyes and pallor. For the first time since I'd met her, she truly looked her age. She was even a tiny bit disheveled: There were a few hairs out of place on her head, and she hadn't matched her jewelry. The gold hoops in her ears didn't go with the silver necklace.

She managed a smile when she saw me. "Hello, Avery. Everything OK?"

I smiled back. "Fine. We're scrambling to catch up. Derek's retiling the bathroom floor. His stepmother and her daughter are painting the bedrooms, and Josh is helping them. Or vice versa. And I'm here." I gestured with the paintbrush to the half-finished cabinets. "When Kate and Shannon get here, I'll have them get started on the cabinet doors."

"I'll send Wilson in here to get some footage," Nina said, but she didn't move, just looked around. This was where we'd been standing two days ago when Melissa and Tony showed up, and I thought maybe she was remembering. Either that or picturing Tony's body on the floor. From imagination or, if she'd killed him, from memory.

"I'm sorry for your loss," I said again. "Were you and Tony close? Back when?"

She forced a smile. "At one time. We worked together and dated for a while. Then things happened, and we went our separate ways. I hadn't seen him in over twenty years."

"That's a long time."

"At first I was shocked to see him, and then upset, because it brought up memories, both good and bad. But it's been so long, and we're different people now. . . . We had a good time at dinner the other night."

"That's nice." I kept painting. Nina kept standing. Since she didn't seem ready to leave, I added, "You can remember that, at least. That you saw him again and things were good."

She shrugged.

"I don't suppose he said anything at dinner? About anyone who might be out to get him? Maybe he'd been working to break some story . . . ?"

Nina shook her head. "We talked mostly about the old days and tried to catch up on everything that had happened to us both since. We had plenty to talk about."

"I know it's personal, but . . . did you talk about getting back together?"

Nina stared at me like I was crazy.

"The police arrested his girlfriend," I explained. "I thought if Tony was planning to throw her over . . ."

Nina smiled. "This was the gorgeous blonde he was with the other day? Your real estate agent? He wouldn't be that stupid. They'd just gotten engaged, or so he said at dinner. Why would he be planning to throw her over? And how would she know if he did? We ate, and then he dropped me off and came here. Unless he stopped at her house on the way, she'd have no way of knowing."

"He might have done that. I just can't figure out why she'd kill him, you know? I've known her for more than a year. Derek's known her for twelve or thirteen. They used to be married, did you know? And he says she couldn't have done it."

Nina nodded, but it didn't look like she really cared. "I'm sure your sheriff will figure it out. He seems capable."

"He is." Even if he wasn't a sheriff. "And I'm sure he will. We haven't had a murder yet that he hasn't been able to solve. I just hope he does it before someone else dies."

Nina blinked. "Why would someone else die?"

"Haven't you noticed how often there's a second victim after the first one?"

"I'm afraid I haven't had much experience with murder," Nina said and turned toward the dining room. "I'll go get Will and the others, and we can get started."

I nodded, wondering if I should tell her to be careful, that she might be the next victim in line, or whether that would just freak her out unnecessarily.

Things got under way after that, with Ted juggling lights and wires and Wilson juggling his camera. Adam was called upon to ask questions and make comments, and he managed to make it through most of the morning without messing up too badly. He certainly did look good, with those glossy brown curls and that tight, open-at-the-neck golf shirt. He'd gone from calling me Ivory to Ivy, and I think I heard him call my boyfriend Tarek once, which was pretty laughable, but other than that, he did all right.

Nina hovered, correcting him with increasingly strained patience when she had to, and I could tell it bothered him. It made me wonder why he didn't just restructure his patter to avoid the words that tripped him up. Like our names. I mean, there wasn't really any reason to start every sentence he spoke to me with, "So, Ivy . . ."

Maybe Josh was right and Adam really was stupid.

Speaking of Josh, he was hanging out in the bedrooms painting and joking with Fae. I could hear her laughter, and Cora and Beatrice's, too. They sounded like they were having a good time in there. After finishing with me, Wilson and Adam and Nina headed in that direction as well, and I tagged along to watch a little bit of the filming.

The bathroom was starting to look good. Derek was on his knees on the floor, and Wilson took the time to stop and film the process for a minute as Derek slapped mortar down on the subfloor, positioned his spacers, and slid another tile into place. And added more thin-set mortar, more spacers, and another tile. Tile laying is time-consuming and tedious and boring to watch, so I contented myself with watching Derek, since my boyfriend's posterior in tight jeans is worth a look, and so are the muscles in his arms under the short sleeves of the blue T-shirt.

Wilson had moved into the bedroom, where Cora was up on a ladder, using a brush to cut in around the ceiling while Josh was applying pale blue paint to the wall with a long-handled roller. There were muscles in his arms, too, that he hadn't gotten from working at a computer. And he looked boyishly charming with his rumpled curls and round glasses and a smear of paint across one cheek. Fae obviously thought so: She was standing in the middle of the room, out of the camera's frame, listening to his banter with a smile on her face.

That was the scene when Kate and Shannon walked in. Shannon took one look at Josh, and at Fae, before she turned and walked back out. Kate looked after her, looked around, and looked at me. I shrugged.

"I'll go after her," Kate said. "In a second." She turned to Nina. "This came for you just as I was leaving the bed and breakfast. I thought it might be important."

She handed over an envelope. As far as I could tell, it looked just like the one that had arrived the day before, and the one they'd told me had arrived the day before that. Small, square, and ecru. There was no reason at all for Nina to turn pale under the carefully applied makeup, but the blusher on her cheeks suddenly stood out vividly.

"Everything OK?" Fae asked, her eyes bright.

Nina looked at her for a second, blankly, before she forced a smile. "Of course. Just a note from an old friend." She slipped the envelope into her Kate Spade bag and pasted a bright, interested look on her face. "Now, where were we?"

—13—

The crew continued working while Kate excused herself to go look for Shannon. Fae had walked over to Nina, and the two of them were standing by the wall in low-voiced conversation, with Fae taking notes on her clipboard. Adam was rehearsing. "Here we are with Laura Ellis . . ." while Wilson had the camera pointed at Fae and Nina. I was just about to disappear, too, when I noticed Josh.

He was looking past me out the door, and the look on his face was perplexed, maybe even a little worried.

"She'll be all right," I said.

"Yeah?"

"Sure. Just give it a few days." Like—say—Sunday. After Fae had left Waterfield.

"OK." Josh went back to painting the wall, but not without another look through the door and into the hallway.

As I went back to the kitchen, I could hear their voices from the small laundry room in the back: Shannon's a little teary, Kate's calm and comforting.

I left them alone and got back to my painting. After a few minutes, they came out, and I asked if everything was all right.

"Sure," Shannon said. Kate shrugged. So I gave them their assignments: Take the cabinet doors and get going on those while I finished painting the cabinet boxes.

"Where should we go?" Shannon asked. Her hair looked like she'd been yanking at it, but she was composed and seemed rather determined to remain so.

"I laid some sheets of plastic on the dining room floor."

"Isn't someone going to paint the dining room? We're painting the whole inside of the house today, right?"

"I hadn't thought about that," I said. "You know, you're right. Maybe it would be better for you to go outside. After the bedrooms, Derek will probably tell Josh to get going on the dining room, and it would be just as well if you weren't there."

Shannon nodded.

She stacked four or five cabinet doors on top of one another and headed out, while Kate gathered the plastic from the dining room and brought it outside, as well. After picking up the rest of the kitchen cabinet doors and carting them into the front yard, they got to work.

The next few hours were quiet. Adam made it through the brief conversation with Cora, once he got it through his head that her name wasn't Laura, and then he and the rest of the team moved into the front yard, where they spent some time filming Kate and Shannon and the new landscaping.

Josh took a break for that, and so did I. I hung out on the porch, watching from a distance. Josh went out on the lawn, but he didn't join Fae, who was hanging out next to Wilson. Instead, he waited for Wilson to finish filming Shannon before he wandered over to her. I don't know what he said, or what she answered, but I saw her nod and saw him put his hand on her shoulder for a second before he headed back into the house. Shannon watched him go, and then she shot a guilty look at Fae, who didn't seem to have noticed. Shannon went back to painting.

The sound of footsteps caught my attention, and I looked out to the street and saw the mailman come up the sidewalk. He stopped at the mailbox, and I thought I might as well grab what mail had arrived, since Tony wouldn't be around to do it.

The mailbox held the usual, which I sifted through on my way back to the house. A couple of circulars, one from the hardware store below Derek's loft and one a coupon flyer from a local pizza parlor. Not Guido's, one of the chains. A couple of bills: one from the electric company—the name on it was Julia Green, not Tony Micelli, so the former tenant had probably skipped out on the final bill—and one for property taxes. A request for money from the March of Dimes. And a small, square, ecru envelope with Tony's name and the Cabot Street address typed in a faded, old-fashioned script on an old, manual typewriter. The *e* was out of alignment.

I changed course and headed for Kate. Making sure I stood between her and Nina, I got her attention, my voice low. "Hey. Take a look at this."

Kate looked up from her painting and shaded her eyes. "What?"

"This just came in the mail for Tony. Look familiar?"

Shannon had caught on now, too, and came to stand next to me. "It looks just like the letters that came for Nina."

"That's what I thought. I didn't get a good look at them, so I figured I'd ask you, since you've seen them better than I have. You sure?"

"Positive," Shannon nodded. "Same shade of dirty yellow envelope, same faded typewriting. What does the postmark say?"

I peered at it. It was faded, too. "Missouri."

Kate nodded. "Same place. Same envelope, same writing. Probably the same person."

"I think we should call Wayne," I said. "I'd take it to him, but I don't have time to leave the house today."

"I'll call him." Kate was already reaching for her phone.

"I'd better get back to work. I'll take the mail inside with me and put it somewhere out of the way. Just in case there's something going on—something to do with the murder—I don't want Nina to see the envelope and catch on. Don't mention it, either. Just tell him to stop by. And when he comes, tell him to come inside and find me."

Kate nodded. As I turned away, I heard her begin to speak. "Hey, Wayne. It's me. Are you busy?"

No one else seemed to have noticed what was going on, although when I walked past her, Fae looked up from her clipboard and sent me a smile. "Everything OK?"

I smiled back. "Sure. Why?"

"No reason. Shannon seems upset."

"Oh." I glanced over my shoulder. Shannon had gone back to work on the cabinet doors, swinging her brush with a vengeance, and she did perhaps look like she was taking out some aggression.

"She's not talking to me today," Fae added, her voice low. "I thought we were becoming friends, and now she won't talk to me. I know she said it'd be OK, but I guess she really didn't like me going out with Josh yesterday, did she?"

I lowered my voice, too. "I think maybe she didn't expect it to bother her as much as it did. They've been best friends for a long time. She worries about him."

"I'm not doing anything to him," Fae protested. "I like him. He's a nice guy."

"I guess maybe she's afraid he'll get his heart broken when you leave on Saturday."

Fae shrugged, and I added, "He told me you have a lot in common. I didn't realize this wasn't your full-time job."

She shook her head. "I study information technology. At Kansas City University. This is just a summer job."

"Nice that you could land such a cushy summer job. Most college students wait tables or work as lifeguards or camp counselors."

"Wilson's my uncle," Fae said.

I glanced over at Wilson, who was talking to Ted, their heads together. "So how do you think things are going today? Is he getting enough footage to put together an episode, do you think?"

Fae shrugged. "He's getting plenty of footage. It all hinges on whether the house will be ready by Friday night, doesn't it?"

On that note, I excused myself and headed back to the kitchen and my painting.

Wayne showed up about an hour later. By then, I'd had what felt like every member of the crew through the kitchen once or twice. Fae had come in to get a water bottle for Nina from the fridge. Then Nina herself had come in to check the progress. Wilson had come in to film the progress. Adam had accompanied him to comment on the progress; he was still calling me Ivy. Derek had popped his head in long enough to ask me to hand him a water bottle, too—I had taken the opportunity to brief him on the appearance of the letter, but he didn't seem to think it was as exciting as I did; I think he was preoccupied with the tiling—and then Fae had come back, this time for a water bottle for Ted. Then Wilson came back to apologize for Adam not being able to remember my name.

"Probably be looking for another gig soon," he confided, while he twisted the lid on his own water bottle. "Nina's getting tense, and who can blame her? I mean, how hard can it be to remember a couple names? Stu didn't seem to have any problems." He lifted the bottle and drank half of it.

"How long was Stuart with the show?"

Wilson glanced around the kitchen. "Three years, give or take. When the show started, we had a different host.

Lasted about a year. Guy named Grant. Looked a little like that Micelli guy. The audience didn't seem to like him. Too slick, if you know what I mean. More suited for anchoring the news than giving renovation tips. Didn't look like he enjoyed getting his hands dirty."

I nodded. Looking like you enjoy getting your hands dirty is a must in that kind of job. Tony had been slick, and perfectly well suited for the news, but I had a hard time imagining him, or someone like him, as the host of a show like *Flipped Out!* I didn't think Adam was quite right, either, to tell the truth, or that he would be even if he were able to remember his lines. This gig required someone more like Derek: a little more casual, even a little scruffy, with easy charm and good looks, but not so much polish. Not that my boyfriend's unpolished, but he's direct and honest and not too concerned with appearances. And gorgeous in spite—or perhaps because—of it. Stuart had been like that. Easygoing and charming, with crinkles at the corners of his eyes and an aw-shucks kind of demeanor that was instantly endearing. I'd enjoyed watching him. To enough of a degree that Derek accused me of having had a celebrity crush.

"Horrible what happened to him. Nina told me he got electrocuted."

Wilson nodded. "Happened just a few weeks ago. House much like this one. Little Victorian in some small town in Kentucky. The electric shoulda been off, but something musta gone wrong, because when Stuart stepped on this wire, it shot electricity through his body. Thought for a second the top of his head was gonna blow off. His hair stood straight up and everything." He took another swig of water.

"Wow," I said.

"Yeah. He got lucky. Shoulda been dead, most likely."

"So what went wrong?"

He shrugged. "No idea. The renovators swore they'd turned off the electric, that they hadn't turned it on again.

Probably they were lying—both of 'em thought the other one'd taken care of it, but no one actually had, and when this happened, they closed ranks—but there's no way of proving it. And it won't make no difference anyway. He'll still be in the hospital."

"How did Adam come to get the gig when Stuart was hurt?"

"Oh, he was hanging around the place," Wilson said with a shrug. "Rubbing up on Nina. Schmoozing. When this happened, she suggested he could step in. Probably his idea to begin with. He used to want to be an actor, I think— can't blame him, with those looks—but he can't remember lines to save his life. If he can't remember your name's Avery, and not Ivory or Ivy, he don't stand a chance of making it in films."

Clearly.

"Guess I'd better be getting back to work." Wilson cast another glance around the kitchen.

I stepped back to appreciate my own handiwork. "Looks good, doesn't it?" All bright and sunny, with the yellow paint.

Wilson nodded. "Sure does. You're doing a good job."

"I think it's going to turn out nice. I just hope we can get it all done in time for you to film the finished product before you leave. I'd hate for you to have wasted a whole week."

"Oh," Wilson said with a grin, "we'll still film the place on Friday before we leave. If it ain't finished, we'll hang you out on TV as not being able to get the job done."

"Great." I made a face. Wilson chuckled and left the kitchen. Just outside the door, I heard him greet someone, and a second later, Wayne's salt-and-pepper curls popped through the opening. "Avery?"

"Hey, Wayne. How are things going?"

"Fine." He looked around the kitchen. "This looks good."

"It does, doesn't it?" I laid the brush down on top of the

paint can, angled so it wouldn't fall off and make a mess, and wiped my hands on one of the wet paper towels I had sitting everywhere. "How are things with you? Did you have a chance to talk to the kids across the street?"

Wayne nodded. "Last night."

"And?"

"They said Tony's car was here when they left around eleven thirty. And so was Melissa's."

"So that's why you arrested her." And why Derek's story about their time spent together hadn't made a difference. Melissa had been here earlier in the evening. Tony might already have been dead when she ran into Derek in his parking lot.

"I didn't actually arrest her," Wayne said. "Just brought her in for questioning. I can hold her for forty-eight hours without charging her, and that's what I intend to do."

"What did she say happened?"

"Nothing," Wayne said. "He was alive and well when she left him."

Just what I'd expect her to say. "Any news on the murder weapon? Or the rest of our tools?"

Wayne shook his head. "Whoever killed him probably dropped them in the ocean. Or tucked them away in his garage or something."

"Melissa doesn't have a garage."

"I know that," Wayne said. "I had Brandon go through her apartment, but there was nothing there. No tools, no murder weapon, no blood. Same thing with the car."

I nodded. "Let's go out in the backyard for a minute. I could use some air. Lots of paint fumes in here." And I didn't want to talk about the letter inside the house. There were too many people wandering around to make conversations convenient.

"Sure," Wayne said and headed for the utility room door. I snagged the stack of mail from where I'd stashed it, out of sight of everyone who'd come through the kitchen, in the bottom of a bank of drawers next to the stove, and followed.

There was some shade in the backyard under a couple of big trees, and we stopped there.

"This came for Tony today." I handed over the mail. The important stuff, anyway; I'd left the circulars inside. "I don't know who else to give it to. Tony won't be able to take care of it, and Derek and I don't own the place. I guess the taxes will become part of the estate, a lien or something, but I'm not sure about the rest."

"Tony had a lawyer," Wayne said. "A guy in Portland. I'll pass this on to him."

"I don't know if Kate's mentioned it to you, but ever since she got here, Nina has been getting letters."

Wayne looked nonplussed. "Lots of people get letters. Even when they're on vacation. Or away from home."

"Not like these. They're small envelopes, sent from Missouri. One every day so far. Kate brought one over for her just this morning that she said arrived just as she was leaving the B and B."

"So?" Wayne said.

"So if you look at what you have in your hand, you'll see that Tony got a small envelope from Missouri today, too. Kate says it looks exactly like the ones Nina's been getting."

Wayne looked down. "This?"

I nodded. "Aren't you going to open it?"

He cut his eyes to me. "It's illegal to open someone else's mail, Avery."

"But you're the police. And he's been killed. Don't you think it might be a clue?"

Wayne kept turning the envelope in his hands.

"I could have opened it myself, you know," I said. "I didn't have to give it to you."

"You'd interfere with the mail?"

"It's not like anyone would ever know. Tony won't miss

his letter. And if I'm right, it's not like anyone's expecting a response."

Wayne gave me a long look.

"C'mon," I pestered. "Open it. I want to see what it says."

Wayne sighed, but he pulled a pocket knife off his belt and slit the envelope. I leaned forward and craned my neck as he pulled out a sheet of notepaper, the same thick ecru as the envelope, and unfolded it.

There was only one sentence marching across the page, typed in the same faded uneven font as the address.

I saw what you did.

So that was one question answered. Yes, it was a poison-pen letter, sort of. But now I had another question. "What does it mean?" I said.

Wayne glanced at me. "I would think that, at some point, Tony did something that someone else knows about, and that Tony probably would have wished they didn't."

I rolled my eyes. "Thank you, Sherlock. Beside that?"

"I have no idea. There isn't anything like that in Tony's past. Not that I know about. No big secrets or anything. He's lived around here practically his entire life. Waterfield and then Portland. Grew up right in this house, went to Waterfield Elementary and High School."

"Did you know him growing up?"

Wayne shook his head. "He was younger than me by five or six years, so I wouldn't say I knew him. Not well, anyway. I knew who he was, and after he went into broadcasting in Portland and I moved up in the Waterfield PD, we ran into one another from time to time. He'd call and ask me for information about cases once in a while, and I'd call him if I needed a description or a missing person's report to get on the air."

"You got along well?"

"As well as could be expected," Wayne said. "He was a local boy, even if he liked to pretend he wasn't. Got out of Dodge just as quickly as he could after high school. We all figured we'd seen the last of him and he'd make a career for himself someplace like New York or LA. He always was ambitious."

"But he didn't?"

Wayne shook his head. "He went to college for a few years and then started working at some small station in the Midwest. Stepping stone to bigger and better, I guess. His mother told everyone in town that he was on his way; it was just a matter of time before we'd see him on *20/20* or *Date-line*. First of the Micellis to ever get a college degree."

"That's nice that his mother was proud of him."

"She was a bit of a stage mother," Wayne said, "from what I understand. And very controlling. I remember old lady Micelli. But yeah, I guess it is nice. She was fit to be tied when he came back, anyway, after just a few months of working out there."

"Any idea what happened?"

But Wayne didn't. "I can't imagine it matters," he said, "since it's so long ago."

"That's where he met Nina. They worked together for a few months on their first job."

"She told me."

"And Nina's been getting these letters, too."

Wayne hesitated, and I could almost hear the gears clicking in his head. After a minute, he turned his head to look at the house. "Is she around?"

"She was. She came with the others this morning, and she hasn't told me she's leaving, so I assume she's still here."

Wayne nodded. "Let's take a walk out front." He headed toward the house before I could say anything, and it was just as well, because he'd said "us," and I wasn't about to dissuade him from the idea that I should come along.

—14—

Inside the house, it was business as earlier. Josh had finished the two bedrooms and was busy rolling paint in the dining room. Beatrice was with him, cutting in. Cora had started the same job in the living room, carefully maneuvering her loaded brush around the stone of the fireplace. Derek was still working on the bathroom floor, but all the tile was laid now, and he was filling in with grout. Wilson was back to filming, with Adam standing by. He had taken to calling Derek Dirk. No one stopped him; I guess maybe because it was closer than anything else he'd come up with so far.

As Wayne and I came through to the outside, Fae was on the porch talking quietly on her cell. I caught just a few words. ". . . anymore. For now, anyway." When she saw us, she turned away and lowered her voice even further.

Kate and Shannon were still on the lawn painting cabinet doors. Usually I prefer a more durable oil-based paint for the sheen and coverage, but since time was of the essence this week, we'd decided to go with quick-drying latex. It was warm in the sun, so the first doors they'd painted had already dried, and Shannon had turned them over and started painting the backs. At this rate, I thought we might almost be able to get everything done by Friday night after all, at least if we cut a few corners along the way. We could spruce up the front of the house, for instance, saving the back and sides until the crew had left and we weren't in such a hurry anymore. That way they'd have a lovely front exterior to film on Friday night, and we could take our time finishing up the rest of the house next week.

Kate looked up when we walked past. She arched her brows at me, and I mouthed, "Nina."

Kate nodded. And watched out of the corner of her eye as Wayne approached the director.

Nina was standing outside the picket fence, a lit cigarette in her hand and a strained look on her face. Wayne's approach over the grass was almost noiseless, so when he greeted her, she jumped. "Miz Andrews."

"Chief Rasmussen," Nina managed. The hand holding the cigarette shook when she lifted it to her mouth. "And Avery." She forced a smile in my direction.

"How are you holding up?" I smiled back. "You seem a little jumpy today."

"It's this situation with Tony," Nina said, taking another drag on her cigarette, deep enough to make her cheeks hollow. "Seeing him again after twenty years and then—poof!— he's gone. Brings back"—she hesitated—"memories."

"I'm sorry for your loss, Miz Andrews. You and Tony worked together once, you said?"

Nina nodded. "Our first job. It didn't last long, though. Just six months or so."

"I remember. He grew up here, you know. I remember his mother telling us about his job, and then just a few months later, he was back in town again. Something happen?"

"Nothing in particular," Nina said, but she avoided looking at either of us.

I would probably have pushed—in fact, I intended to do a little online research tonight to see what I could dig up; both about Nina's past and about Tony's—but Wayne just nodded. He put his hand in his pocket and pulled out the letter. Tony's letter. Unfolded it and handed it to her. "I need you to tell me about this."

For a second, I was afraid that Nina was going to drop into a dead faint. What little color she'd had drained from her face and she wobbled. The cigarette in her hand shook hard enough to dislodge the inch-long piece of ash that had been hanging off the end.

When the ash fell and hit her toe in the open sandal, she seemed to come back to reality. She looked at the cigarette for a second, her expression disgusted, and then she dropped it on the pavement and stepped on it. Before squaring her shoulders and looking at Wayne. "Where did you get that?"

Nina obviously thought this was one of her letters. Wayne did nothing to dissuade her from that belief, either. "I'll ask the questions, if you don't mind. My wife tells me you've been getting these for the past few days. Ever since you and your crew arrived here in my town."

Nina nodded. No reason not to admit it when Kate had seen the letters. Or at least the envelopes.

"Did it start this week, or has it been going on longer?"

"It started a few weeks ago," Nina said. She glanced around to make sure no one else was in hearing distance. Kate and Shannon were still on the grass, but Fae had disappeared off the porch. "At first it was just one. I didn't think anything of it. I mean, these things happen, right? Prank calls and e-mails and letters once in a while is just part of the business."

Maybe so, I thought. Or maybe not. The talent, sure, they're in the public eye, and it stands to reason they'd sometimes catch the attention of some wacko or other, but the director, someone who spent her time behind the scenes . . . ?

Wayne didn't ask, though, just nodded for Nina to continue.

"Then another came. Exactly the same as the first. And a few days later, another. In the past week, they've been coming every day."

"Any idea who's sending them?" Wayne asked.

Nina shook her head. "If I did, don't you think I would have put a stop to it?"

"I don't know." Wayne's voice was bland. "You might not want to confront someone who claims to know something you did. Something the letter-writer seems to think you'd want kept quiet."

Nina didn't answer, but she flushed.

"Would you mind telling me what the unknown writer thinks you did?"

"I have no idea," Nina said. "I've done a lot of things in my life. I can imagine quite a few of them might have upset someone. You flirt with someone's husband, you inherit someone's job, you take someone's parking space. Things happen every day. Isn't that the case for most of us?"

Wayne shrugged, but I had to agree. We all do things that affect other people all the time, and sometimes, if one of those people is more on edge than the rest, he or she might resort to poison-pen letters. Like Derek had said, it needn't even be something that anyone else would consider a big deal.

"I was an investigative reporter for a while," Nina continued, "and I discovered things about people. Little secrets, things people wouldn't necessarily want the neighbors to know. Nothing stands out, though. I didn't do criminal investigations, just public-interest things."

"Anything else come to mind?" Wayne had pulled out his little notebook and was scratching in it.

Nina hesitated. Just for a second, but I noticed. So did

Wayne. He leveled a stare at her. She buckled. "I wondered . . ."

"Yes?"

"The first letter arrived just a few days after the accident."

"Accident?" Wayne said.

"Stuart's accident?" I asked. Nina nodded.

Wayne looked from one to the other of us. "Who's Stuart and what happened to him?"

Nina explained. Her explanation matched Wilson's in every particular. Wayne, however, was not happy. "Why didn't I hear about this?" he demanded.

Nina glanced at me. I shrugged. "I guess no one thought it was important. You have enough to deal with, with Tony's death."

"Besides," Nina added, "there's no possible connection between them. Stuart never met Tony, or heard his name, even. And what happened to him was an accident. Totally unforeseen and tragic, but an accident."

"But you knew both of them," Wayne said. "That's a connection."

Nina blanched. "What are you saying?"

Wayne got right back in her face. "That two men close to you have met with violence in the past few weeks, and that from what you're saying, it sounds as if Stuart was lucky he didn't die as well."

"So?"

"So it's a connection. And something I needed to hear. You can't possibly know what's connected and what's not. You should have told me."

"Sorry," I said, since I'd known about Stuart, too, and hadn't thought to tell Wayne, either.

"So when the letter came just after Stuart's accident"— Wayne brought the conversation back on track—"you thought that perhaps the writer was accusing you of having had something to do with it?"

Nina shrugged. "It crossed my mind."

"And did you?"

She looked offended. "Of course not! I liked Stuart. He was a joy to work with, and he made *Flipped Out!* what it is today. We would never have let him go voluntarily. As it is, we're all hoping he'll make a full recovery and come back."

"That's not likely, is it?"

Nina shook her head. "But I'm not going to start a search for a new host until I have to. We'll just have to put up with Adam for the time being." She turned to me. "I'm sorry he keeps botching your name. But he photographs like a dream, and the camera loves him. I'm sure that knowledge doesn't make it any easier for you, but for now, we'll just have to deal."

Wayne cleared his throat. "Would you mind letting me see the letter you have in your bag?"

Nina looked surprised, and her eyes flickered to the letter in Wayne's hand.

"This isn't it," Wayne said as Nina dug into her purse to make sure he was telling the truth. She came out a second later with her own envelope, still unopened.

"You tricked me!"

Wayne shrugged unapologetically. "Not really. You just assumed it was yours. Fear, I'd guess, and perhaps a bit of guilty conscience?"

Nina didn't answer. Wayne added, "Open it, please. I'd like to compare it to this one."

"It'll look exactly the same," Nina said, as she tore at the envelope with long fingernails. "All the others did."

"I'd still like to see it. If you'll allow."

"It's not going to do me any good to refuse, is it? Here you go." She handed him the letter from her purse, without even glancing at it. It did indeed look identical to the one Wayne already had in his hand.

"May I keep it?" he asked.

"Sure. I burned the others, but they were all exactly like this, too. I was going to burn this one."

"And you have no idea who's sending them to you? The postmark says Missouri."

Nina shook her head. "I don't know anyone in Missouri. It's more than twenty years since I worked there for just a few months, and I didn't make any connections in the community. As for my coworkers, we're all over the map now. It was the kind of midsize market that's a stepping stone to bigger and better, and we've all moved on."

For a second, it looked like she was going to add something, but she must have changed her mind. "Sorry I can't be more help."

"That's all right," Wayne said. "Thank you."

Nina nodded and turned halfway around. Then she turned back. "Just out of curiosity . . . if that isn't my letter, whose is it? Is someone else on the crew getting them, too? Because then, maybe it *does* have something to do with Stuart's accident."

"I'm afraid not," Wayne said, shaking his head. "This arrived here, for Tony."

When Nina just gaped at him, he added, "Give it some thought, would you? And if you can come up with something that happened in Missouri that involved you and him, perhaps you'll be so kind as to let me know?"

He didn't wait for an answer, just walked off across the grass again. I smiled apologetically to Nina and followed.

Wayne stopped by Kate's side and watched her work for a few seconds before he stated his intention to go back to the police station. "I'll have to have Brandon do fingerprints on these. I doubt he'll find anything, but it has to be done."

"Brandon said he was going to stop by the Waymouth Tavern last night," I said. "To see if anyone remembered Nina and Tony eating there. Do you know if he did?"

"He didn't," Wayne said. "We got busy with Melissa last

night, so he didn't have time. I'll remind him to do it tonight, when they open."

"No need. I'll get Derek to take me there for dinner. I'll let you know what they say."

"You know I can't take your word for it. . . ." Wayne began, and then he admitted defeat. "Sure, Avery. Do what you want."

"Dinner at home?" Kate asked, batting her eyes up at him. "Just the two of us? I'll make enchiladas."

"Great." Wayne relaxed, grinning. Shannon looked up.

"I forgot. I'm going out tonight, too. At eight. That's OK, isn't it?"

"Sure," Kate said. "If anyone has an emergency, they can walk across the grass to the carriage house to find me. You go out and have a good time, honey."

"Thanks." Shannon grinned. Adam must be growing on her if she could smile like that at the thought of going out with him.

• • •

So Wayne headed back to his police cruiser, and I headed back to work. For about an hour, until it was time for lunch. Fae had found the circular from the pizza parlor, and she had ordered a half dozen pizzas to be delivered. "Expense account," she said when I thanked her. "It seems the least we can do after bringing all this trouble your way."

"Don't be silly." I smiled at her. "None of this is your fault. You just came here to do your job. It's not like *you* killed Tony."

Fae shook her head, her lips tight. "I didn't even know him. Just met him that one time on Monday. It has to be a coincidence that he was killed just when we got here. Don't you think?"

"I'm sure it was," I said, although it would have to be a huge coincidence, if so. That didn't necessarily mean that anyone on the crew had killed him, of course. Their arrival could have precipitated the murder in other ways. I kept coming back to Melissa. Maybe Tony had carried a torch for Nina for twenty years, and now that he had seen her again, he'd known he couldn't possibly go through with marrying Melissa. Maybe little Miss Melly had gotten her nose out of joint when he took Nina to dinner. Maybe she had followed the two of them. When he dropped Nina off, she had gotten his attention and they'd ended up here at the house. And when he told her he couldn't go through with the marriage, Melissa had gone for the screwdriver. And then she'd panicked. And she had gotten Derek to come upstairs to her loft and had kept him there half the night, thinking it would give her an alibi.

No wonder Wayne had arrested her and refused to let her go. If I'd been in charge, I would have arrested her, too.

But what had she done with the murder weapon? There was no ocean between Cabot Street and Main that she could have dropped it in, and if Brandon had gone over her apartment and her car . . .

"What are you thinking?" Fae asked, from far away. I shook myself and managed a smile.

"Nothing. Or at least nothing pleasant. Hey, listen—"

"Yes?"

"You seem to have known Stuart well. Can you think of any reason anyone would have wanted him dead? Or out of the way?"

Fae turned pale. "What a horrible thing to say!"

"Sorry. It's just that two bad things have happened recently to people associated with this show, and I thought maybe you could think of something. Like, a rival show is trying to get *Flipped Out!* off the air or something."

"That kind of stuff just happens on TV," Fae said. "I can't think of anyone who would have wanted to hurt Stuart. He was a really sweet guy, very humble, not full of himself at all."

Unlike Adam, then.

"There was nothing going on in his personal life that I know of. He didn't really have one. No girlfriend or wife. The crew is on the road so much . . ."

"Were you there when it happened?"

"Oh, yes." She shuddered. "It was horrible. At first I thought he was dead. Electricity shot right through his body, and made his hair stick straight up. He convulsed and everything." She swallowed. "Ted ran to turn off the breaker, and when the electricity went off, Stuart fell all in a heap. And we were afraid to touch him, you know?"

I nodded. Derek had lectured me on electric shock, because it's one of the possible hazards of home renovation, and he had told me that a current can be passed from body to body. After the power has been turned off, there's no danger, though.

"Then Ted came back and he kept Stuart alive until the paramedics got there," Fae said. "They said he'd been lucky, and that if Ted hadn't given him mouth-to-mouth resuscitation, he probably would have died." There were tears in her eyes now.

"Are you sure it was an accident? That someone didn't turn the power back on deliberately?"

"I don't know," Fae said, with a helpless shrug of her thin shoulders. "Everyone just assumed it was an accident. That both the renovators thought the other one had turned the power off when really, no one had. I just can't imagine why anyone would want to hurt Stuart. He was the sweetest guy in the world!"

Tears were rolling down her cheeks now, and I felt like an enormous jerk for making her cry. "I'm sorry," I said. "I'll . . . um . . . just go tell everyone that lunch is here, OK?"

"OK." Fae sniffed, wiping at her cheeks. I made myself scarce.

The pizza was on the porch, and a few minutes later, everyone was out there eating. Derek, Kate, and I sat down on the porch steps. Shannon, meanwhile, took her pizza back to the plastic sheet in the yard and was eating there. After a minute or two, Josh joined her. Fae had latched on to her uncle, and they were standing at the other end of the porch talking in low voices. Fae still seemed teary.

"What's going on there?" Kate asked me, with a toss of her head.

I made a face. "I upset her. Nina said she originally thought those letters she's been getting might have had something to do with what happened to Stuart, the former host of the show. He was electrocuted when he stepped on a live wire, and I suggested to Fae that maybe someone had staged the accident. She didn't like that idea."

"I don't like it, either," Derek said. When I turned to him, he added, "If it could happen at someone else's work-site, it could happen here. Maybe someone will try to get rid of Adam."

We all turned to Adam, who looked like a male model— for pizza—standing in the front yard, sleeves rolled up to the shoulders so the sun could gild all his visible muscles. I was surprised he hadn't taken his shirt off entirely. But maybe he was just trying to maintain his tan, and not, in fact, trying to show off his assets.

Or maybe he was trying to listen in on Nina and Ted's conversation. They were over by the fence, where Nina had stood earlier, when Wayne and I talked to her.

"Josh said murders come in twos," I remarked, "although he seemed to think Nina was the next logical victim."

Derek looked at me, brows raised. I ran through it for him while Kate nodded.

"If that's the case," Derek said, "we ought to be safe. If Stuart was the first intended victim, then Tony was the second, and we shouldn't have any more."

I hadn't thought about it like that. "That's actually promising."

He shrugged. "That's if you're right and there's a connection. What happened to Stuart might have been an accident."

"Nina doesn't think so," I said, watching her holding forth to Ted, her hands waving and her face intent. He was listening and nodding.

"Well, I'm not sure there's anything we can do except wait and see. And take precautions. From here on out, I'm checking everything myself. Twice." He got up to get another slice of pizza out of the box. "Avery? Kate?"

I shook my head. "I've had enough, thank you." Kate nodded, her mouth full.

"You know," she said once she'd swallowed, "what this place needs is a porch swing. There's not enough seating out here."

"I know. I was planning to get one. But the lumber depot was out when I was there last week. I was planning to paint it turquoise and put lots of pillows on it. But now I don't know if I'll have time to track one down. I doubt Derek will let me go off on a porch swing hunt anytime soon."

"You got that right," Derek said, sitting down next to me again with two more slices of pizza on his paper plate. "This is good pizza." He filled his mouth.

"The porch needs something, though," Kate said. "A couple of chairs, if nothing else. Or you could make your own swing."

"That'd take more time than driving to Portland to buy one."

She shook her head. "Not necessarily. I saw an article in a magazine once where someone had made a porch swing out of an old door."

"A door?"

"It was more of a hanging chaise lounge, really. A wooden door with chains at each corner, and a head rest, sort of, added on. Plus a bunch of pillows. It looked kind of cute. And I don't think it'd be difficult to make."

Derek swallowed. "Drill holes at the corners. Hook chains to the ceiling. Put some scrap wood on for the head rest. Paint the whole thing. An hour or two at the most. We can do it tonight."

"You're taking me to the Waymouth Tavern tonight."

He arched a brow. "I am?"

"Wayne told me that Brandon didn't get up there yesterday, what with talking to the teenagers and picking up Melissa. I told him we'd ask about Nina and Tony. Just in case someone noticed something." Like Melissa skulking in the parking lot, watching the couple through high-powered binoculars. Or a particularly homicidal gleam in Nina's eyes.

"I see," Derek said. "OK, then. You can make the porch swing tomorrow. After you put all the kitchen cabinet doors back on."

"I thought we weren't going to be able to work inside tomorrow."

He shook his head. "We'll have to, Tink. We can come and go through the back door. I'll poly the floors tonight before we leave, and again in the morning, and then we can work on the kitchen and utility room. I'll hang the laundry room cabinets while you make your porch swing. There are a couple of old doors out in the shed behind your aunt's house that you can use."

"Sure," I said happily.

—15—

And so it went for the rest of the day. We painted. By now, Derek had finished tiling and grouting the bathroom floor, and it had to sit and dry for at least twenty-four hours before anyone could step on it. Painting the bathroom would be a task for Friday. One of those last-minute cleanup tasks, ridiculous as that sounded. Luckily it was a small room, with lots of tile in it, so it wouldn't take much more than an hour to paint.

I finished painting the kitchen cabinets, and Kate and Shannon finished the doors. Then all three of us started on the kitchen and laundry room walls. The utility room would be yellow, bright and sunny, to pick up the color in the kitchen cabinets. The kitchen itself would be a warm shade of creamy white, to pick up the speckles in the new countertop we'd be putting in tomorrow.

While the rest of us painted, Derek loaded Wilson and Adam into the truck and drove to Portland to pick up the kitchen counter. Wilson thought it was a good idea to get some footage of Derek at the granite depot, and of Derek and Adam flexing their muscles getting the slab of granite we'd ordered into the back of the truck. Adam was less thrilled about the whole thing. He seemed to want to hang around the house, although I wasn't sure whether it was Shannon, Fae, or Nina who was the draw. But it didn't matter anyway, since Wilson snapped his fingers at him, and Adam had to jump.

By the time they got back, it was going on dinnertime. Cora, Beatrice, and Josh had finished painting the living room and dining room while Shannon, Kate, and I had just a little bit left to do on our area of the house. We had to stand aside while Wilson filmed Derek and Adam, aided by Josh, wrestle the slab of granite into the utility room. Muscles strained under short sleeves, and all us women stood still for a minute and enjoyed the show. Including Fae, who had stuck around although Nina and Ted had gone back to the B&B.

"She wasn't feeling well," Fae said, with a flip of her hair.

"I'm sorry to hear that."

Fae shrugged, which seemed a little uncaring, I thought.

The last thing we did before we left was put a coat of polyurethane on the hardwood floors. I passed through the two bedrooms with the big shop vacuum, and then Wilson filmed Derek spreading poly while I moved into the living room and dining room. Specks of dust in the polyurethane makes for an uneven finish, and Derek is rabid about vacuuming and mopping before starting to spread poly on the floors.

Once he was done, we cleared out, stopping in the front yard to turn around and look at the house. After the pressure washing, and with the new shrubs and bushes in place, it already looked a lot better. With a porch swing with some pillows, and Derek's window boxes, and the planters on the porch, it would look even better.

"Not bad for three days' work," Derek remarked, putting an arm around my shoulders.

I nodded. "We've managed to do a lot, even with losing a lot of yesterday. Doing the outside work instead helped."

"I'm glad we did this—the TV show—but I don't think I ever wanna do it again. The next time I renovate something, I want to take my time. Do it right. Enjoy the process."

I nodded. Me, too. This was a lot more stressful that I'd wanted it to be. Of course, that was partly because we didn't just have the stress of the renovations to deal with; we had the stress of a murder, and poison-pen letters, and Derek's ex-wife ending up in jail. . . .

"Can we stop by your place before we go to the Waymouth Tavern?" I asked Derek.

He looked surprised. "Why?"

"Don't you want to change into something more presentable? And less dirty?"

He glanced down at himself. "I guess that might not be a bad idea. You want me to drop you at your place on the way? Give you a little extra time to get ready?"

I shook my head. "I want to come with you."

He chuckled. "To watch me change?"

Not exactly. Not that I don't usually enjoy that particular experience. But in this case, I had something else in mind.

"You go on up," I said when Derek had pulled the truck into the parking lot behind the hardware store. "I'll wait down here."

"You sure?"

"Positive."

"Suit yourself." He jogged toward the door to the stairs. I waited until he was inside, and then I turned around and surveyed the terrain.

If I had just come back from killing my fiancé, and I needed somewhere to hide the murder weapon in a hurry, where would I put it?

The lot was fairly small, tucked behind the hardware

store and the yard of the building on the next street. It only had a dozen spaces, and two of them were taken up by a big Dumpster that belonged to the True Value store. Derek's truck was parked in his customary slot, and there were a couple of other cars sitting around, too; they probably belonged to people who were inside the store, either shopping or working. There was a big bin over by the wall, with a lid on it; it looked like an oversized, old-fashioned salt-box, and it probably contained either gravel or salt or sand for the winter months. It looked like a great place to hide a screwdriver—just shove the tool in and bury it—but the bin had a padlock on it.

I sighed. The only other option was the Dumpster, and I'd really hoped to be able to avoid that. But as it seemed I had no choice, I wandered over and peeked in. It was full of cardboard boxes and bags of trash from the hardware store. Derek threw his kitchen trash into it, too, I knew. There were flies buzzing around, and things didn't smell too good. I really had to do some fast talking to convince myself to crawl in.

A couple of minutes later, I heard Derek's voice. "Avery?"

I raised my own. "Here."

"Where?"

"Dumpster."

His face appeared in the opening above me. "What happened? Did you fall in?"

"Hardly. I'm looking for your screwdriver. And the rest of the tools."

He gave me one of those eyebrows that told me to go on, so I did. "If Melissa killed Tony—and I know you don't think she did, but go with me here—if she was there, and she killed him, she took the murder weapon with her. We're thinking the screwdriver was the murder weapon, right?"

"The wounds were consistent with a round instrument," Derek said.

"A screwdriver. Or something else, but we're missing a

screwdriver, so let's just go with that. And let's go with Melissa, just for the time being. She kills Tony with the screwdriver, and then she takes it with her, because she knows her fingerprints are all over it. She takes the other tools, too, to make it look like a break-in gone bad. But she didn't leave the stuff in her car, because Brandon checked, and she didn't take it upstairs to her apartment, because he checked that, too—"

"I think I would have noticed if she pulled a bloody screwdriver out of her purse while I was there," Derek said. "Especially if it had my initials on it."

"Exactly. So she got rid of the screwdriver and everything else sometime between when she left the house on Cabot and when you saw her. Right here."

"Shit," Derek said, following my train of thought.

"What better place to put it? It's yours, so no one would think twice about it being here. And the Dumpster belongs to the hardware store; they deal with tools all the time."

He shook his head, his mouth set. "Have you found anything?"

"Not yet. There's a lot of stuff in here." I ducked back out of sight to keep rooting through the garbage.

"You want me to come in there and help you?"

"You just changed. I've got it." I moved a crumpled bakery bag out of my way. "And I doubt she crawled in and actually hid it. She probably just tossed it through the opening."

"Makes sense," Derek said, just as the bakery bag hit the side of the Dumpster with a click. "What was that?"

"Something that shouldn't have made a sound. Unless this half a scone is really, really stale." I reached for it. Yeah, there was definitely something in there that wasn't baked goods.

"Gimme," Derek said, reaching a hand into the Dumpster. I handed him the bag. He opened it and looked in.

"Yep, that's it. My screwdriver and a handful of bloody napkins. Plus a coffee cup with lipstick on it."

"Don't touch anything. There's probably fingerprints. Or DNA."

"Do I look stupid?" Derek said and put the bag gently on the ground. "Can you see any of the other tools?"

I shook my head.

"Let me give you a hand out."

"I'm not sure you want to touch me right now. I smell kind of ripe."

"I'll take you home for a shower before we go to dinner," Derek promised, ignoring the filth to help me out of the Dumpster. "But first I want to take this to the police."

"I'm right behind you." I headed for the truck, brushing myself off as I went.

The Waterfield jail turned out to be a one-room cell in the new police station on the Portland Highway. Back in the old days, the Waterfield PD was housed in one of the historic buildings off Main Street, but some fifteen years ago or so, the town—and nearby Portland—had grown enough to necessitate more space for officers, computers, and other equipment, so the town built a brand-new police compound on the western highway, a few miles outside of town. It was a just a few months since I'd been there to look at some clothes Wayne had taken off a drowning victim in an effort to try to identify the girl.

Everything looked the same way it had then. Ramona Estrada, the police secretary, was long gone, home to her husband and grandkids, but a young man, someone even younger than Brandon, was manning the front desk. "Ma'am," he said politely when I walked in, "Sir."

"Hey, Connor," Derek said. "Avery, this is Connor Estrada. Ramona's grandson." He turned to the young man. "What are you doing here, Con? I thought you were at school."

Connor's face had relaxed. "Home for the summer. I needed a part-time job, so Grandma talked Chief Rasmussen into taking me on. It frees up one of his deputies. Usually, one of them has to ride the desk when Grandma isn't here." He smiled.

He was a good-looking young man, with his grandmother's dark hair and eyes, and a ready smile.

"You looking for the chief?" he asked now.

Derek shook his head. "We're looking for Brandon. This"—he put the bakery bag on the counter—"seems to be the screwdriver that killed Tony Micelli."

Connor's brows arched. "Where'd you find it?"

"Dumpster behind my apartment," Derek said. "I want Brandon to check it for fingerprints."

"Sure." Connor appropriated the bag, very carefully. "He's gone home for the day, but I'll make sure he gets it in the morning."

"You've also got my ex-wife locked up in your dungeon. I'd like to see her."

Connor glanced at me. "Both of you?"

"Melissa and I are old . . ." I hesitated for a second, looking for the right word. When none was immediately apparent, I settled for the old standby, "friends."

Connor shrugged. "Visiting hours ended long ago, but I don't think anyone would mind. C'mon. I'll take you back."

He moved out from behind the counter, and that was when I realized he was sitting in a wheelchair. It was a surprise, not at all what I'd expected from such a young, healthy-looking man, and I guess I must have shown it, because he glanced up at me in passing. "Traffic accident."

"I'm sorry."

"Me, too." He shrugged. "It's down here."

He wheeled and we walked into the bowels of the building, past the offices—including Wayne's, where I'd been this spring; it was dark and quiet now—and down a set of stairs to the lower level. The stairs were equipped with a lift, which took Connor and the wheelchair down while Derek and I walked.

Yes, the "dungeon," as Derek had called it, was in the basement. But it didn't look anything like a dungeon. And Connor Estrada was certainly no old-fashioned jailer. He knocked politely on the door before he inserted the key card in the lock and hit the button for the intercom. "Miss James? You decent?"

"Yes, Connor," Melissa's voice floated back. "You got something for me?"

"Visitors. They're coming in." He removed the key card—it was the kind of lock you find on hotel room doors, with a light that flashes green, along with a no doubt super-secret code he had to enter on a keypad—and pushed the door open.

I looked in, into a small room, only about eight by eight feet, with a bed—bolted to the wall—a desk or table—ditto—and a chair. It had carpet on the floor and the walls were painted an inoffensive off-white, something like the grayish yellow ecru of Nina's poison-pen letters. The bathroom wasn't in the cell itself, the way you see on TV; it was in a separate room off to the side. There was no door between them, but it wasn't like this little space would be shared by more than one person at a time, anyway. It didn't look like somewhere I'd want to spend more than a few hours, but it didn't look too uncomfortable, either.

Melissa was sitting on the bed, legs tucked sideways, flipping through a home-and-garden magazine. And for being in jail, she still managed to look pretty damn good. Her hair was brushed and gleaming in the fluorescent ceiling light. Her makeup was perfect, and she made jeans and a cotton top look like the height of fashion. There were even diamonds sparkling in her ears, as well as on her finger. When she saw Derek, she jumped up. "Thank God! Have you come to get me out?"

Derek shook his head. "Afraid not. Wayne isn't ready to release you yet."

Melissa pouted, and the pout got even more pronounced when she saw me coming through the door after him. "Oh. Hi, Avery."

"Melissa." I managed not to smile too broadly, but I must admit that seeing Melissa in jail—even a fairly comfortable jail—had gone a long way toward making my day. Even if she managed to look stunning through it all, and even though I—after a long, hard day of manual labor and my crawl through the garbage—surely looked (and smelled) anything but.

And all right, yes, there was the chance that she'd actually killed Tony. Derek seemed to think she hadn't, and I found it hard to reconcile it in my own mind, as well, but with what we knew right now, it seemed awfully possible. Which went some way to mitigating any glee I felt. Along with the fact that, if she hadn't killed him, she'd just lost her fiancé.

So I focused hard and managed to sound sympathetic when I added, "Is there anything we can do for you?"

"Get me out of here?" Melissa suggested and threw herself petulantly back down on the bed. Derek offered me the room's only chair, but I declined. He sat, and that left me the choice of sitting on his lap, sitting next to Melissa, or standing. I chose to stand.

"I can't stay away from the desk too long," Connor said, heading back to the lift. He added over his shoulder, "I'll be back in fifteen minutes. That enough time for you?"

"Plenty," Derek said.

Melissa must have noticed that he was pretty brusque, because she refrained from any comment about his not wanting to spend time with her. Instead, she just smoothed her hair behind one ear with a talon-tipped finger. The diamond sparkled. "What are you doing here, if you're not coming to get me out?"

"You lied to me," Derek said. "I want to know why."

Melissa huffed. "I didn't lie."

"You didn't tell me you'd been at the house on Cabot Street the night Tony was killed."

"You didn't ask," Melissa said.

"Oh, I was supposed to ask? Excuse me for not realizing that!"

They stared at each other.

"What were you doing there?" I cut in, trying to become the voice of reason.

Both of them looked at me, as if for a moment they'd both forgotten I was in the room. I arched a brow at Derek, who made a face, before we both turned to Melissa. She rolled her eyes.

"He asked me to meet him."

"When?"

"He sent me a text."

"Why didn't he just stop by your place?" I asked.

Melissa shrugged. "No idea. I didn't talk to him."

"Didn't you think to ask?"

She huffed. "Have you ever texted anyone, Avery? It's not really suited for long conversations, OK? He said he was back, he wanted to talk, could I meet him?"

"And you . . . ?"

She tossed her head. "I said yes. And drove over there."

"To the house on Cabot?"

She nodded. "It was about eleven thirty. I didn't want to rush, because I wanted him to know that I wasn't happy about him going out with Nina, even if he told me they were just old friends and it was her idea. And besides, I thought maybe he was going to tell me that he wanted to break off the engagement, and I wasn't in any hurry to hear that."

Couldn't blame her there.

"What happened when you got there?" I wanted to know.

"We talked for a few minutes. Then I went home."

"Try again," Derek said. "We just found the screwdriver. In a bag in the Dumpster behind my loft. I always thought it was strange that you were there that night. If you'd been in your apartment, you would have been able to look across the street and see that my lights were off."

Melissa had turned pale under the perfect makeup. "You found the screwdriver?"

"Did you think we wouldn't? It was pretty obvious when you think about it."

"So what really happened?" I asked. "That night? Tony texted you, and what?"

All the bravado had gone out of her, and her voice was low, so I had to step closer to hear. She wouldn't meet my eyes. "I knocked on the door. He didn't answer, but I knew he was there, because his car was parked at the curb. So I tried the door, and it was open. I walked in, and then . . ." She swallowed noisily. "I saw him lying there."

"Dead?"

"Of course dead! You think I would have left him if he wasn't? I was married to a doctor for five years, Avery, I know how to tell when someone's dead!"

"Sorry," I said.

She deflated. "It's OK. I checked. He was dead. Stabbed with that stupid screwdriver that I stupidly touched. I just wasn't thinking, you know? It was sticking out of his chest, and I pulled it out. I was just trying to help!"

Derek muttered something, probably to the effect that if she'd been married to a doctor for five years, she should have known that it would have been better to leave the screwdriver where it was. Melissa didn't seem to hear.

"Why didn't you call nine-one-one?" I wanted to know.

She looked at me as if she couldn't believe I had to ask. "I thought they'd say I'd killed him. That he'd told me he wanted to end the engagement and I'd been so upset that I'd grabbed the screwdriver and stabbed him."

"So you took the murder weapon and ran?" Derek said. "Christ, Melly . . . !"

Melissa sniffed and tossed her head.

"What did you do then?" I wanted to know, and she turned her attention to me.

"I drove back home. With the screwdriver on the seat next to me. Inside the bakery bag. I'd picked up a coffee and a muffin in the morning. But when I parked, I realized I couldn't take it upstairs. It had Tony's blood on it, and Derek's initials, and what if the police came and searched my place? So I decided to put it in Derek's truck, after I wiped it clean."

Derek sputtered. "*My* truck? What the hell . . . ! What were you trying to do, make it look like *I'd* killed him?"

"Of course not," Melissa said. "It's just . . . you have so many tools, I thought you wouldn't notice that this was the same as the one from the house. All tools look alike, right?"

Derek look of disgust eloquently expressed his opinion of that question, and of Melissa's intelligence.

"Not exactly," I answered. To a carpenter or a handyman, someone who works with his tools every day, each screwdriver is distinctive and different. If this screwdriver had shown up in Derek's truck, he would have known right away that it was the screwdriver from the house on Cabot Street. Even if all of Tony's blood had been wiped away.

Melissa shrugged. "Well, the truck wasn't there anyway. So I started to go home again. But then Derek drove up, and I had to say something to explain why I was there. So I tossed the bag with the screwdriver into the Dumpster behind the hardware store. When he asked me what was going on, I told him I was upset about Tony going out with Nina and asked him if he could come upstairs with me for a while."

Derek snorted. He was obviously rather outdone with his ex-wife at this point. "Christ, Melissa, you should have just called the police when you found him. It would have been better than running away and taking the murder weapon with you."

"Wayne doesn't like me," Melissa said. "You don't, either."

Her eyes were filling up with tears, and as she turned to me, they spilled over and ran down her cheeks. "You have to help me, Avery. I know you've dealt with this kind of thing before. You have to figure out a way to prove to Wayne that I didn't do it. Please!"

—16—

Had the circumstances been different, I might have felt rather gratified at that point. Melissa, perfect, fabulous, do-no-wrong Melissa, was in way over her head and begging for my help. My help in keeping her out of the slammer, which made it all the sweeter.

I couldn't quite bring myself to enjoy the situation as much as I might, however. Partly because she seemed very sincerely distraught, and partly because I really couldn't wrap my brain around the fact that she might have killed Tony. Much as I disliked her—and yes, I did, especially after hearing her say that she'd been trying to foist the murder weapon off on my boyfriend!—I couldn't see her as a murderess. Stupid enough to run away with the murder weapon, sure. Manipulative enough to try to rope Derek into providing an alibi for her. But not crazy enough to stab Tony to death with a screwdriver. At least not over something idiotic like a dinner date with Nina.

We walked out of police headquarters shortly after I

promised her I'd do my best to exonerate her. Connor came back to ask if we were ready to go, and escorted us upstairs and to the front door. "Everything go OK?" he asked, his face worried.

"Everything went fine," I said. Derek's silence was eloquent.

I had thought he'd be happy about me saying I'd help Melissa, since he'd been trying to convince me all along that she didn't do it. He didn't turn out to be. Happy, I mean. When we were in the truck on our way toward the Waymouth Tavern later, I asked why.

"You have to ask?" He gave me a look that was somewhere between incredulous and angry.

"I thought you wanted Melissa out of jail."

"I don't care if she spends the rest of her life in jail," Derek said in a modified bellow, "especially after she tried to frame me!"

After a moment, he added, in a calmer voice, "Although I'd feel better if she was actually guilty. And I don't think she is."

"So why aren't you happy that I'm helping her?"

He shot me another boy-you're-stupid look. "There's a murderer running loose. I don't want anything to happen to you."

"Nothing's happened to me before." Any of the other times I'd gotten involved in Wayne's murder cases.

"Lots of stuff's happened to you before!"

Point taken. "But I always came through it OK. I never even got hurt!"

"Then," Derek said. "This time you might."

"I won't. I promise. I've got you and Mischa to protect me. What could go wrong?"

"A whole lot," Derek said.

"Well, I don't have a choice. I promised her I'd try."

He shook his head, exasperated. "Only you, Avery. You don't even like her! Why would you go to all this risk and trouble for Melissa?"

"Because she asked. And because she didn't do it." Or so she said. "And because if she didn't, then someone else did. And if Melissa goes to jail for it, then that someone else gets off."

And besides, I liked the idea that Melissa would be indebted to me. You never know when something like that might come in handy.

"I don't like it," Derek said.

"I'm not going to do anything stupid. I promise. For starters, I'm just going to ask the staff at the Waymouth Tavern whether they noticed Nina and Tony the other night. And after that, and after dinner, I'm going to go online and see if I can find anything about the TV station they worked at in Missouri. If someone from there is sending them both letters saying 'I know what you did,' they must have done something."

"It would seem that way," Derek agreed as he pulled the car into a parking space outside the Waymouth Tavern, next to a small, blue Honda. "Looks like Josh is here, too."

"Probably having dinner with Fae again." That wouldn't make Shannon happy.

"Stay out of their business," Derek warned as he helped me down from the car.

I'd felt pretty icky after going Dumpster diving, and seeing Melissa looking stunning even in jail while I looked like something one of the cats had dragged in had made me even more eager for a shower and clean clothes. I had made Derek stop at Aunt Inga's house for thirty minutes to let me get clean and changed into something more appropriate for dinner. Part of the appropriate attire was sandals with high heels—perfect for showing off the nail polish I indulge in on my toes!—and I guess he thought I could use some assistance. Little did he know I'd spent my formative years—teens and twenties—wandering around New York City in shoes that were a lot less practical than these. This pair had ankle straps and platform soles, and I was perfectly comfortable getting in and out of the truck in them. That didn't mean I eschewed the help; I'll take any excuse to snuggle up to my boyfriend when he offers.

He helped me down and then held me for a moment, looking down at me. "I just don't want anything to happen to you, Avery."

"I know. And I appreciate it. I'll be careful." After a second, I added, with a grin, "Josh won't hurt me if I interfere in his love life."

"I didn't mean Josh," Derek said, into my hair, "and you know that very well."

I did. And since it was nice to be wanted and nice to be held, I didn't try to be funny anymore, and just enjoyed standing there until he let me go and headed for the door to the restaurant, an arm around my shoulders.

I couldn't resist keeping an eye out for Josh and Fae on the way to our table by the window, and spied them over in a dark, romantic corner on the very opposite side of the tavern. Josh's attention was focused on his companion, and all I saw of her was a fall of long, black hair fastened with a couple of sparkly star-shaped clips. Neither of them noticed us going by on the other side of the room.

"Did you work two nights ago," I asked the hostess as I slid into my own side of the booth, with a quick glance at her name tag, "Cali?"

She nodded. "I work Sunday through Thursday. Someone else works Friday and Saturday."

"Do you know who Tony Micelli is?"

Another nod. "He comes in all the time." And then she corrected herself. "Used to come in all the time."

"Monday?"

"Sure. He had someone with him. Not the fiancée. Someone else. She was a little older, but she was another blonde. I guess he must like those." She shrugged, tossing her own blond hair.

"You heard what happened to him, right?"

She nodded. "Oh, sure. It was on the news last night."

"I don't suppose you noticed anything about him and the blonde? Anything they talked about? Anything in particular that seemed off or wrong? Did they argue, maybe?"

But Cali shook her head. "I don't see people for very long," she said apologetically. "I just seat 'em, you know? And then I leave, and the waiter takes over. I can get the waiter who took care of them on Monday for you, if you want."

"That'd be great. Thanks."

"Here are your menus. Someone will be with you shortly." She bustled off, a Candy lookalike, but in a short, black dress and high heels, and with stick-straight hair down around her shoulders.

"I can't believe Wayne's letting you question people for him," Derek said, opening his menu. "Next you'll want to be deputized. You know what you want?"

I didn't bother checking the menu. "We've been here enough. I'll probably have what I always have. And it isn't like I won't tell Wayne anything I find out, you know."

"I know. Crab cakes?"

"At least I know they're good."

"You don't have to justify yourself," Derek said. "I'm having what I always have, too."

Burger and fries, in other words. It's always struck me as funny that he lives here on the craggy coast of Maine, where lovely seafood abounds, and he'll order a hamburger and French fries when he goes out to dinner. Then again, he goes to the little deli in downtown and has a lobster roll at least once a week, too, so it isn't like he's not getting his share of omega-3s.

"So at least we know that Tony and Nina really were here the other night," I said.

"Was there any doubt?" Derek answered.

"I guess not. Wonder if the waiter noticed anything?"

"Why don't you ask?" Derek indicated the white-shirted young man approaching.

"Hi." He stopped beside the table. "I'm Grant. Cali said you wanted to talk to me?"

A stray thought buzzed through my brain for a second, but I didn't have the time to chase it down. "Hi, Grant. Did you wait on Tony Micelli when he was here on Monday night?"

Grant, a persnickety-looking blond in his midtwenties, looked from me to Derek and back down the full length of his nose. "Who wants to know?"

"Actually," Derek said, "the chief of police does."

"You're not the chief of police. I know him."

Grant and everyone else in town.

"No," I said, with a glance at Derek, who was grinning, "but he sent us. Or rather, when we told him we were coming here, he said to ask."

Grant pondered for a moment. "All right," he said eventually. "Yes, I waited on Tony Micelli the other night. So?"

"You heard what happened to him, right?"

"Sure. It's all over the news."

"We . . . I mean, Wayne . . . that is, the chief of police wanted to know whether you'd noticed anything when he was here. Did he say anything that stuck out to you? Did anything happen that was unusual?"

Grant pondered. "Can't say it did."

A man of few words. I tried to sound as official as I could. "Maybe you could tell me about it? In your own words?"

Derek smothered a smile, and I grimaced at him across the table.

"Sure," Grant said, with an elegant shrug of his narrow shoulders. "They got here around seven thirty, I guess. Tony and a blonde. Not the Realtor, another one. Older. Very well dressed. Out-of-towner. They sat over there." He pointed to a booth farther up the row.

"He had the surf and turf, no starch. Watching his weight, I guess. She had the salmon Caesar. And a bottle of wine."

"By herself?"

Grant shrugged. "The bottles aren't that big."

"Did they have dessert?" Derek asked.

"Black coffee for her," Grant said. "Cappuccino for him."

Sounded like they were both dieting. The curse of working in television, I guess. Tony had to keep trim for the camera, and for Nina, it was probably just habit.

"Did you hear anything they said?"

"They stopped talking whenever I got close," Grant said. "It seemed deliberate. She actually hushed him once. I only caught a few words: 'never meant for it to happen.' "

"Never meant for what to happen?"

"No idea," Grant said, with another shrug. "I told you, I only caught a few words."

"Well, did they seem to get along? We're they arguing? Flirting? Acting like old friends?"

Grant thought for a moment, his head tilted to the side, birdlike. "They weren't flirting. He's engaged, you know."

Was, rather. "Yes, I know," I said.

"And they weren't arguing. Although the conversation did seem intense. Their body language was a little stiff, but they didn't seem uncomfortable with each other. Old friends, maybe. Used to be close, hadn't seen each other for a while."

Bull's-eye. "But you have no idea what they were talking about?"

"I just heard the one sentence. At one point, I thought she said Rory, but it could just have been 'sorry,' I guess."

Or Corey. Laurie. Or Maury. Or Tory or Glory. Maybe gory.

"How about when they left? Were they still getting along OK?"

"Seemed to be," Grant said. "He paid. Opened the door for her when they left. Put his hand on her back on the way across the parking lot." He shrugged. "What can I get you guys to drink?"

Derek ordered a beer, I ordered a Diet Coke. And since we were ready, we also ordered our food. Grant said he'd be right back and left us there.

"So that was a whole lot of nothing," Derek said.

I nodded. "But at least we know that Nina wasn't acting murderous when they left here."

"She could have turned murderous in the car."

"I suppose. Although he dropped her at the B and B before he went to the house on Cabot."

"So she says," Derek said. "No one actually saw her come in."

"He texted Melissa, though. He wouldn't have asked her to meet him if he still had Nina in the car." I thought for a second and added, "If he did text Melissa."

"What do you mean?" Derek said. "Wayne would have checked that, don't you think? Made sure she really did get a text message asking her to go to the house?"

"I'm sure he did. I was thinking more along the lines of it maybe not being Tony who sent the text, but whoever killed him."

"Ah." Derek sat back on the seat. "Go on."

"Well, Tony and Melissa may have been in the habit of sending each other text messages. Some people are. But wouldn't it make more sense for him to call her? Or even just stop by? It was late. She wasn't working, so he wouldn't be interrupting anything. And she might not hear a text coming in, but she'd hear the phone ring. So calling would have been safer if he wanted to make sure to get hold of her."

"That's a good point," Derek said. "Unless he was hoping *not* to get hold of her, but he wanted it to look like he tried."

"True. But someone else could have texted, hoping she'd think it was Tony, to set her up. Get her to the house on Cabot to implicate her."

"What else?" Derek wanted to know.

I shrugged. "Just a thought that buzzed through my brain earlier. When Nina and Wayne and I were talking about those letters, she said at first she thought they might be from someone who blamed her for what happened to Stuart. The former host."

"So?"

"I had this idea that someone might be trying to ruin the show. I even suggested it to Fae, and she laughed at me."

"Yeah?"

Grant brought our drinks, and Derek nodded his thanks.

"Wilson told me the show had a different host before Stuart. His name was Grant, and he was fired after the first season. Not personable enough."

"Grant?" Derek said, looking after the waiter's back as he bustled toward the back of the restaurant. "Not that Grant?"

"I'm sure it isn't. Wilson said the guy looked like Tony, and the waiter doesn't look anything like that. But the name reminded me."

Derek tipped the bottle up and took a swig of beer. "So what are you saying? The former host of the show arranged the accident so he could get his job back? Or just out of spite because they fired him?"

"If he wanted his job back, I think he would have approached Nina, don't you? It was probably just to ruin the show. They fired him, so he didn't want them to be successful."

"He took his time about it, then. They've been on the air for three or four seasons, haven't they?"

"Four, I think. It would have been three years ago that he was fired. Or his contract wasn't renewed, or however they do things in television. That does seem rather a long time."

I swirled my straw around in the Diet Coke, watching the ice cubes dip and bob. "This is frustrating. If Melissa didn't kill him, who did? And how do the letters fit in? Melissa didn't send them; she didn't even know Nina existed until a couple of days ago. Unless Tony talked about her, but I don't really think he would. Maybe Tony did it?"

"Sent the letters? To himself?"

"He could have done that to divert suspicion. If something happened twenty years ago, he'd be the logical person to know about it, since he seems to be the only one who knew Nina back then. Maybe *he* sent her the letters. Via a friend he made in Missouri back when he lived there. And maybe on Monday night he told her he did. Maybe he threatened to go public with whatever it was he knew unless she paid him."

"Blackmail?" Derek said, interested. "Why? He had plenty of money."

"Maybe he wanted revenge. Maybe she dumped him back then. But she realized that as long as he knew, he'd always be a threat to her, and so she decided to get rid of him instead of paying him off. Maybe he waited for her outside the B and B so she could get her checkbook, and when she got back in the car, she insisted he drive her to the house on Cabot. She may even have had a gun."

"If she had a gun, why didn't she just shoot him?"

I shrugged. "Ballistics? Afraid someone would match the bullet to the gun? Or that the police would check and find out that she has a gun license for the same caliber weapon? And then she remembered the conversation we had earlier in the day, about thieves and empty houses, and she decided to kill Tony and take the tools to make it look like a robbery gone wrong."

"And Melissa?"

"Tony could have texted her while he sat in the car and

waited. On the sly, so Nina wouldn't notice. Or Nina could have done it after the murder to frame Melissa. In case the robbery story didn't pan out."

"That makes a certain amount of sense," Derek admitted.

"Well, who else is there, after all? Fae was hanging out with Shannon. Ted and Wilson went to Portland together."

"Adam," Derek said.

"Why on earth would Adam kill Tony?"

"He was having a sordid affair with Nina and got jealous? Or he had seen Melissa and been overcome by passion?"

"I suppose that's possible. Although it doesn't seem like a good enough reason."

"I was kidding, Tink," Derek said. "Here's the food. Can we talk about something else while we eat? Not that I'm queasy—I've seen a lot worse than Tony in my day—but murder just doesn't make for nice dinner conversation."

"Sure," I said as Grant put my crab cakes and Derek's burger and fries on the table. "What do you want to talk about?"

"How about the weather? That's always safe."

"If that's what you'd like." I lifted my fork. "It's been nice the last few days, hasn't it? Hopefully it'll last for the rest of the week. If we run into rain tomorrow or Friday—especially tomorrow—we'll be in trouble."

Derek nodded and took a bite of his burger.

We spent the rest of the meal in idle chitchat and plans for the rest of the week. All in all, things at the house were not going too badly, even with being behind schedule. I wouldn't have time to go hunt down a porch swing, but we figured out the details for how I could make my own, and Derek suggested I could take the old Adirondack chair in Aunt Inga's garden shed and do something with that, as well. It needed paint, obviously, but if I cleaned it, and painted it—the same color or a complementary color to the door and/or swing—it would look great sitting on the porch.

"Ooooh!" I said, excited, "I know what I can do! I saw this in a magazine once—"

"The same magazine where Kate saw the porch swing?"

"I have no idea. But . . ." I stopped and squinted at him. "Are you making fun of me?"

"Wouldn't dream of it," Derek said, but not without a twinkle in his eyes. "Your projects always end up looking great, even if they sound crazy at the outset. If anyone can make a porch swing made from an old door look good, you can. So tell me about the chair."

"I saw this in a magazine. It was an Adirondack chair—new and unfinished, but I don't think that matters—that someone had drilled holes in and then painted yellow. It looked great. Like—"

"Cheese," Derek said. "You want to make the chair look like it's made of Swiss cheese and put it on the front porch."

"I can, can't I?"

"Like I said, you can make anything look good. So go ahead. I trust you."

I smiled. I love my boyfriend.

We ended up sharing a whoopie pie for dessert—whipped vanilla cream between two soft chocolate cakes; a Maine delicacy and a favorite of mine—and then we headed outside and home. Josh's car was already gone, I noticed. Maybe he was taking Fae for another drive up the coast to "talk" more.

It was a lovely summer evening, nice and cool now that the sun had set, and with just a faint sparkle of stars up above. The horizon was still light, orange just fading to peach and then purple where the sun had set. The entire Atlantic Ocean was spread out to our left as Derek maneuvered the truck down the ocean road toward Waterfield. A few of the islands had summer homes on them, so lights blinked here and there, and there were also a few pleasure boats floating across the water, some of them with strings of colored Christmas lights festooning their masts, like strands of brightly colored beads moving through the darkness.

When I was five and visited Waterfield for the first time, my mother had warned me about the cliffs. Here and there along the coast, there are tall cliffs that go pretty much straight down into the ocean. A few old houses sit on them, and I knew from experience that at least one of them— Cliff House, sitting empty now while the Historical Society prepared to open it as a part-time museum—had smuggling tunnels and secret storage rooms carved into the rock underneath.

Anyway, I've always had a healthy respect for the cliffs, instilled in me at an early age. When I drive myself along the ocean road, I drive slow. Derek doesn't, but he's driven these roads his whole life, so I wasn't worried. I leaned back, my head against the seat, my eyes half closed as I watched the scenery fly by.

And then I scared Derek into practically running off the road when I shot up straight and shrieked, "Stop the car!"

"What!" For a few seconds we fishtailed, before he got the car under control and slid to a stop at the side of the road. "God dammit, Avery, don't do that! Did you forget your purse at the restaurant?"

I shook my head. "Go back."

"Back where?"

"Back up the road. I thought I saw something. Back up. Slowly."

Derek arched his brows, but he did it. Put the truck into reverse and moved carefully back the way we came, his arm slung over the seat and his eyes out the back window. I, meanwhile, was staring out the window on his side, scanning the shoulder of the road. Until . . .

"Stop. Stop! You see it? There." I pointed.

Derek breathed a very bad word before he jumped out of the truck and ran toward the cliff, between the two tire tracks leading directly off the edge.

—17—

By some miracle, or maybe just Josh's ability to maneuver the runaway car down the curving ocean road until he got to this spot, the car hadn't flown off into nothingness, Thelma and Louise style, before plunging like a rock toward the ocean below. Instead, there was a somewhat less than gentle grade that ended in a few jagged stones down at the water's edge. Still, it could have been so much worse. The small Honda must have picked up quite a lot of speed on the way down, but even so, Josh had managed to keep control of it for long enough to avoid hitting the big rocks and to aim for a spot where he could shoot straight into the water. They hadn't crashed into anything. And because the water wasn't that deep right here, the car hadn't sunk. Not yet, anyway. When we hurtled over the edge of the road and started sliding down the steep grade, we could see that Josh had made it around the car and was trying to open the passenger-side door. After a moment of wrestling, he wrenched the door open and leaned in.

"Seat belt," Derek said breathlessly. I tried to nod, but it was hard to do, what with running flat out down an unstable forty-five degree hill and trying not to topple. And in platform shoes, too. Derek was hauling me along, and I was slowing him down. I twisted my hand out of his.

"Go. Help him. I'm gonna call nine-one-one."

Derek dropped my hand and picked up speed, slipping and sliding in the dirt, sending small avalanches of pebbles and sand down with him. I turned and started crawling back up in the other direction, literally on my hands and knees, trying to catch my breath before I got to the car and the phone in my purse.

As soon as I had connected with 911 and told them where to find us—"On the ocean road a few miles outside of town; look for the black truck with its hazard lights on!"—I slipped out of my shoes and headed back down to the water again. A lot faster this time.

By the time I got there, the Honda had slipped farther into the water to where it was almost submerged, but Josh and Derek had gotten the unconscious Fae out of the car and had laid her on the dirt at the water's edge. I plopped down on my knees next to her, breathless. "How is she?"

And then . . . "That's not Fae."

For a moment the world spun dizzily, and if I hadn't already been sitting down, I think I would have been reeling. Bad enough while I thought it was Fae lying there, unconscious and bleeding. Worse when I realized it was Shannon.

Josh shook his head. He was sitting a few feet away, shivering, his arms around his knees and his glasses missing but his myopic eyes glued to the still form next to me. I tossed him one of the blankets I'd grabbed from the truck. Derek keeps an emergency stash behind the seat: flashlight, a couple of blankets, a small spade, and a bag of kitty litter. Here in Maine, you mostly expect to need those things in the winter, but there was no denying the supplies came in handy right now.

"It was Shannon you were with at the Waymouth Tavern?"

"Obviously," Josh managed, pulling the blanket around himself. I turned to Derek.

"How is she?"

"Knocked out. She'll probably turn out to have a concussion. And the seat belt bruised her some. But she'll be all right. I don't think there are any internal injuries."

He didn't look up at me as he said any of it, just concentrated on taking care of Shannon. She had a bleeding gash on her forehead that looked like it might need stitches. Josh had a few scratches on his face, too, I noticed, one of them rather close to his eye. It was bleeding, but not profusely.

"What about you?" I wanted to know.

Josh didn't look away from Shannon to answer me. "Glasses broke. Seat belt hurt me some. I twisted my ankle on something in the water. Don't think anything's broken, though."

"I called nine-one-one. They're on their way. So is your dad."

Josh nodded.

"So . . . um . . . what happened?"

"No idea," Josh said. "The car was fine when we drove out here earlier. And I didn't notice anything wrong when we left the restaurant. It wasn't until we hit the hills that the brakes didn't work. By then there was nothing I could do."

Been there, done that. "Did you try the brakes at all between the Tavern and here?"

Josh shook his head. "Can't be sure. I think I would have slowed down to get on the road, but maybe not. You go pretty slow in the parking lot anyway, and if I saw that there weren't any cars coming . . ."

He thought for a second, and then added, "And I did. I remember looking and there was nobody coming in either direction, so I'm not sure I put my foot on the brake then. And there's no real need to brake between the Tavern and here. Not until you get to the downhills . . ."

And by then it would be too late. "When was the last time you had the car serviced?"

"Two or three months ago," Josh said. "In the spring. My dad's pretty rabid about safety. And Kate knows I drive Shannon a lot."

Unlikely the brake lines would have unraveled on their own, then. Or whatever brake lines do. And, I realized, it said rather a lot about what my life had become over the past year that I should immediately jump to a conclusion of foul play rather than natural or mechanical failure.

The chain of events was suggestive: Stuart's accident, Tony's murder, and now another accident that might very well have become fatal, too, had Josh not known the road well enough to steer the car to the only place along the coast where he wouldn't plunge the pair of them directly into twenty-plus feet of water.

In the distance, I could hear sirens approaching, and then we could see the flashing lights of the ambulance moving up the ocean road toward us. A pair of headlights followed close behind, probably Wayne and Kate. Both cars screeched to a halt on top of the cliffs, and a few seconds later, powerful flashlight beams started playing over the hillside. They focused on our little group, and then several dark forms started down, causing scree to rain down on us.

A few minutes later, the situation was under control. The paramedics had lifted Josh—who couldn't walk on his twisted ankle—and Shannon—who was still unconscious— up the steep hill to the road. Derek had provided the same service for me, since I'd come down here barefoot the second time, and the soles of my feet had taken a beating. Kate had visibly paled when she saw her only daughter, while Wayne had been rigidly professional, his lips and jaw tight and his eyes hooded and angry. Law enforcement personnel tend to take it very personally when someone targets their families, and that seemed to be the case this time.

He asked Josh the same questions I'd asked, and Josh

gave the same answers. Wayne went on to ask Josh whether he'd noticed anyone in the parking lot when he came out of the restaurant earlier, and Josh said no. He also hadn't seen anyone he knew inside, and had never noticed Derek and me. He'd been too preoccupied with Shannon to notice anything or anyone else. He didn't say that, but it was definitely the impression I got.

"What about you two?" Wayne turned to us, standing at the edge of the road while the paramedics were busy getting Shannon situated in the back of the ambulance and while Josh sat in the open door waiting his turn.

"I didn't notice anyone."

Derek shook his head.

"We did ask the staff about Nina and Tony," I added.

"Anything?" Wayne asked.

"Not much. The waiter said they seemed to get along reasonably well. They weren't arguing but their conversation seemed 'intense.' He only caught a few words. Someone never meant for something to happen, and the name Rory. Or maybe Corey or Laurie."

"Except he said he could have misheard and it might have been 'sorry,' " Derek added.

"If it's Rory," Wayne said, "or Corey or Laurie, that would help."

"When we leave here, I'm going to go online and see what I can discover about the TV station in Missouri that Tony and Nina worked at twenty years ago, and anything that might have happened then. I'll keep an eye out for the name Rory. Or Corey or Laurie. Unless you need us to go to the hospital with you?"

I glanced from him to Kate, sitting next to Shannon inside the ambulance. Kate didn't seem to have heard me, but Wayne shook his head. "I'll make sure she calls you when something happens. You two both look like you should go home and get cleaned up. We've got this."

I nodded. Derek and I both looked a little worse for

wear. His jeans were stained and dirty and had a rip at the knee from sliding down the hillside, while the soles of my feet were scratched and bloody, and my skirt was torn to shreds. Silk and tulle are lovely materials, but they aren't meant for crawling around in the dirt.

"Whoever did this," Derek said, "wasn't Melissa."

Wayne looked at him in silence for a moment. "Let's make sure it was deliberate before we go making pronouncements, yeah?"

"Fine. But if it was deliberate, and we both know that's the most likely explanation, Melissa didn't do it. She wouldn't know how anyway, but she's been in lockup since last night."

"And she'll stay there," Wayne said, "until I say otherwise. Thanks for finding the murder weapon, by the way. Connor called."

"My pleasure." Well, sort of.

"Now, if you'll excuse me, I've got more important things to worry about."

He stalked away, already on the phone with Peter Cortino, the local mechanic, making arrangements to have the Honda pulled out of the water and taken to Peter's shop, where Peter would determine whether the brake failure had been mechanical or induced.

"Shall we?" Derek said. I nodded and turned to Josh, who'd been watching the exchange between his father and Derek from the open back of the ambulance.

"Tell Kate we're going, would you? I'm not sure she can hear me right now. And remind her to call me when Shannon wakes up."

Josh said he would, and Derek picked me up again and carried me to the truck and put me inside. A minute later, we were on our way down the ocean road toward Waterfield and home at a much more sedate pace than earlier. There's nothing quite like a really bad scare to make you face the fact that bad stuff can happen anytime, anywhere.

Mischa was lying in wait in the hallway at Aunt Inga's

house and launched himself at Derek the minute we walked inside, growling menacingly. I unhooked him and lifted him to my face, where I buried my nose in his soft fur. He immediately began purring.

"He's looking at me," Derek said with a scowl, hands on his hips.

"So?"

"He looks like he thinks he's won. What does he think this is? A competition?"

"Probably. I'm his human. You're another guy. It makes sense that he'd be jealous."

"He wasn't like this on the island." He'd preferred me there, too, but he hadn't been openly hostile to Derek. Not like now.

"This is my home," I said. "That he's sharing with me. He probably thinks you're an interloper."

"He'll have to get over that. I'm not going anywhere." He leaned in to kiss my cheek and pulled back when the kitten hissed. "Stupid cat. I'm gonna take a shower. After that, you should soak in the tub. Make sure all the sand and dirt gets out of your scratches. I'll bandage your feet when you're done."

"You're so nice to me."

"I love you," Derek said. "Cat and all."

He blew me a kiss and headed up the stairs, two steps at a time.

Still holding Mischa, I wandered down the hallway toward the kitchen and utility room, wincing as my feet protested with each step I took. In the back of the house, I made sure that Mischa, as well as Jemmy and Inky, had food and water before I put Mischa down and made my slow way back to the front hall and up the stairs.

Jemmy and Inky were curled up on the love seat in the parlor. Inky twitched her tail in greeting and Jemmy opened an eye to look at me as I went by, but that was the only reaction I got. They were getting used to Mischa, though. He had learned to stay off "their" love seat, and as long as he didn't try to eat their food—which he did, occasionally, still being a growing boy—they got along just fine. They weren't friendly, but they weren't unfriendly, either.

A lot like Nina and Tony, according to Grant the waiter.

That thought brought me back to what had just happened tonight, and as I dragged myself up the stairs and into the bathroom and slipped into the tub of hot water that Derek had drawn for me, I thought about the car accident on the cliffs and what might so easily have happened had Josh been a worse driver and less used to the roads in and around Waterfield.

If I'd been on my way down the ocean road last fall when my brakes gave out, I didn't think I'd have been able to do what Josh did. I hadn't lived here long enough to know where to turn off from the road, and I probably wouldn't have been able to keep the truck under control on the way down, either. I'd grown up in New York City, and although I'd had a driver's license and had made sure I kept it up, I was a far from experienced driver. Josh was only twenty-one, but he'd been driving these roads for years and had been riding with his dad before that. Whoever had done this had either counted on Josh's inability to handle the car or hadn't realized that Josh knew the roads as well as he did.

Had the accident been meant to kill them, then? But if so, which of them? Or did that even matter? Who in the world would want to kill either Josh or Shannon? They were perfectly harmless, rather lovely young adults who had never done anything to anyone. True, Josh had helped his dad dig up evidence on a few cases, but surely that wasn't reason enough to want to kill him? And as for Shannon . . .

Now, if it had been the other way around, and it had been Fae in the car instead of Shannon, and I hadn't known Shannon as well as I do, I might have postulated—for just a second, in a completely unbiased, impersonal way—that maybe Shannon had been trying to get rid of Fae. Not that she'd do anything like that, of course, and wouldn't have, even if Fae wasn't going to be leaving town in a few days. Not Shannon. But someone who didn't know her the way I did might think so, perhaps.

Fae . . .

When I'd seen Josh at the Waymouth Tavern, I'd assumed he was having dinner with Fae again. She and Shannon did look alike, especially from the back, which was all I'd seen. Fae's hair was jet-black, obviously dyed, while Shannon's was a deep black cherry with red highlights, but that difference wouldn't be obvious in the romantic dusk of the restaurant. And those sparkly stars she'd used to hold her hair back on one side looked like something Fae might own.

Was it possible that someone had sabotaged the car, thinking they were getting Fae, while really, they were getting Shannon?

"Why would someone want to get Fae?" Derek asked when I was out of the tub and lounging on the bed in shorts and a T-shirt while he applied salve and Band-Aids to my feet. He had pulled on a clean pair of jeans from the small stash he keeps in a drawer of my bureau for occasions like this, but he was still bare-chested, and the view was distracting. Nice, but distracting. "This isn't too bad. You might be a little uncomfortable walking for a day or two, but it's no big deal. Just shallow scratches. Nothing deep. Stay there." He got to his feet.

"Why?"

"I'm gonna get you a pair of socks. They'll make your feet feel better."

I stayed where I was while I answered his earlier question. "I have no idea why anyone would want to get Fae. But that seems more likely than that someone would want to get Shannon. Fae's part of the TV crew, and someone did get Stuart. And Tony."

"Tony wasn't part of the crew," Derek said, coming back with a pair of the fluffiest socks he could find. After he had pulled them on my feet, I wriggled my toes luxuriously.

"No, but he was part of the renovation. If someone wanted to sabotage the show, they might have decided to target Tony, since the house was his. Or wait a minute—"

"Yeah?" Derek said, helping me to stand.

"What if Tony drove by the house on Cabot on his way home from dropping off Nina, and he saw someone there, someone who was staging some sort of accident? And then that person killed him, so he wouldn't tell?"

Derek blinked. Once, then once more. "That actually makes sense."

"Don't sound so surprised. Someone from the crew, then, since whoever is staging these things was around when Stuart was electrocuted, too."

"It's a small suspect list," Derek said. "Nina. Fae. Wilson. Ted. Adam."

"None of them had an alibi, that I know of."

"Wilson and Ted were together, weren't they? In Portland?"

"So they say," I said, "but they could be in it together, right? It doesn't have to be just one of them, it could be two of them working together, too." Although if Wilson was working with someone, surely it was more likely to be his niece. "Fae watched movies with Shannon and then went to her room. Nina said she came home at ten thirty, but no one saw her. And I have no idea where Adam was."

Derek nodded. "Didn't you say you were planning to do some research on these people?"

We started down the stairs to the first floor, me walking very gingerly but really liking the feel of the fluffy socks on the abused soles of my feet. Since they were quite slippery, I held on to the banister with one hand and to Derek with the other. My great-aunt had died from tumbling down these stairs, and I had no desire to follow in her footsteps.

"Not specifically on these people," I said when we got to the landing, "but now maybe I will. I was more interested in that time twenty years ago when Nina and Tony worked together. But I'll see what I can find out about the rest of the crew as well. And Grant."

"Maybe he's had cosmetic surgery and he's really Adam," Derek suggested, depositing me safely on the floor in the entry.

"Or he's had a sex change and he's really Fae." I padded toward the front parlor. "Do you have something to keep you busy while I do this? It could take a while."

"I thought I might have a go at that old Adirondack chair in the shed. Get the drill out and give you Swiss cheese."

I smiled. "Sounds like fun. Knock yourself out."

"I'll just drill the holes tonight. Tomorrow, we'll take it over to Cabot Street and you can use the leftover paint from the utility room to paint it."

"Works for me." I sat down at the desk and pushed the button to boot up the computer. Meanwhile, Derek went to the window behind me and lifted the bottom sash.

"This way we can talk," he explained.

I nodded, already preoccupied with how to best tackle the Internet search.

I'm fairly computer literate. I'm on a nodding acquaintance with Google and I'm familiar with most of the big social networking sites. I'm not a computer genius, though. For anything more complicated than the basics, I rely on Josh, who knows ten times more than I do. Or Ricky, but he was back in Pittsburgh with his family and with Paige. And, of course, Josh was at the hospital. Looked like it was up to me this time. I cracked my knuckles and set to work.

Behind me, outside the open window, I heard Derek moving around. A big sort of hollow thump was the sound of the Adirondack chair from the shed being dumped on the wooden slats of the porch floor. Derek moved around some more—pulling out the electric drill and plugging it in—before I heard the whirring of the drill itself being tested. Then the sharp whine as the drill bit into the wood and the occasional muffled swear word floating in through the window screen when something didn't go Derek's way. Every so often, he'd stop—I realized later it was to change the drill bit; Swiss cheese needs holes both big and small—before the drill started up again.

Meanwhile, I let my fingers do the walking on the keyboard, with varied results.

Since it seemed logical—and easy—I started by googling each of the members of the crew by name, and coming up with the expected information. Adam and Fae both had Facebook and Twitter accounts; Wilson, Ted, and Nina did not. She had a LinkedIn profile, and so did Adam, but none of the others did. She was mentioned in a couple of different articles over the years—nominations for Emmy awards, presence at award shows and industry functions—and so were Wilson and Ted. There were pictures: Wilson with his lovely wife, whom I recognized from the photo he kept in his wallet; Nina and Ted individually and sometimes together. Adam was mentioned a few times in the cast of low-budget films and the equivalent of off-off-Broadway theater productions. Once he'd landed a recurring role in a cable TV show, but his part had been cancelled, or not renewed, after just four episodes. That wasn't what he'd told me that first day I met him, when he told me his life story while Derek went home for another T-shirt. Then, he'd made it sound like it had been his choice to leave the cable TV show to go on to bigger and better opportunities.

I found a couple pages of photos of him: He photographed extremely well, of course, and had quite the six-pack tucked away underneath those tight T-shirts. In several of the pictures, he was lifting the shirt to show off his abs, which I found more than a little icky, especially since he glistened as if he'd rubbed himself with Crisco for the occasion.

Fae had no professional presence at all; from what I could make out, she was just your average college student who happened to have landed a summer gig in television, thanks to her uncle Wilson. She studied at Kansas City University, but then I already knew that. What I didn't know, or didn't realize, was that Kansas City U happened to be located in the great state of Missouri.

All right, yeah, I knew there were two Kansas Cities. Somewhere in the back of my head, from a geography class years ago, I remembered that. I just hadn't realized that when Fae said she was from Kansas City, she was actually from the state of Missouri, not the state of Kansas.

"Hey," I called out to Derek through the window; this realization happened to strike during a lull in the drilling, so he could hear me. "Josh told me yesterday that Fae's a college student. This is just a summer job. And guess what? She's studying at Kansas City University."

"Missouri or Kansas?" Derek called back.

I made a face. Of course he'd catch that immediately, when I hadn't. "Missouri."

"That's interesting." He leaned down so he could look through the window and see the computer screen.

"I thought so. But that's about the only interesting piece of information I've managed to find. Adam's struck out repeatedly in pretty much every career direction he's tried. Theatre, TV, movies. Nina has won a few awards, and I discovered that she moved to *Flipped Out!* from another series at the same network, which was cancelled. It was called *Burb Appeal.*"

"As in 'suburb' appeal?"

"I guess so."

"No wonder it was cancelled," Derek said. "What about the old host? Grant? And Stuart, the guy in the hospital?"

It hadn't crossed my mind to search Stuart, but now I did. And found very little. He'd been a rank nobody when he landed the gig as the host of *Flipped Out!*—a charming, aw-shucks young man from somewhere in Oklahoma who'd sent an audition tape to the network. He didn't get picked then, but a year later, when Grant had failed out, he was offered the job. I read that in a press release the network had published to explain the changeover. It also gave Grant's last name—Cummings—and said he'd left due to "creative differences."

Stuart's accident last month got a mention on the *Flipped Out!* blog, followed by a few hundred comments, most of them from women offering wishes for a rapid recovery and a few other things I won't mention, and they probably shouldn't have, either. There was no mention of foul play.

Grant Cummings was all over the Internet. He had a Facebook page, a MySpace page, a LinkedIn profile, a Twitter handle, a website, and a fan page, and after checking all of them, I could say with a lot of certainty that I was pretty sure he hadn't had anything to do with Stuart's accident or anything that had happened here in Waterfield. Unlike Adam, he really had gone on to bigger and better. After hacking around Hollywood for a year or so, doing very little—or very little I could find—he had landed a small, recurring role on a soap opera and had managed to translate it into a two-year run. His Facebook page said his contract had just been renewed for the new season. So he clearly had no time and less reason to want to sabotage the show that had dropped him.

"Bummer," Derek said.

"It was just a thought. I suspected all along this had something to do with Nina and Tony and Missouri, not Grant. But it's good to be able to eliminate him."

"Come have a look at your chair. How many holes do you want?"

"Enough to look like Swiss cheese," I said, but I got up and padded outside. My feet felt a little better after the bath and the bandaging, and with the soft, fluffy socks. The chair didn't look so hot right now, old and covered with dirty paint, but I could picture the finished product in my head, and it would look awesome. "How come the wood didn't split or crack when you drilled this?" I ran my finger around the inside of a hole that overlapped two boards.

"You need a guide board," Derek said, holding one up. It was a thin piece of plywood with a hole drilled into the middle. "You just clamp it to the front of the chair and drill through it. It's easier to get the hole started that way. It helps with the biggest holes and the ones that are between two boards."

"Maybe a couple more? And a few on the armrests?"

"I don't wanna put too many on the seat," Derek said, "since it might compromise the structure. But I can add a few to the backrest and the arms."

"I'm gonna go look up Missouri."

He nodded. "I'll be in when I'm done with this and I've cleaned up."

I padded back inside and sat down at the computer again. Mischa had entered the parlor now, too, and had jumped up on the windowsill, where he sat and stared out at Derek, tail twitching.

—18—

Nina's resume on LinkedIn told me where she'd started her career and gave me the call letters of the television station in Missouri where it had all begun. I even knew the time she'd worked there: six or seven months twenty-one years ago. I started there.

And unfortunately, came up pretty empty. Neither Nina nor Tony were mentioned anywhere on the station website. And no wonder, considering how many years it had been since they worked there and that neither of them had stayed very long. There were no mentions of previous employees at all, unless something bad had happened to them. Like one young woman, Aurora Jamison, who must have died suddenly, and who had gotten a road named after her. Aurora Lane, the road heading up the hill to the transmitting tower. But since both Nina and Tony had been alive and kicking when they left Kansas City, there was no mention of either of them.

I've had occasion, in the past, to look into Waterfield

history, and I usually start with the historical society and the local newspapers, the *Waterfield Weekly* and the daily *Clarion*. Kansas City probably had a historical society, but this wasn't something they'd be able to help me with, being fairly recent in historical terms. The newspapers, on the other hand . . .

The big newspaper in those parts seemed to be the *Kansas City Star*. Its news archives didn't go back twenty years, but some of its content did. When I googled Tony Micelli + Nina Andrews + KRBQ, the call letters for the station, I lucked out and found myself staring at an obituary. For none other than Aurora Jamison, who had given her name to the TV-station road.

There was a picture at the top of the obit, showing me that Aurora had been a beautiful girl in her early twenties. From the name, I had expected a blonde—Sleeping Beauty's name was Aurora, maybe that's what threw me—but this Aurora was a brunette. Curly hair, big eyes, sweet smile. Something about her was familiar, although I couldn't put my finger on what.

She had started at KRBQ less than two years before she died, but the hometown girl had quickly become a viewer favorite, as well as a favorite with the powers that be at the station. There were plans for making her the host of a new midday show they were putting together. That news hadn't been made public yet, and several of the other young reporters associated with the station were in contention for the spot, as well. But at the time she died, Aurora was the front-runner.

And then she had been in a car accident on her way to work in the super-early hours of the morning. Nobody was around to see what happened, but the postmortem showed that she was DUI, and she ran off the road and crashed the car. By the time paramedics got to her, it was too late.

That information wasn't in the obituary, of course. I found that by googling Aurora's name. And where the *Star* didn't have their news archives online for twenty years back, one of the smaller Kansas City newspapers did. They quoted Nina, another of the TV station's up-and-coming young reporters, who had been called in to work to replace Aurora in that morning's broadcasts, as saying that everyone was in shock and nobody could believe it had happened. There was no mention of Tony except for his name in the obituary with her other colleagues. I scanned the list, just in case there was a Rory or Corey or Laurie on it, or even a Roderick or a Lauren, but no such luck. The closest I came was Frederick, but it was difficult to imagine how Grant could have turned that into Rory.

"Find anything?" Derek asked, coming into the parlor to lean over my shoulder. He dropped a kiss on the top of my head on his way down, and then swore as Mischa launched himself at him. I let Derek unhook the kitten from his jeans on his own this time as I focused on the computer.

"Check out this article about a woman named Aurora Jamison, who worked at the same TV station as Nina and Tony. She died while they were in Kansas City."

"Rory," Derek said, putting Mischa back on the windowsill. "Damn cat."

"Excuse me?"

"I hate this cat. He's always getting on me. Oh. Rory. Short for Aurora."

"Really? I've never heard that."

"I knew a Rory once whose name was Aurora." When I slanted a look at him, he was smiling.

"Old girlfriend?"

"Summer fling. I was sixteen. So what happened to this Aurora?"

"Car accident. Late at night. DUI and probably hurrying to get to work on time."

"Hard to imagine how that could be anyone else's fault," Derek said.

"I know. If she and Nina were close friends, I suppose Nina might have felt bad about it afterward. But bad enough to leave a good job at a TV station? The article said she ended up taking over Aurora's job on the early news."

"Maybe she felt guilty. If she'd wished Aurora out of the way, and then Aurora died."

"Someone sent the letters, though. And it wasn't Nina."

"You don't know that," Derek said, "but no, it probably wasn't. Did Aurora have any family?"

"If she did, they're not mentioned here. I can keep digging. There's probably a regular obituary somewhere, too. A personal one. Not this fancy one from the TV station."

"Tomorrow," Derek said. "It's time for bed. You need to rest your feet."

"You're kidding, right?" They were scratches. And not even deep scratches.

"Are you questioning my medical expertise?" He picked me up bodily, straight out of the chair.

"But Kate hasn't even called yet. Don't you want to wait to hear from the hospital?"

"Bring the phone upstairs. We've got another early morning and another long day tomorrow. We both need sleep."

And that was it. He didn't even give me time to shut down the computer, although I did reach out and flick off the light on my way out the door.

Kate didn't call until the next morning at the ungodly early hour of 5:45. We were up by then, dressed and downstairs in the kitchen, waiting for the coffee to brew. My feet felt better, but I was still wearing fluffy socks and comfy sneakers, in spite of the hot weather. And I was tired. So was Derek, his eyes dull as he watched the coffeemaker go through the motions. Kate sounded tired as well, even if the relief in her voice was palpable.

"She's awake. She woke up for just a minute last night, and then went to sleep. But it was after midnight, so I didn't call."

"She's all right?" Derek asked. I'd put the cell on speaker so we both could hear and talk to her.

"She's fine. She's got a concussion, like you said, but she can remember everything up until running off the road. The last minute or two of heading down toward the water are gone, but the doctor says it's no big deal; people with concussions often have minor memory loss of things that happened right before they hit their heads. And besides, we know what happened."

Derek nodded.

"She's going to stay in the hospital until tomorrow. Josh will be released today, but I don't think he'll be able to come help you guys. His foot is bandaged."

"Twisted?"

"Broken. Some little bone near his ankle. He'll be fine, too, but the ER doctor said to stay off it as much as possible for a few days."

"What about you?" I wanted to know.

"Oh, I'm fine. I'm on my way home to take care of the crew before they head out to work. After that, I think I'll take a nap. I didn't get much sleep overnight."

"Look at their reactions when you tell them what happened," Derek instructed. "Just in case one of them says or does something suspicious."

"Wayne told me the same thing. He'll be there, too."

"Tell him to give us a call later. There's something I need to tell him. And let us know how it goes."

She promised she would, and we hung up.

"That's most of our work crew gone," Derek said.

I nodded. "You don't think that's the reason for the accident, do you? Someone trying to sabotage our project?"

"Who'd care that much about a TV show?" Derek answered. "And killing Tony is taking things pretty far, wouldn't you say? If someone truly hated us that much, wouldn't they just try to kill one of us? It'd be simpler."

"Don't say that!"

He shrugged. "We've never done anything to anyone to deserve that. And besides, if someone disliked either one of us enough to go to such lengths to ruin our first TV appearance, don't you think we'd know who it is? That kind of crazy is hard to hide."

He had a point. The only people I could imagine might dislike either of us enough to kill were the folks we'd helped put in jail, and they were all where they were supposed to be, as far as I knew. In lockup.

"And," Derek added another qualifier, "that doesn't explain the accident in Kentucky that put Stuart in the hospital. Or the poison-pen letters."

"So we're back to someone who's trying to ruin the show itself. Or trying to ruin Nina."

"One of the crew," Derek said. I nodded. "Well, at the moment, we're gonna ruin our own chances of being on TV if we don't get moving. We won't have much help today, so that means we'll have to do more of the work ourselves. Let's go."

"The coffee . . . ?"

"Take it with you," Derek said and headed outside to load the holey Adirondack chair into the back of the truck.

. . .

By the time the television crew arrived at the house on Cabot, we were hard at work. Derek was finishing up the second coat of polyurethane on the wood floors, and I was putting the doors back on the kitchen cabinets and screwing the new door handles and drawer pulls onto the doors and drawers. It all looked great and would look even better when the kitchen counter was in.

Ted and Adam helped Derek maneuver the counter in place while Wilson filmed. Meanwhile, Fae pushed me into the utility room, Nina on her heels. "We heard about Shannon and Josh. How horrible!"

I nodded. "They were lucky. Things could have been so much worse."

"What happened?" Nina asked. "Kate said they'd run

off the road on the way home from dinner yesterday, and she'd been at the hospital all night."

"Basically, that's all we know. The brakes on Josh's car failed. No idea why yet, but I'm sure we'll find out when the mechanic has taken a look at it. Luckily, Josh managed to find a place where they didn't fly off a cliff and drop like a rock straight into the ocean, so it turned out all right. He has a broken bone in his foot. Shannon has a concussion. Other than that, and some cuts and bruises, they're both fine."

"Oh, my," Nina said, and grabbed Fae's arm. "That could have been Fae!"

"If it had happened the night before, sure. Although there are no cliffs on that side of town." I hesitated for a second, calculating a plan of attack, before I continued, "But really, they were very lucky. People die in car accidents every day. Young people no older than Josh or Shannon. Or Fae. You had a friend who died in a car accident, didn't you, Nina?"

Nina paled, and she dropped her hand from Fae's arm. "How do you know about that?"

"It's public knowledge, isn't it? KRBQ in Kansas City named a road after her. Aurora Lane, right?"

Fae was looking at Nina now, too, while in the kitchen, Derek had started the process of screwing the kitchen counter to the cabinets. From the other room, we could hear Adam explain the process to the camera. "What Dick is doing now . . ."

"His name is Derek, Adam," Wilson said. "Start over."

In the utility room, all were silent. Fae was watching Nina, a guarded expression on her face. Nina looked like she had trouble breathing.

"I went online," I said. "Last night. Something's going on here. People are dropping like flies around this production, and we're lucky Tony's been the only fatality so far. I wanted to know why. So I did some research."

"And you found out about Rory?" Nina's voice was hoarse.

I nodded and chalked up a point for Derek, who had postulated the nickname. "She died during the time you worked for KRBQ, right? You and Tony?"

Nina nodded, her face still several shades too pale. She was twisting her fingers together.

"Did you have something to do with it?"

"I didn't kill her," Nina said. "It was an accident. I wasn't even there that night. And I had no idea she'd get in the car and try to drive to work even though she'd been drinking. That was just stupid!"

"Maybe she was afraid that if she didn't show up, you'd take her job," Fae suggested, her voice low but with an underlying sharpness. "That's the way it is in television, isn't it? So many reporters, so few jobs?"

Nina looked stricken, and I followed up with another question. "You did take over her job, didn't you? Afterward?"

She swallowed. "Just the newscasts. Not the midday show. They decided to shelve that when Rory was killed. And I didn't stay there much longer, anyway. Just a month or so after she died."

"Guilty conscience?" Fae suggested. Nina turned on her.

"I didn't do anything! I wasn't even there when she left. Sure, she was the favorite, and we all knew it, and we all wished she'd mess up or be late or do something stupid so the rest of us could get our chance, but we didn't want her dead!"

Fae snorted.

"Who did she go drinking with that night?" I asked, and Nina looked at me, her eyes haunted.

"Tony."

"She and Tony were dating?"

I'd thought Nina and Tony had been dating, but maybe I'd misunderstood the situation. Although that *was* what she'd said, wasn't it?

Nina shook her head. "Tony was with me. God knows why, because she was much prettier than I ever was, although I didn't look too bad back in those days, I guess." She shrugged. "Rory had a baby, though, and Tony didn't want to be tied down. He wasn't looking for anything permanent. I always knew our relationship wouldn't last beyond Kansas City. Tony had too much ambition. So did I. Rory didn't, but things just seemed to work out for her. You know?"

I nodded. I knew the type. "So what was she doing with him that night?"

"She always liked him. He'd never given her the time of day before, but that night he asked her out. And to go home with him afterward. She said yes."

I wrinkled my brows. "How did you feel about that?"

"I asked him to," Nina said.

"You what!"

This was Fae, and Nina turned to her. "I asked him to do it. To take her out and get her drunk and take her back to his apartment. I thought it would make her sleep through the two A.M. alarm, and she wouldn't make it to the TV station in time to do the morning broadcasts. Or if she did, she'd be too drunk or too hungover to go on the air. I made sure I was there so I could do it instead."

"You asked your boyfriend to take advantage of her?"

"It wasn't taking advantage!" Nina said. "I told you, she liked him. She said yes, didn't she? And all I wanted was to make sure she couldn't go on and do the morning news. I didn't want anything to happen to her!" Her eyes had filled with tears.

"What did happen?" I asked, making sure my voice was gentle.

Nina blinked. Hard. "I don't know. Nobody does. Tony slept through it. He didn't wake up until I banged on his door hours later. He didn't even realize she'd left. Maybe she tried to wake him up in the middle of the night, or maybe she didn't. Nobody knows. I don't know why she didn't just call a cab, if she was bound and determined to get to the studio. She wasn't supposed to drive!"

The tears overflowed and spilled down her cheeks, and she dug in her handbag for something to wipe them with. I tore off a sheet of paper towel and handed it to her, and she buried her face in it. Fae watched her for a second before she slipped off into the kitchen to join the others, I guess maybe to give Nina some privacy. I would have liked to have done the same, but I still had questions.

"Do you think this is the reason you've been getting the letters? Someone knew what you did?"

"But I didn't do anything!" Nina said again. "I didn't want anything to happen to her, I just wanted her out of the way for a couple of hours so I could take her place. That's all! I felt horrible when I heard what had happened. But we never intended for her to try to drive herself to work in the dark!"

"I get that." And I did. She seemed too distraught not to be telling the truth, and besides, it wasn't like she'd stayed at KRBQ after the accident to take advantage of Aurora's passing. Both she and Tony had been out of Kansas City within a few months and hadn't been in contact with one another for twenty years. Those weren't the actions of people who had planned to kill. "Did anyone else know? Or just you and Tony?"

"Ted," Nina said.

"Ted was there?" I hadn't noticed his name in the obituary, but then they may just have listed the talent, not the lowly tech guys. Or maybe Ted wasn't really his name. Maybe it was Theodore or Edward or something.

"He was new, too. We were friends. Could have been more, maybe, if it hadn't been for Tony."

"And he knew what happened? Could he be the one sending you the letters?"

"Ted?" Nina said with an amused smile on her face.

"Not in a million years. He'd never do anything to hurt or threaten me."

"Are you . . ." I hesitated, not quite sure how to phrase the question.

She smiled. "Off and on. Between other things. He was married for a while. I've had a few relationships since Tony. But we always seem to end up back together."

"That's . . . nice." It was, sort of. Unusual maybe, but nice. And possibly it was just the way they did things in show business. "Does he know about the letters?"

"I haven't told him," Nina said. "He worries."

"Right." I thought for a moment. "How did he and Tony get along? Back in Kansas City?"

"Ted didn't like Tony," Nina said readily. "Tony pretty much didn't know that Ted existed. I'm not sure he recognized him when he saw him this week."

I nodded. So Ted had wanted Nina twenty years ago in Kansas City when Tony had had her. Then Tony dropped off the face of the earth for twenty years, and Ted got Nina. At least on and off, when they weren't involved with other people. Which—OK—was a little strange, but to each their own, right? And now they were here in Waterfield, on again, off again, and then Tony shows up. Tony, whom Nina had been involved with before. At a time when she could have had Ted, but had chosen Tony over him. So what were the chances that Ted thought Nina might get involved with Tony again?

Probably pretty good, I figured.

What were the chances that Ted had killed Tony to keep that from happening?

Probably not so good, I admitted to myself. If he'd been married himself, and he'd been OK with Nina's other relationships through the years, he might not care if she had another fling with Tony, especially if the crew was only here in Waterfield for five days. They hadn't tried to make a long-distance relationship work last time, so chances were they wouldn't this time, either. Still, it bore looking into, perhaps.

Ted had said he and Wilson had been in Portland together the night Tony was killed. Or maybe it was Wilson who'd said it? I couldn't remember anymore. I did remember hearing it, though. Maybe I should double-check and make sure they were both onboard with that explanation.

Unless they'd been acting together and neither had been in Portland.

Or they'd both been in Portland but had stopped by the house on Cabot on the way back.

Or something.

"How did Ted find out about what happened to Aurora? Did he plan it with you?"

Nina shook her head. "I came up with the idea and got Tony involved. Ted had nothing to do with it. But after Rory died, Tony and I couldn't keep our relationship going. Too much guilt, I guess. It was her choice to drive drunk, nobody made her do it, but we knew if it hadn't been for us, she wouldn't even have been drinking that night. It got to where we couldn't look at each other anymore. But I needed someone to talk to, and Ted was there, so I talked to him."

That made sense. Rebound relationship.

"So you left Kansas City, and so did Tony, and until this week, you didn't see him again."

She shook her head. "It was a shock, too. At first I wanted nothing to do with him. It brought everything back, things I hadn't thought about for years. But then I got back to the B and B and found the letter and realized it had followed me here. And that was the first time I thought that maybe the letters had something to do with Rory. Up until then I thought maybe someone was blaming me for what happened to Stuart."

"So you agreed to go to dinner with him. And you talked about Aurora. And maybe the letters, too?"

She nodded.

"Was he getting them, as well?"

She shook her head. "He said no. The one that the chief of police showed me must have been the first."

And it had been sent after the crew had arrived in Waterfield. After someone had realized that Tony had known Nina in Kansas City and might have had something to do with Aurora's death, as well. Unless Tony had lied, of course.

"And then he drove you home?"

"Like I told you."

"But you can't prove it, can you? Nobody saw you. And you didn't see anyone."

Nina shook her head. "I didn't kill him, Avery. Why would I? He was as complicit in Rory's death as I was, and everyone agreed he wasn't to blame. He told the police what happened, you know. That they'd been drinking and they'd fallen asleep and he didn't wake up until morning. She was already long gone by then. Everyone agreed it wasn't his fault."

"Did he tell them about you, too?"

This time her cheeks flushed. "No. He kept that part out of it. When we broke up after it happened, everyone assumed it was because he'd cheated on me with Rory."

"What if he had threatened to tell now?"

"What if he had?" Nina said. "We didn't kill her. We didn't even want her to die. We just wanted her to oversleep and miss her on-air time. That's all."

And that really was all. Sure, what they'd done was probably unethical, and it was certainly unpleasant. But it wasn't illegal. Nobody had made Aurora Jamison get into that car. She could have called a cab to take her to the TV station. What happened to her, ultimately, was her own fault. Even if someone seemed to think it was Nina's. And Tony's, if that person had killed him because of it. And it was starting to look that way.

"You need to be careful," I said.

"I've already figured that out," Nina answered.

—19—

After Wilson filmed Derek installing the kitchen counter, we all moved outside to the front porch.

I wasn't sure how many of the others had heard Nina's and my conversation in the utility room, but I thought a few of them looked at her sideways. Nina didn't seem to notice, or if she did, she pretended otherwise. I exchanged a look with Derek while Ted moved next to Nina in a silent show of support.

Fae really seemed to enjoy my Adirondack chair, especially after I started painting it yellow. It did look amazingly like Swiss cheese, and it would look adorable sitting next to the front door. Maybe I could find a pillow with the Jarlsberg logo, or at least something burgundy and dark blue, to approximate it. Stamped with the number of the house, maybe. Fae wanted to know how to make the holes, so Wilson filmed me painting the chair while I explained— to Adam—that we'd cut the holes with a drill and different drill bits in different sizes. This morning, Adam's name for me was Evie, so it took twenty minutes to get the thirty-second segment in the can.

While we were doing that, Derek hauled out the old door we were planning to make into a porch swing and we got to work, drilling holes in the corners to attach chains and nailing on the small headboard. Wilson filmed that, as well.

In the middle of the day, we broke for lunch. The crew dispersed, and Derek turned to look at me. "Wanna take a break?"

I stood and stretched my back. "I wouldn't mind driving over to Cortino's Auto to see if Peter's had a chance to look at Josh's car."

"We could just call," Derek suggested.

"I'd rather just go."

"You just want an excuse to look at Peter," Derek said, but he was grinning. I grinned back. Peter Cortino is probably the best-looking man in Waterfield, although Derek runs a close second. Except for this week, when Adam's polished good looks might have them both beat. Personally, however, I find both Derek and Peter infinitely more attractive than Adam, with his gym-rat muscles and high-gloss veneer. There was nothing real about Adam, while neither Derek nor Peter are afraid of getting their hands dirty by doing an honest day's work.

"What did you and Nina talk about in the laundry room earlier?" Derek wanted to know as he drove the car down Cabot Street in the direction of Cortino's Auto Repair. "I caught a few words, but between the drilling and the camera and Adam screwing up the words, I couldn't keep up."

I gave him a rundown of what had been said, and he whistled. "Fae looked pretty disgusted when she came into the kitchen."

I nodded. "What they did to Aurora Jamison was despicable. But it wasn't criminal. I really don't think they meant for her to die."

"Probably not," Derek admitted. "And Tony didn't deserve to die for it, either. If that's what happened."

"Don't you think it was?"

"Twenty years is a long time to wait."

"Maybe it was—" I stopped as a thought ran swiftly through my head and out the other side.

"What?" Derek said.

"Something Nina said. That Aurora had a baby. That's why Tony wasn't interested in her; he didn't want to get tied down."

"So?"

"If Aurora had a baby twenty-one years ago, that baby would be around twenty-two now."

"Or a few years older," Derek said. "Some people call them babies until they're at least three or four. And if Nina and Aurora weren't close, she might not have known exactly how old the child was. Aurora probably didn't bring it to work."

"You just want it to be Adam."

He looked at me. "Don't you?"

"I'd rather have it be Adam than Fae," I admitted. "I like her. But I think he's probably too old. Would Fae have the strength to stab Tony several times with a screwdriver, though?"

"I imagine she might, if the incentive was big enough. And he'd be less likely to worry about being alone with her, too."

True. "I can't remember where either of them are from. Fae's attending Kansas City University, but I don't know if she was born there. And Adam . . . I just can't remember. But neither of their last names are Jamison. Adam's is Ramsey, and Fae's is . . ."

"Cameron," Derek said, and swung the truck into the lot in front of Cortino's. Waterfield is such a small town it takes only a few minutes to get anywhere. "Aurora sounds like a single mother. The baby may have had the father's name."

"Or Jamison could have been a stage name. Or TV name."

"Let's get this out of the way first, and then we can try to figure out where they were born and whether either of them could have been Aurora's child. One thing at a time." He got out of the truck and slammed the door. I did the same.

Jill Cortino nee Gers was Derek's high school sweetheart, and through the ordeal of his marriage to Melissa and hers to Peter, and everything that had happened since, the two of them had managed to remain good friends. It's Peter's former loft on Main Street that Derek lives in, and it was the Cortinos' little boat we'd used to get back and forth to Rowanberry Island for the past four or five months.

Jill was in the office when we walked in, and lit up when she saw us. Getting up from the stool she'd been perched on—with a little difficulty—she made her way around the counter and over to us to hug us both. "It's so good to see you!"

"You, too," I said, while Derek put a hand on Jill's stomach.

"How are things in there?"

She beamed. "Just fine. Due date is still November."

"Do you know what it is yet?"

She turned to me. "Another girl. Now we'll have two of each."

"What's her name going to be? Petunia?"

The other Cortino children are called Peter Jr., Paul, and Pamela. Petunia seemed a logical, if unlikely, choice.

She made a face. "God forbid. Peter wants to name her Portia. I'd prefer Penelope or Polly. Or maybe Piper."

"Lots of pretty *p* names out there."

She nodded. "We still have a few months to figure it out. So what can we do for you two?"

"Wanted to see if Peter had had a chance to look at Josh Rasmussen's car," Derek said, glancing through the window in the door into the shop itself, where a couple of cars were sitting high up on lifts while men in greasy overalls walked underneath. "It drove off the road into the ocean yesterday."

Jill nodded. "Peter pulled it out last night. Took the biggest tow truck up there, with the longest hook and line he could find, and pulled it all the way up to the road. It spent the night drying out, and he's been looking at it this morning."

"And?"

"Ask him." She opened the door to the shop and yelled for her husband. A few seconds later, he came running and burst into the office, eyes worried.

"What's the matter, *cara*?"

I mentioned Peter's good looks earlier. He's Italian, with curly black hair, velvety brown eyes, and the kind of bone structure Michelangelo used to carve. He's also wonderfully devoted to his wife, who doesn't look like the type who ought to have ended up with a gorgeous specimen like Peter. Jill's a little dumpy, with fluffy blond hair, a plain face, and too much junk in the trunk. Peter adores her. As evidenced by their rapidly expanding brood.

That's where the worry lay, of course. Jill was pregnant, and Peter treated her like she was made from spun glass. When she called, he came running, just in case something was wrong.

"Oh," he said now, smiling as he noticed us, "it's you two. What can I do for you? Truck need servicing?"

Derek shook his head. "Just wondered about that car you pulled out of the Atlantic last night. Have you figured out what was wrong with it?"

"I already called the chief of police. Brake lines were cut. Simplest way in the world to cause an accident." His brown eyes glanced off mine. I shuddered. Yes, I knew. It wasn't that long since we'd been here, hearing the same news about Derek's truck.

"Foul play?" Derek said.

Peter shrugged. "Doubt anything that wasn't a knife could have cut 'em that cleanly."

"Thanks."

"That all you wanted to know? You coulda called for that."

"We've spent every waking moment over at the house on Cabot Street," I said. "We needed a change of scenery."

Derek grinned and put an arm around my shoulders. "We'll get outta your way."

"How are things going at the house?" Jill wanted to know. "We heard about Tony Micelli. How awful!"

Peter put his arm around his wife, as well. "Any idea who did him?"

"We're working on it," I said.

"Same guy who cut the brake lines on Josh's car?"

"That's the assumption."

"Be careful, then. That could easily have gone much worse."

"I need to talk to Wayne," I said when we had left the auto shop and were back in the truck. "Tell him everything Nina told me. And tell him to keep an eye on her. If someone killed Tony because of what happened in Kansas City, then Nina has to be next. Don't you think?"

"Seems that way," Derek agreed. "Unless whoever killed Tony did it for a different reason."

"What reason could that be? Given the anonymous letters, isn't Kansas City the most logical explanation?"

"It's logical. But it doesn't explain Stuart. Or Josh's brake lines. Unless someone thought Josh was taking Nina to dinner."

I sat back on the seat. "So maybe someone's just trying to ruin the show. Maybe Tony caught someone in the house trying to rig another accident, and then she had to kill him to keep him quiet."

"She?"

"Fae is the logical person. She's the right age to be Aurora's daughter, and she's got a connection to Kansas City. I think maybe Wayne needs to put her in the cell next to Melissa's. That would protect her, too, if Josh's brake lines were cut to get Fae."

"In that case, I guess Nina was the one who cut them," Derek said. "She realized that Fae knew about what happened to Aurora, and that Fae had been writing the letters, and that Fae had killed Tony. So Nina sabotaged Josh's car thinking that he'd taken Fae out to dinner again. If she was upstairs, and saw Josh drive up, and saw—from the third floor—Shannon get into the car, she might have thought Shannon was Fae."

I shuddered. "Now we *really* need to talk to Wayne. Before anything can happen to anyone else. If Nina tried to kill Fae, and Fae is planning to kill Nina . . ."

"I'm on it," Derek said, and stepped on the gas.

. . .

We found Wayne at the police station, struggling with paperwork. He looked relieved when we interrupted him, although that passed as soon as he heard what we had to say.

"Fae?" he said, looking dismayed. "That sweet little thing? You really think she could have stabbed Tony to death?"

This was directed at Derek, who shrugged. "Rage can give people extra strength. Fear, too. And she'd have surprise on her side. Tony wouldn't expect it."

"Or," I said, having just thought of something, "maybe she didn't do it. Maybe Wilson did. He's her uncle."

"How do you know that?" Wayne turned to me.

"Someone told me. Josh, I think. She's a college student at Kansas City University in Missouri, and this is just a summer job."

"Nice work if you can get it."

I nodded. "That's what I said. And Josh told me that Wilson is her uncle and he set it up for her."

"No one mentioned that to me," Wayne said.

"Maybe they didn't think it was pertinent."

"Like hell it isn't!" Wayne said.

"Wilson and Ted told me they were together the night Tony died. In Portland. Did you confirm that?"

"You thinking they might be working together?"

"Shades of Agatha Christie," Derek contributed, mouth quirking.

I shrugged. The thought had crossed my mind, briefly. *Murder on the Orient Express* and all that. "These people all seem to be connected. Fae and Wilson are family. Ted and Nina are friends, sometimes with benefits. They both worked with Tony, as well as with Aurora. If Fae is Aurora's daughter, then Wilson is Aurora's brother, or brother-in-law."

"Not necessarily," Derek said. "He could belong to the other side of the family. Fae's father's family."

I shook my head. "I don't think so. That picture of Aurora looked familiar when I saw it. I think she may have looked like Wilson's wife. He showed me a picture of her a few days ago. Her name is Veronica. Beautiful woman. Dark hair, brown eyes."

"Like Fae," Derek said.

I nodded. "Maybe she's the one sending the letters. They've got Missouri postmarks."

"Think I'm gonna have to talk to Fae," Wayne said. "And Wilson, too."

"We were thinking it might be a good idea for you to keep her overnight."

Derek went over our reasoning with regards to Fae either being in danger or being a danger to someone else, specifically Nina. Wayne nodded.

"But don't keep Wilson," I added. "We need him to finish filming the renovation."

"If he killed Tony," Wayne said, "I'm keeping him."

"What about Melissa?" Derek wanted to know. "You still holding on to her?"

"The murder weapon has her fingerprints all over it. Hell yeah, I'm still holding on to her. At least until I have someone else I can lock up instead."

Wayne scowled, but after a moment, he relented. "If this idea with Fae and Wilson works out, she might be out by tonight. I can't keep her for more than forty-eight hours, without charging her anyway, and if there's a chance that someone else did it, then I don't wanna do that. All it takes is reasonable doubt to get her off, so if I charge anyone, I want it to be watertight."

"You going to talk to Fae and Wilson now?" Derek asked.

Wayne nodded. "Guess I'd better."

"Let us know how it goes." He grabbed my arm and pulled me out of the police station, leaving Wayne to get on with it.

We ended up back at Aunt Inga's house, where we shared tuna sandwiches and chips. Derek had to dodge Mischa, who spent the entire time—after I peeled him off Derek—on my lap, purring hysterically. Once we'd eaten, we filled the bed of the truck with the window boxes and planters Derek had made the other night, along with the pillows I'd stitched, and headed back to Cabot Street.

It turned out to be a quiet afternoon. Derek went back to work on finishing my porch swing, while I pulled out a gallon of exterior paint and started painting the front door. Tony had put vinyl siding all over the house at some point in the last few years, so we couldn't change the color of the house itself, but we could liven things up by adding some splashes of color. Namely, the cobalt blue door and—Derek decided—some new shutters.

"Batten board," he said. "Or board-and-batten."

"In English?"

I'd taken mandatory architecture classes at Parsons back in the old days, so I knew the basic home styles of the past few hundred years, but he knew a lot more about the specific details than I did, especially when it came to the construction of things.

"It's a type of siding or paneling that has wide boards and narrow wooden strips, called battens. A lot of Tudor houses and beach cottages have board-and-batten shutters. So do brownstones; you probably saw them in New York. They're real easy to make; you just put three boards together, and then nail two battens near the top and bottom."

"Oh!" I said. "I know what you're talking about!" I had indeed seen them, both in New York and up here in Maine. "That style would look great on this house!"

Derek grinned at my enthusiasm. "Why don't I run to the lumber depot and pick up some boards? It won't take but thirty minutes to put them together. Then you can paint while I start hanging them."

"Pick me up one of those bristly doormats, too," I said. "I saw them last time we were there. Everyone's been tracking dirt all over the house, and I want a mat here by the time we open the front door tomorrow. I'll paint a pattern on it to make it match the front door."

Derek said he would, and headed for the truck. It wasn't until he drove away that I realized I was all alone.

. . .

I'd like to be able to say that something awesome, significant, or even scary happened, and that I singlehandedly solved the case while I stood there, paintbrush in hand, but alas, no such luck. The only thing that happened was that the (much reduced) crew came back to the house, and there was nothing awesome, significant, or scary about it. They just parked the van at the curb, wandered through the yard, and stopped when they got to the porch.

And only Nina, Ted, and Adam returned to explain that Fae and Wilson were talking to Wayne.

"Do you know what's going on?" Nina wanted to know.

Her eyes were puffy, but she looked calmer than earlier. I noticed she was sticking close to Ted. Maybe they'd decided to go "on again." When I glanced at him, he gave me a tiny smile.

"I think he just had some additional questions for them," I said. "They hadn't mentioned being related, and I guess maybe he thought that if they'd kept quiet about that, they may have kept quiet about other things, as well."

Nina and Ted exchanged a look. "Like what?"

I circumvented the question, since I really had no idea. Or rather, I had a lot of ideas, but no solid facts. "Would you happen to remember whether Aurora Jamison's baby was a boy or a girl? And was it really a baby? Could it have been a toddler? Two or three years old, say?" Or six, if we were talking about Adam.

He had taken up position with his back to one of the porch posts. I avoided looking at him.

"God." Nina shook her head. "It was more than twenty years ago, Avery. How do you expect . . . ?"

"It was a girl," Ted said. "And she was less than a year old."

We all stared at him. And I guess we must have been thinking the same thing, because Nina's expression changed to one of dawning realization while Adam slapped Ted on the back with a grin. "My man!"

"Don't be a jackass," Ted said, moving away. "Nina . . ."

Nina stared at him as if she'd never seen him before. "You and Rory? You never told me that. Even after she died, when we spent all that time talking, you never told me you'd been involved with her. And—God!—that her baby was yours . . . !"

"It didn't matter," Ted said.

Nina looked like she wasn't quite sure how to take that, and frankly, I wasn't, either. Ted must have realized it, because he tried to explain. "It didn't last long. Our affair. Just a few weeks. I wasn't devoted enough to her. She was really insecure, always looking for someone who'd give her whatever she felt was missing in her life. She had this older sister that she was always talking about, who had everything Rory wanted. . . ."

"Name?" I shot in.

Ted shrugged. "It was twenty years ago. Who the hell remembers?"

"Could it have been Veronica?"

"Might have been. Why?"

"That's Wilson's wife's name."

They'd both finally caught up, and I watched Ted's sallow skin turn pale. "Fae? Fae is Rory's daughter? My daughter?"

"There's a good chance. It all hangs together, right?" And now that I examined Ted up close, something I hadn't really done so far, there were hints of Fae in his eyes and the shape of his face.

"You never wanted her?" Nina asked, and Ted turned to her.

"I was twenty, Neen. So was Rory. It was before I met you, and before Tony came to work at the station. I wanted her to have an abortion. She said no. I guess maybe she thought a baby would fill that hole she had inside that nothing else ever could." He was silent for a moment before he continued, "I must have made it clear I wasn't interested in being a daddy, because she didn't put my name on the birth certificate. I don't think I saw the baby more than a half dozen times, and always by accident. I wasn't a part of her life, and I didn't want to be."

"But when Rory died . . . ?"

"I thought about it," Ted said. "But I didn't think I'd be able to take care of a kid. We were all so young, and we wanted so badly to make it big. . . ."

Nina nodded.

"I went to see Rory's parents afterward. Told them I thought I was the baby's father but that I didn't feel I could take care of her. They were just fine with me giving up any rights to her. She was all they had left of Rory; they didn't want to share her with anyone."

"And you haven't seen her since?"

Ted shook his head. "She doesn't look like Rory. Fae doesn't."

"She looks a little like you, though," I said. He turned to me, surprised. "The eyes."

"Huh." He thought for a second, then shrugged. "Too late now, I guess. So you think she's the one who's been sending Nina the letters?" Nina must have clued him in during the time they'd been gone, because when I'd asked her earlier in the day, she'd told me she hadn't confided in Ted about what was going on.

"I think there's a good chance," I said. "She and her auntie Veronica. Or maybe her grandmother. Someone who's still in Missouri."

"Veronica's not in Missouri," Nina said. "Wilson and Veronica live in California." She shook her head. "How would they know about me? I mean . . . targeting Tony I could understand; he was the one who was with her that night—but why me?"

"You took over her job?" I suggested. "They blamed you?"

"I told them about you," Ted added. "That time after the funeral that I went to them to talk about the baby. I told them that you and Tony were both really sorry about what happened. I guess they put two and two together."

Nina nodded, pale. "I deserve it, you know. The letters. Being scared. I can forgive her for that, if she's the one who's been sending them. But Tony shouldn't have had to die. He didn't deserve that. We didn't force her to get in her car that night. Rory made that choice."

There were tears in her eyes. Ted moved to comfort her, and for a second, it looked like she might reject him. But then she smiled, and I guess decided to let bygones be bygones. It wasn't like she was without blame, after all. There was enough of it to go around.

"I'll take you back to the B and B," Ted said. "You don't have to deal with this today. Without Wilson, we can't film anything anyway. Let's just see how it goes."

He steered her down the porch steps and through the yard, toward the van. I glanced at Adam, who was still leaning against the porch post, muscular arms folded across his chest, the better to emphasize his biceps.

He caught my eye and winked, flashing that smile that someone at some point had probably told him was irresistible. "That was real," he said.

I shrugged.

"So Fae is Ted's daughter? And Nina and Tommy—"

"Tony."

"—did something to her mother when she was a baby?"

"Not really. She died in a car accident. After going out drinking with Tony."

"And Fae's been sending Nina letters?"

I nodded.

"Wow," Adam said as a calculating look entered his pretty blue eyes.

I'm not particularly devious or underhanded myself—I tend to be more naive and believe the best of people until I have proof otherwise—but I'd decided I really didn't like Adam, and in this case, I had no problem following the direction of his thoughts. In a word, blackmail. Adam was trying to figure out how best to take advantage of this new knowledge, and probably to put the screws on Nina not to fire him for incompetence once they got back to Los Angeles.

"Well, we've all done things in our lives that we aren't too proud of," I said.

Adam looked at me. "I guess."

"I'm sure you've got something you'd just as soon no one ever brought up again. Right?"

Adam nodded.

"In that case, it would probably be best if you just left

this one alone, don't you think? In the interest of fairness, and all that."

Adam hesitated. But then Ted laid on the horn and Nina leaned out of the car window and raised her voice. "Are you coming, Adam?"

Adam turned back to me. I smiled sweetly. Out at the street, Derek's truck pulled up and my boyfriend jumped out. And Adam gave up the fight. "I guess," he said.

Attaboy!

I thought about saying it, but I didn't. Instead I just smiled again. "I'll see you later."

"Right," Adam said, and headed for the van.

•

—20—

Derek and I spent the rest of the day alone, tying up a whole lot of loose ends with the renovations. He finished the porch swing and hung it, and it did look pretty cool, if I do say so myself. I couldn't wait to show it to Kate, whose idea it had been.

We hung the batten board shutters Derek had nailed together and I had painted, and we planted flowers in the window boxes after hanging them, too. I arranged pillows on the new porch swing and in the Swiss cheese Adirondack chair, and I painted borders and "Welcome" on the prickly doormat Derek had brought from the lumber depot, and put it in front of the freshly painted door. We stepped back to look at the front of the house.

"The curb appeal is great," Derek said. "The house looks really good."

I nodded. "As long as Wilson doesn't film the sides or the back of the house, nobody will ever know that we only spruced up the front."

"And the inside. Don't forget that."

I shook my head. No chance of that. "We'll finish that up tomorrow, right? On the surface, anyway. And then we'll do the rest next week. Paint the back door to match the front and put a planter back there, too? Make it look nice for when Melissa puts it on the market?"

"If Melissa gets to put it on the market," Derek said. "But sure." He put his arm around my shoulders. "I'll hook up the kitchen sink and install the waterline to the freezer then, and do all those other little things that aren't gonna show up on camera tomorrow if they aren't done."

I nodded. We'd been cutting corners left and right this week, focusing on making things look good on the surface while planning to go back and actually do them right once the crew had left. The new kitchen sink was one of those. Right now it was where it should be, looking pretty, with faucets and everything in place, but nothing worked. There was no water line hooked up to the kitchen, and no sewer line going out from the sink, either. It looked beautiful, but only until you started trying to use it.

But the camera wouldn't know that, and it was one less thing we had to do before the crew did their final shoot tomorrow night. The job—at least this week—was all about slapping lipstick on the pig and making it look pretty for the camera.

And all in all, I didn't think we were doing too bad of a job, even with the time constraints. Sure, we were running a little short on sleep—and a little long on stress—but we'd found time to eat, and the cats were taken care of, and even if we had precious few moments to ourselves, we had managed to sneak in some personal time here and there. And we'd still gotten a whole lot done over the past couple of days. Thanks to our friends—Kate and Cora and Bea, Josh and Shannon—who'd pitched in and helped, but also thanks to our own hard work. We'd done good.

I said as much, and Derek grinned down at me. "Told you we could do it."

"I know you did. Although we're not done yet."

"What could go wrong?" Derek asked expansively.

I arched my brows. "A whole lot. Someone else could get murdered, or almost murdered. The house could burn down overnight. . . ."

"Don't even say that," Derek said with a shudder. He turned toward the street, his arm still around my shoulders. "Nothing more is going to happen. Wayne's got Fae and her uncle under wraps. Nina's safe. So is Fae, in the event that Nina was actually trying to kill her and hurt Shannon instead. Nobody else is in danger. Josh is fine and Shannon's getting there. . . ."

"Can we go see her?"

"Sure," Derek said, and let the garden gate slam shut behind us. "Bet we'll find Josh at the hospital, too, even if he's been released."

I shook my head as he opened the truck door for me. "No bet."

. . .

Josh *was* at the hospital, and so was Kate. "He's been sitting here all day," she confided to me in the hallway as the two of us took a walk for some fresh air. "Not that I'm surprised. He's always been devoted. But he hasn't stirred from her bedside all day. They released him this morning, and instead of going home, he went to Shannon's room. He's been there ever since."

"He loves her."

Kate nodded. "He's not trying to hide it, either. Before, he's always been friendly toward her more than anything else. I could always tell he felt more—we all could, including Shannon—but he never acted on any of it. Now it's in everything he does and everything he says."

I glanced at her. "Does that worry you? I mean, I know you love Josh. . . ."

"He's my stepson," Kate said. "And Wayne's son. I'd

love him because of that. But I met him before I met Wayne, and I loved him because he made Shannon feel at home in Waterfield when we first moved here. He stood by her when her father died. He introduced me to Wayne. He's family on a whole lot of levels, even apart from the fact that he's in love with my daughter."

That didn't actually answer my question, and I said so.

Kate shrugged. "It could be awkward. If he's in love with her and she isn't in love with him. Our whole family dynamic would be affected."

"But . . . ?"

She glanced at me. "This whole situation with Fae seems to have affected Shannon. I think she assumed Josh would always be there. Even though she didn't want him, I'm not sure she ever considered that he'd find someone else. It was always the two of them and Paige. Josh took Paige to prom, and Shannon knew there was nothing between them. This was the first time Josh had gone on a date with someone he might actually fall for, and I think it shocked Shannon. I don't think she ever considered that she might lose him."

I nodded. Shannon had essentially told me the same thing.

"And then the accident happened," Kate said, with a barely suppressed shiver. "It could have been so much worse, Avery. Either of them—both of them—could have died last night. Josh saved their lives. And I think they both realize it. That they could have lost each other, in a much more permanent way."

"So you're OK with it? With them?"

"They haven't asked me," Kate said, with a shrug. "I'm not even sure they've talked about it. Mostly they just sit there and chitchat. They've played cards and watched TV and talked, but not about anything important. Just the things they usually talk about."

"You can tell that something's different, can't you?"

I had been able to tell just in the minute or two I'd spent in the room with them both before I whisked Kate off for some air and a conversation. It was in the way they looked at each other. And I thought Kate was probably right: The fact that they'd almost lost one another permanently last night had been a shock and a wake-up call for both of them. Josh had decided to stop pretending, and Shannon . . . well, Shannon's wake-up call might have happened earlier, when Josh went out with Fae, and last night's accident simply brought the possibility of losing him home with even more of a vengeance.

"They'll be all right," Kate said. And added, "I won't be surprised if we end up with another wedding in the family within the next year."

I nodded. I wouldn't be surprised, either.

We went back into the room and spent thirty minutes chatting with Shannon and with Josh, who did not take the opportunity to get himself some fresh air while we were there. It seemed he'd rather be next to Shannon than anywhere else, and who could blame him? She looked at him with absolute adoration in her eyes, and that had to be a nice change.

She didn't look bad at all. A little pale, maybe, and with a big, white square of gauze on her forehead, but otherwise not bad. "Five stitches," she told me when I asked what had happened to the gash on her head. "The doctor said it wasn't too bad. Clean edges, easy to sew. I might end up with a scar, although I guess I can just wear bangs for the rest of my life."

"What about everything else?" I wanted to know. "Any other injuries?"

Shannon shook her head. "Just the concussion. My head hurts when I don't take pain pills, and I get dizzy when I try to get up. But it'll go away."

"You were lucky."

She shook her head and reached out to take Josh's hand. "It wasn't luck. It was Josh. He saved my life."

"Does that make it mine now?" Josh wanted to know, grinning. He twined his fingers through hers. Shannon blushed.

"That was sweet," I said to Derek when we were back in the truck on our way toward home again.

He grunted.

I looked at him. "What's the matter?"

"Nothing."

"It doesn't sound like nothing."

He shrugged.

"Seriously. What's the matter? You're happy for them, aren't you?"

"Ecstatic," Derek said.

"You don't sound ecstatic."

He shot me a look. "They remind me of me and Melissa. Really young and crazy about each other, but with no clue about anything."

I shook my head. "It isn't like you and Melissa. They've known each other for seven or eight years. Josh has probably been in love with her for six of those. It isn't anywhere close to the same situation."

"Maybe not," Derek admitted, "but just the way they're looking at each other . . ."

"It isn't the same. Josh and Shannon will be fine. They know each other. She's not going to decide, five years down the line, to divorce him because he decides he wants to change careers."

Derek opened his mouth, but before he could say anything, his phone rang. Instead of continuing the conversation with me, he pulled it out and looked at the display. "Speak of the devil."

"Who?"

Derek answered the phone, and then quickly turned it to

speaker in time for me to catch the last of Melissa's statement. ". . . might be able to give me a ride home."

Speak of the devil. Right.

"Wayne's letting you go?" I said.

There was a second's pause, and then Melissa's voice came back. "Avery?"

"Derek put the phone on speaker," I said. "He's driving."

"I see." Melissa sounded pissy about that. Or maybe it was just my imagination. She could have been upset about the situation in general and not the fact that she wanted Derek's undivided attention and didn't get it. "Apparently he doesn't have enough evidence to charge me."

"That's . . ." Lucky for Melissa, but too bad for Wayne.

"I was wondering if Derek might swing by the police station and pick me up," she said now, smoothly. "It wouldn't be out of his way at all. After all, he lives just across the street from me."

As if I wasn't already too aware of that.

I opened my mouth to tell her what she could do with her apartment right across the street from Derek's and with her need for a ride, but before I could, Derek spoke over me.

"We'll be there in ten minutes." He shut the phone off.

I turned to him. "Why did you do that?"

He spared me a glance as he turned the nearest corner. "What?"

"Why did you agree to go pick up your ex-wife from jail and take her home?" To her apartment right across the street from his?

"She needed a ride?"

Well, duh. "Why couldn't she call someone else?"

"Like who? She doesn't have any family here. Her fiancé is dead. My family doesn't want anything to do with her, and she's not good at making friends. . . ."

No kidding, I thought. Derek added, "She doesn't have anyone else."

"That doesn't mean *you* need to run to the rescue! She

could have taken a cab, for God's sake. Or asked Wayne for a ride. He would have given her one."

"Probably too prideful for that," Derek said. "You would be, too, if the situation was reversed."

He might be right. Not that I'd ever find myself in the situation Melissa found herself in right now—God willing—but even if I did, it would still be different. I'd have no qualms about asking Wayne for a ride. We were friends. He'd probably offer, because he wouldn't want me to find my way on my own. And the realization that Derek was right—Melissa might not have anyone else—did make me feel just a twinge of sympathy for her. It couldn't be much fun being all alone in the world, or in Waterfield, surrounded by her ex-husband, his family, his new girlfriend, and a bunch of people who all thought she might have murdered her fiancé.

And it would only take a few minutes. We'd drive her home and drop her off and that would be it. I sat back and prepared myself to be nice.

Melissa was waiting outside the police station when we got there, still looking just as glamorous as the night before, in the same jeans but another shirt and sandals with high heels, with her makeup firmly in place and her hair sleek and moonlight pale. She had an overnight bag at her feet, so obviously Wayne had been courteous enough to let her pack a few necessities for her stay at the police station. Or perhaps she had barreled right over Brandon Thomas, if he'd been the one to pick her up, and had insisted he let her gather what she needed before he hauled her off to jail. Either way, she didn't look anything like a released prisoner. She looked more like we were picking her up from an overnight trip to Boston.

When Derek pulled the truck up to the stairs where she stood, she minced over to the cab and pulled the door open. "Hi, Avery." She gave me a big, fake smile as she stowed the overnight bag at my feet. I scooted closer to Derek. She slid onto the seat next to me, and then spoke across me. "Hi, Derek. Thanks for coming to get me."

"Nice of Wayne to let you go," I said.

Melissa smiled back, insincerely. "I think he realized I couldn't possibly have done this horrible thing, Avery. Tony and I were getting married. I adored him."

"Right," I said. "I don't suppose you know who inherits, do you? Seeing as he died before you guys tied the knot, and he had no other family."

Derek glanced at me.

"I imagine I do," Melissa said.

"No kidding."

"Oh, no." She shook her head. "He made a will. As soon as we decided we wanted to spend the rest of our lives together, we each made one in the other's favor. Of course, I don't have much to leave. The money from the sale of the house I shared with Ray went to buy the loft, and when Derek and I separated, I was making more money than he was." She smiled at him in a way that did its best to exclude me.

"So you inherit everything? The house on Cabot Street? The condo in Portland? The car? Whatever is in his bank accounts?"

"I imagine so," Melissa said.

"And Wayne let you go anyway?"

Derek shook his head, resigned, eyes on the road. We were entering downtown Waterfield, with its cars and thousands of tourists clogging every sidewalk. In another minute or two, we'd be on Main Street. And none too soon for me.

"I was under the impression he had arrested someone else," Melissa said, a tiny wrinkle between her perfect brows.

"What gave you that idea?"

She looked politely puzzled. "When I was told I could go, young Brandon Thomas said they were exploring other avenues. And when I questioned why Wayne couldn't be bothered to release me himself, Brandon said Wayne was interviewing another suspect."

"I'm not sure they're really suspects. . . ." I said, partly because I didn't really want them to be, but more because I didn't want to give up on the idea that Melissa might be guilty. Sure, killing Tony for the house on Cabot Street and the condo in Portland and whatever was in his bank account didn't sound like something Melissa would do—not when she could just marry him and get it all anyway—but I was upset with her, and for that matter with Derek, and although I realized I was being somewhat ridiculous, I just couldn't seem to let it go.

"I'm just repeating what Brandon Thomas told me," Melissa said sweetly.

"Well, maybe Brandon shouldn't have told you that! And just because they let you go now doesn't mean they can't come after you later, if things change, you know. Just because Wayne isn't willing to press charges right now, since there are other people involved who look like they may have had motive and opportunity, too, doesn't mean you're not still a suspect!"

"Avery," Derek said.

I ignored him. "You still could have killed Tony. The screwdriver has your fingerprints all over it, and if you inherit everything, that's motive and means, and we both know you had opportunity, because you were there that night!"

"Avery," Derek said again.

"So I wouldn't feel too confident if I were you. Just because you're out of jail right now doesn't mean you won't be back there tomorrow, or the next day."

"Avery!" Derek said.

I turned to him. "What?"

"Give it a rest."

I blinked.

He added, "She didn't kill Tony. I was married to her for

five years, and if she didn't kill me, she wouldn't have killed him. OK?"

I nodded, speechless. Melissa smiled, very much like a cat with a big bowl of cream. Derek drove on, seemingly unaware that he'd just taken his ex-wife's side against me and that I wasn't happy at all about that.

As soon as he pulled the truck to a stop in the parking lot behind the hardware store and Melissa slid off the seat and grabbed her bag; I jumped out, too, without waiting for Derek to catch me.

"I'm going home."

"Avery . . ."

I shook my head. "Not in the mood."

"The mood for what?" Melissa inquired, sweetly.

I rounded on her. "Stay out of this. It's none of your business."

"Avery . . ." Derek tried again.

I shook my head again. "Just leave me alone. I'll see you tomorrow."

"But, Tink . . ."

Going for the nickname was a super-low blow. Still, I walked away. I halfway expected him to follow me, but only halfway, so it didn't come as a huge surprise when he didn't. When I glanced back just as I rounded the corner onto Main Street, he was standing there watching me, a puzzled look on his face, as if he had no idea what he had said that bothered me.

—21—

I worked up quite a head of steam climbing the hill from downtown. Some of it was exertion—Waterfield is a steep little town, and it was the end of July and hot as Hades—but a lot of it was annoyance, too. How dare he take Melissa's side? And in front of her, too! He had no right to treat me like that. And not only because he was my boyfriend and he was supposed to stick by me, especially in front of his ex-wife, but because I was right, dammit.

All right, so maybe she hadn't killed Tony. I didn't really think she had, to be honest. Derek knew her better than me—the bastard—and he didn't think she had, either. But she'd been there at around the time Tony was killed. She'd had reason to kill him—both for the money and because he might have been thinking of dumping her for Nina—and the bloody murder weapon had her fingerprints all over it. I wasn't out of line for thinking—or even suggesting—that she wasn't out of the woods yet. Fae and Wilson had less reason for killing Tony than Melissa did.

Nina was right: She and Tony hadn't been responsible for Aurora Jamison's decision to drive under the influence. They weren't the cause of her death. Sure, they probably felt culpable, and morally, maybe they were, at least partly, but it was her own choice. She chose to drink, to go home with Tony, and to try to drive to work in the middle of the night, tanked on whatever he had served her. And besides, it was twenty-plus years ago. If Fae and her uncle were harboring murderous intentions and were determined to kill the people responsible, why choose Tony instead of Nina, and why wait so long? Wilson had had access to Nina for years, and getting Aurora drunk and unable to work had been her idea in the first place. Fae had had access to Nina for at least a month or two. Yes, the two of them had probably been sending the letters, but letters are passive-aggressive. I'm sure they'd wanted Nina to suffer and to feel horrible about what she did, but they didn't necessarily want her dead. Stabbing Tony with a screwdriver was active aggression: Someone wanted him out of the way and that someone had made sure he'd been dispatched. And I couldn't get that someone to match up with Fae and Wilson.

By the time I'd huffed down to the end of Bayberry Lane, where Aunt Inga's house was, the T-shirt was sticking to my back, and the hair on my neck and around my face was damp and frizzy. Sticking the key in the lock, anticipating the coolness of the air-conditioning, Murphy's Law kicked in and I had to twist the key back and forth several times before it would let me open the door and tumble into the foyer. If I hadn't known better, I'd have wondered if we'd forgotten to lock up this morning. We had been in a bit of hurry, so it wouldn't have been surprising.

A lot of people in Waterfield leave their doors unlocked all the time. In New York City, such a thing wouldn't have crossed my mind, but here, where everyone pretty much knew everyone else, it didn't seem like that big a deal. I'd gotten into the habit of keeping everything locked up tight early on, though, back when I'd just moved to town, when someone desperately wanted me gone and wasn't above sabotaging my house and trying to kill me to do it. I admit it, I did grab a heavy candlestick from the sideboard in the dining room and carried it around with me as I walked from room to room, making sure that I was alone and that nothing seemed to be missing or rigged to kill me.

After five minutes of creeping around my house, from basement to attic and everywhere in between, I decided that everything seemed to be in order. Nothing was out of place, and there was no sign that anyone had been inside. Either we had forgotten to lock up this morning, or I'd temporarily lost my mind in the upset over Derek and Melissa, and I'd thought I'd had a problem with the front door when I had, in fact, just been twisting the key back and forth for no reason other than that my hands were shaking with anger. There was nothing wrong here. My laptop was on the desk in the parlor, my jewelry box was on the bureau in the bedroom, all my designer clothes—the ones I'd made myself—and my designer shoes—that I hadn't—were in the closet where they belonged. The TV and DVD player were in the living room. There was no sea of broken dishes on the kitchen floor, the way it had been the time I walked in here and someone had broken all of Aunt Inga's china in an effort to scare me off. All my replacement dishes were neatly stacked on the shelves behind the doors trimmed with Aunt Inga's never-used wedding veil. Even the basement stairs were safe and sound. Everything seemed normal. I went to the fridge, removed some cold cuts and a roll, and began to put together a sandwich.

It was then that I realized that something was indeed missing. The cats were gone. And whereas that wasn't unusual for Jemmy and Inky—they came and went at will all day and night through the cat flap in the back door—Mischa hadn't shown much inclination thus far to wander. After being on his own for a while before we found him, scrounging for food and warmth through the cold Maine winter, now that he had a place and a warm lap of his own, he tended to stick close to home. He certainly was diligent in protecting it, and his human, from intruders.

Every once in a while he'd go outside to do his business, however, having never gotten used to a litter box. As I sat down at the kitchen table, with my sandwich and a DIY magazine, I expected to hear the sound of the cat door slapping at any moment.

It didn't, and after I had finished eating and had rinsed off the plate and glass and put them in the dishwasher, I decided that maybe I'd better go look for him. He'd only lived with me a few weeks, and he wasn't used to Waterfield yet. On Rowanberry Island, he'd mostly hung out under the front porch and—as he got more comfortable with us—on the porch and sometimes inside the house while we worked. Here, he'd done the same. I hated the idea that he'd wandered off and couldn't find his way home. Or that he'd gotten into something he couldn't get out of. Like, he'd climbed a tree and couldn't get down, or he'd wandered into Aunt Inga's garden shed and couldn't find his way out.

Derek had been in the shed the other day, first to get me the Adirondack chair that was currently sitting on the porch of the house on Cabot Street, and then to pick up the old door that had been turned into a porch swing. What if he'd forgotten to close the door all the way? He'd been carrying things. And what if Mischa had squeezed through the opening and into the shed, and the door had closed behind him, trapping him there? He wasn't strong enough to push it open again, if it had.

Drying my hands on a dish towel—one I had designed myself, with giant bluebells all over it—I slipped on a pair of flip-flops and ventured back out into the evening.

Maine is far enough north that the sun stays up late in the summer. It was still up, but low in the sky, and the clouds to the west had taken on a peachy hue, fading to pale lavender behind the pine trees. The shadows were long and dark across the grass. There was no sign of Mischa or, for that matter, of Jemmy or Inky.

I wasn't too worried about the two of them. They'd grown up here and knew their way around. Mischa was another story. He was still small, he couldn't defend himself very well—his attacks on Derek notwithstanding, and right now, I was still angry enough with Derek to applaud those. He could have gotten lost, he could have treed himself, he could have been hit by a car, he could have gotten into trouble with a fox or a raccoon or a loose dog. . . .

I walked into the street but saw no sign of him. The Beetle was parked at the curb, and Mischa wasn't inside it, nor was he crouched underneath. So I wandered around the house instead, into the yard, calling his name. Gooseberries and currants are prohibited in Maine, because they're host plants for something called the white pine blister rust, which attacks pine trees, but down at the bottom of the yard, there were neat rows of raspberry bushes between stakes and strings. I spent a few minutes walking through each row, peering under the leaves and picking the occasional ripe raspberry and popping it in my mouth. I enjoyed the dessert, but Mischa wasn't there. When I got out of the raspberry patch, I stopped, hands on my hips, and surveyed the yard.

The shed was left, down in the corner. It was a small clapboard building, painted the same robin's egg blue as the main house, with the same ochre trim, and from where I stood, I could see that the door was closed. It wasn't likely that Mischa was inside—he wouldn't have been able to close the door behind him, and there was no wind tonight that could have pushed it shut—but I wandered in that direction anyway.

When I first came to Waterfield, I'd found someone's

bicycle in the garden shed, a discovery which had eventually helped Wayne solve a missing person's case. Of course, it had helped when I'd found the body of the missing person, as well, a few weeks later. But that's beside the point. The shed is full of cast-offs and odds and ends: Aunt Inga's tools, some wood and nails, a snow shovel, a spade and a pitch fork, some empty flowerpots, the old bike Derek brought me from Cora when I'd just moved in and didn't have a car . . .

The shed door wasn't just closed, but bolted. I didn't see any reason to open it, since there was no way Mischa could have moved it to get into the shed, let alone closed it from the inside once he was there. And last year, when Derek and I had renovated the main house, we'd used the excess lumber to replace any rotted boards on the shed, as well, before we painted it. There were no big gaps or holes Mischa could have squeezed through. And besides, if he had crawled through a hole into the shed, he could have just done the same thing to get out again. So there was no way he was inside.

I had turned and was heading back to the main house when I heard a crash from inside the shed, followed by a terrified squeal.

The crash sounded as if one of the flowerpots had fallen—or been pushed—off a shelf onto the concrete floor. The squeal sounded like Mischa. Or one of the other cats—the Maine coons have surprisingly soft, kittenish voices for their size—but most likely Mischa. I ran the couple of steps back to the shed, pushed the bolt out of the way, and yanked the shed door open, peering into the dark.

Everything happened really fast after that. It took my eyes a second to adjust to the darkness inside the shed, and that was all the time it took for Mischa to spy the open door. He shot through the doorway and between my legs, running flat out toward freedom. I staggered, and in that one or two seconds, I heard a rush of feet behind me. The next moment, a strong push between the shoulder blades sent me stumbling forward into the shed, landing with a crash and an "Ooof!" against the shelves on the opposite wall. They weren't built to withstand a hundred twenty-plus pounds of female at sixty miles an hour, and collapsed, and I fell to the floor in a heap of broken planks, terra-cotta flowerpots, garden tools, and bags of fertilizer.

In the minute or two it took me to catch my breath and push all the broken pieces of this, that, and the other off my body, the door had been slammed, the bolt pushed across, and I could hear a sort of splashy noise outside.

I tried to push against the door, of course, even though I knew that it was bolted. I also hammered on it and screamed obscenities and demands that whoever was out there open the door and let me go. I didn't expect to get an answer, and I didn't get one. The splashy noise continued for another minute, all around the shed, and then I heard a soft *thunk*, as of something hollow hitting the grassy ground. A different noise followed, a sort of small, repeated scratch.

Uh-oh.

As I stood there, I could smell the gasoline. The scratching had to be the sound of a match struck against the side of a matchbox. Repeatedly, as if whoever was outside had a hard time getting the match to work.

Unfortunately, it didn't take long enough; I'd barely started feeling around for something I might be able to use to break out when the match lit, and then there was the crackle of flames, starting at the front of the shed but moving quickly around in both directions. Whoever poured the gasoline had obviously done a thorough job and covered every side of the shed, maybe even the sides and roof.

Yep, there it was; the beginning of another fire up above. At this rate, it wouldn't take long for the whole shed to burn to the ground with me inside it. And just wait until the fire reached the sacks of fertilizer; they were flammable, weren't they?

Outside, footsteps were hurrying away. At this point, I didn't honestly care too much who was out there. Obviously I'd seriously upset someone's equilibrium today for them to go to such lengths to get rid of me, but damned if I could imagine who it might be, and right at the moment, I had more important things on my mind. If I didn't think of a way out of here, and in the next few seconds, I'd burn to a crisp.

Things were heating up, and I mean that literally. The damp heat from hustling up the hill earlier, when the sweaty T-shirt had stuck to my skin, was nothing compared to the heat I was feeling now. My skin felt parched, tight, like it was cracking from dryness, and I had the sensation the moisture was being sucked right out of my hair. Flames were crackling all around the shed, licking at the walls and the roof. I had maybe a couple of minutes before the whole thing went down in a smoking heap.

So I did the only thing I could think of and felt around for a spade. When I found it, the handle was almost too hot for me to grip, so I wrenched my T-shirt off—what's a little modesty compared to certain death, and it wasn't like anyone could see me anyway—and then I wrapped it around the handle and started hacking at the door. After a few stabs, though, I realized that the door might not be the best place to attack: That was where everything was reinforced, with a door frame and everything. So I switched my attention to the nearest corner instead, and started slamming the spade against what I assumed were the weakened planks at the bottom of the shed, where the flames had been licking the wood.

Yes, I did realize, somewhere in the back of my mind, that if I knocked a hole in the bottom of the wall, the roof was likely to cave in on top of me. But it didn't make any sense to attack the top of the wall, where the wood was stronger. And besides, I'm short. I figured my chances were better close to the ground.

The shed had started to fill up with smoke, so I crouched in what was supposed to be the slightly cleaner air near the ground and continued to slam the edge of the spade against the wood of the shed wall. Flames were licking around the spade, too, now, and there was a roaring sound from the fire. My ears were roaring, as well, and I was coughing and gasping for air. If I didn't make it out soon, I'd pass out from the smoke inhalation, and then it'd be over. So I'd hold my breath for as long as I could before gulping another mouthful of smoky air.

If the shed had been in better shape than it was, I never would have made it out. As it was, I focused on the oldest boards in the wall, not the new ones Derek had nailed up last summer, and threw all my strength into breaking one, and then breaking another. By the time I'd made enough of a hole to crawl through, I had very little strength left to actually crawl. I let the spade fall from hands that were blistered from the heat and the labor, and dropped to my hands and knees, ready to try to squeeze through the small hole and the flames outlining it. And that was when the door was wrenched open.

—22—

I fumbled for the spade as I squinted through the smoke with stinging eyes. If whoever had put me in this situation had come back to make sure I was dead, he—or she—was in for a surprise.

But then I relaxed when I heard a familiar voice breathe a couple of words I'm not going to repeat. The next second, Derek had stooped through the smoke to grab me and drag me out of the shed to a safe distance, where he put me down on the cool grass. His voice sounded rather frantic. That could have been my imagination, I suppose, but I don't think so. "Avery? Are you still with me?"

I coughed and that must have convinced him I was still alive.

"Lay still." I could feel his hands, wonderfully cool, move all over me, checking for fire damage. "Are you burned anywhere?"

"Don't think so," I croaked. Trying to talk made me

cough again, and this time I couldn't stop, at least not until I'd coughed up some icky black slime.

Derek sat back on his heels. "What the hell happened? No, don't answer that. Just let me get you inside. You're starting to shiver."

The air and grass had felt wonderfully cool just a minute ago after the searing heat of the shed, but now it had turned chilly.

"My shed . . ." I managed as he scooped me up in his arms.

"I'll build you a new one. The fire department will put out the fire." I could hear sirens coming up the street as he started for the house, cradling me in his arms like a child, or like a most treasured possession. His voice was hoarse, too, although nowhere near as bad as mine. "God, Tink, I thought I'd lost you. When you weren't in the house, and then I saw the shed about to go down in flames . . ."

"I thought you'd lost me, too," I managed. "I was so scared, Derek." I started to cry; amazingly, there was still enough moisture left in my body to produce a few tears. Just a few; after that, the pipes were dry.

"Who did it?"

He strode in through the back door, which he must have left open in his rush to get to the shed earlier, and kicked it shut behind him. On the floor, I heard mewing, and when I looked down, I saw that Mischa had joined us. Amazingly, he wasn't trying to attack Derek. When we headed through the kitchen and down the hallway, he fell in behind and trotted up the stairs after us.

Derek opened the door to the bathroom and set me down. "Get undressed. You have to go into a tepid bath to get your body temperature down, and then I'll bandage your hands and any other parts of you that got burned." He turned away to start the water running into the claw-footed tub. Outside, I could hear the sirens come to a stop, and then the sounds of running feet and loud voices as the firemen aimed their hoses at the burning shed.

I didn't think any other parts of me had gotten burned—I hadn't actually touched any flames; it was just that the spade handle had been so hot—but I didn't bother to tell him so. Instead I concentrated on stripping down to my skin and sliding into the tub.

The cool water felt ice cold against my overheated skin, and I gasped. Derek's lips twitched. "You'll feel better in a minute. It isn't actually that cold. And if you have any burns, the cold water will stop them from developing."

"Like pasta," I managed, through chattering teeth.

"Excuse me?"

"Stops cooking when you rinse it in cold water."

"Right," Derek said. "Pasta." He turned back to the medicine cabinet, rooting around for burn salve and bandages.

Pretty shortly he turned back around and got a wash rag that he used to apply cool water to my face and to rinse my hair. The latter came clean in black streaks from the soot and smoke, which was disgusting, but which made the water dirty enough to obscure the view. Not that he hadn't seen me before, but it was different sitting here in cool water up to my shoulders, with nothing to hide any part of me.

Pretty soon he decided I'd been cooled down enough, and I got out of the tub and was wrapped up in a warm terrycloth robe with a soft, fluffy towel around my head to contain my dripping hair. Thus I padded over to the bed and sat down on the edge.

"OK," Derek said, surveying me with his hands on his hips, "where do you need bandaging?"

"Not a lot of places." My throat was still scratchy, and every once in a while I'd cough up some soot-streaked phlegm, but otherwise I seemed to be doing pretty well. "Mostly my hands, I think. From the spade." I showed them to him.

"Damn," Derek said and got to work, his hands gentle

as he slathered my palms with salve and wrapped them with gauze. "Your face is a little pink, and I think you'll have some blisters coming up by tomorrow. But you look pretty good, everything considered."

I cleared my throat. "I feel pretty good, too. Everything considered."

"Let's get you downstairs and get some liquids into you, and then we'll talk." He picked me up from the bed and carried me down the stairs, although there was nothing whatsoever wrong with my feet. Nothing new, anyway, although I still had the scratches from the other night. It seemed to be my week for getting hurt.

Mischa trotted behind, as if determined not to let me out of his sight. Again, I was amazed that he didn't try to attack Derek, not even when Derek picked me up, something that would have given Mischa all sorts of fits yesterday.

Downstairs in the kitchen, he deposited me on the same chair I'd sat on an hour earlier to eat my sandwich, and then he went to the fridge to get me a glass of lemonade. With a straw, so I wouldn't have to hold the glass in my bandaged hands to drink. After opening a fortifying beer for himself, he sat down across from me. "Who did it?"

He'd asked that earlier, when he first carried me into the house. I hadn't known the answer then, and I didn't now. "Whoever it was, was hiding. When I opened the door to the shed and Mischa ran out, he—or she—ran forward and gave me a great, big push. And bolted the door behind me. I never saw who it was."

"Ideas?" Derek asked, his lips tight.

I shook my head. "Although I guess I can try to figure out who it wasn't."

"Go ahead."

I took a sip of lemonade to soothe my throat and make it easier to talk. "I don't think it was Melissa. Whoever did this set it up before I got here, and she wouldn't have had time. What happened, anyway?"

"Earlier? She went to her apartment, I went to mine. I have no idea what she did, but I took a shower and changed my clothes and grabbed a sandwich. Figured I'd give you some time to simmer down before I showed up to apologize."

"You were going to apologize?"

"'Course." His eyes were very blue looking into mine. "I should have supported you, at least in front of Melissa. Even if I didn't agree with what you said."

"Thank you."

He shook his head. "That's what a good boyfriend does. Although for the record, I don't think she killed Tony. Seriously, with the fights we used to get into, she would have been more likely to kill me, and she never did."

"I know," I admitted. "I don't really think she did it, either. I just couldn't resist giving her a hard time. She bothers me. The way she's always snuggling up to you . . ."

"She does it because she can tell it bothers you," Derek said. "Just pretend it doesn't, and she'll stop."

"I'll try that next time."

He nodded. "God, Avery . . . When I realized you weren't here, and the shed was burning to the ground, possibly with you in it . . . I swear my heart stopped beating."

I smiled, although my eyes were filling with tears again. I must have rehydrated sufficiently. "Anyway, I don't think it was Melissa. It probably wasn't Fae or Wilson, either, since I'm guessing they're still at the police station with Wayne. At least they were when Melissa was released, and if she didn't have time to set this up, then they wouldn't have, either."

Derek nodded. "Who does that leave?"

"Other than the rest of Waterfield? If it has to do with the house on Cabot, and with Tony, I guess it leaves Ted and Nina and Adam."

"Any idea why any of those three would want to kill you?"

I shook my head. I'd had a little time to think about it

while I was soaking in the tub, and I had come up with zilch. Zip. Nada. No reason at all why anyone would want to get rid of me.

"We should check with Wayne," Derek said when I reiterated as much, "just in case he let Fae or Wilson go. We should report the fire to him, anyway."

"I'm sure the fire department has already done that. In fact, I'm surprised he's not already here."

"I'm sure he's coming," Derek said. "So Ted and Nina and Adam. Any reason you can think of why one of them would want to kill you?"

"Not really. Ted is Fae's father, although I'm not sure she knows it. Nina didn't even know it until this afternoon. But maybe he's developed a late conscience and hates me for turning her in to Wayne. Or maybe he lied, and they've both known it all along, and Ted's been working with Fae and Wilson in driving Nina crazy."

"He seems genuinely devoted," Derek said, "but then again, I guess he'd have to. But he's known Nina for years. Ever since Aurora died. If he was going to drive Nina crazy, or kill her—or Tony—don't you think he'd have done it already?"

"Probably. What about Nina? What if she killed Tony because she thought he was writing the letters? He knew exactly what she'd done, and I don't think many people did."

"Possible," Derek admitted. "We'll have to have Wayne check her alibi, try to figure out where she was this evening. Could it have been Nina who pushed you?"

I shrugged helplessly. "I guess so. It was a pretty hard push, but I'm small and she's a lot bigger. So yes, probably."

"Maybe she thought that guy, Stuart, was sending the letters, and so she arranged a little accident for him, too. But then the letters kept coming, and so she thought she'd made a mistake and Tony was sending them. And she killed him, but the letters kept coming again. So she tried to kill Fae, and got Shannon instead. And now the cat's out of the bag, and Wayne knows about Fae, so Nina can't get at her. But why kill you? Does she think you know that she killed everyone else?"

"I suppose she might," I said. "I don't, though. Know it. She hasn't said anything to make me think that. I don't suspect her any more than I suspect anyone else. And I'm sure I haven't given her any indication that I think she's guilty. . . ."

I would have gone on, but now there was a knock on the door. Or rather, a fusillade of knocks. Derek hurried toward the front door, admitting not only Wayne, but Kate, too. She pushed past both the men and got to the kitchen first. Her face was pale underneath the freckles. "Avery! Are you all right?"

"I'm fine," I croaked.

"But your voice . . . and your face and hands . . ."

"Smoke inhalation," Derek explained behind her. "She was trapped in the shed while it burned to the ground. Her hands are blistered from trying to get out, and her face is parched from the heat. So is her throat. Other than that, there's nothing wrong with her. No burns. Nothing that won't heal itself in a few days."

"Thank God." Kate sat down at the table, as if her legs suddenly gave out. "What happened?"

"I'd like to know that, too," Wayne growled, taking the chair opposite from her, his jaw tight. "Tell me everything, Avery. From the beginning."

Derek found a couple of glasses in the cabinet and poured lemonade all around, topping off my glass as I went through what had happened from the time we left the hospital earlier to when Derek hauled me out of the shed. "Were the firemen able to save anything?"

Wayne shook his head. "The shed's a total loss. If you'd been in there, you would have been, too. There's nothing left but cinders and ashes and a few pieces of twisted metal."

"Thank God we both got out." I tried to pet Mischa, who had curled up in my lap, but it didn't work. With the bandages on my hands, I couldn't feel his fur, and besides, it hurt. He opened his eyes and looked at me and didn't seem to mind.

"So the cat was in the shed," Wayne prompted.

I nodded. "He wasn't in the house when I came home, so I went looking for him. I didn't think he could be in the shed, because it was locked, but then I heard a crash inside. So I opened the door, and he ran out, and someone pushed me in. And splashed gasoline all around and lit a match."

"But you have no idea who it was?"

I shook my head. "It all happened too fast. And it was getting dark. Mischa startled me when he ran between my feet, and then someone came from behind and pushed me. I never saw who. Or anything about them. Not even whether it was a man or a woman."

"That's too bad," Wayne said. "I'll have to have a look around tomorrow morning, when the sun comes up, although between the water and most of the fire department tramping through your yard, I'm not sure I'll find anything."

"There might be another way," Derek said. We all turned to him.

"What?"

"He—or she, whoever did it—put the cat in the shed, right? So he—or she—must have walked into the house to get the cat."

I nodded. "I thought there was something funny about the front door lock when I got home, but I thought maybe we'd forgotten to lock it this morning."

He shook his head. "We didn't forget. I watched you."

"So what if our arsonist walked into the house?" Wayne asked impatiently. "What does it matter? He probably had enough sense to wear gloves. Most burglars do. Most fire starters do, too. They don't want to get gasoline on their hands."

"I don't care about that," Derek said. "If this guy walked into Avery's house, chances are Mischa attacked him. That cat attacks me every time I walk in, and he likes me. If someone else walked in, I'm sure Mischa would have attacked them, too."

"So? If he was wearing gloves . . ."

"Mischa goes for the legs," I said, hoarsely. All this talking was messing with my voice. "Derek has tiny little puncture marks all up and down his calves."

"So what do you suggest? We make everyone on the crew wear shorts to work tomorrow?"

"You could go to the B and B right now and ask them all to show you their legs."

"You're not serious?"

I shrugged. I was serious, sort of, but if he couldn't do it, then he couldn't do it, and that was that.

"Where was everyone tonight?" Derek wanted to know. "Fae and Wilson were in jail, right?"

Wayne shook his head. "I released them both this evening. They admitted to sending the letters to Nina and Tony—Fae's grandmother, who is Wilson's mother-in-law, in Kansas City put them in the mail—but they're alibied for Tony's murder. Wilson was with Ted, and Fae was with Shannon."

"But what about the letters? Is it legal to send poison-pen letters to someone?"

"It wasn't blackmail," Wayne said. "They didn't ask for money. And no one's filed a complaint. There's nothing I can do."

"Nina and Ted went to dinner earlier," Kate added. "At least that's what they said they'd be doing. They were still gone when I left the B and B just now. Adam went for a run and never came back. That must be a couple of hours ago."

"Gosh," I said, "I hope he's all right." What if whoever was behind all this craziness had hurt Adam, as well? Someone had tried to kill the previous host of *Flipped Out!*

after all, so what was to keep that someone from doing the same to Adam?

Kate shrugged. "He probably stopped somewhere for something to eat. Or maybe he met a girl. He could have come back without my seeing him, too. I was in the carriage house cooking dinner for Wayne."

"So any one of them could have set your fire," Derek said.

We sat in silence for a few seconds, all of us thinking.

"Why you?" Wayne said eventually.

"Excuse me?"

"Why would someone want to get rid of you? It doesn't make any sense. You're not involved with the show, other than this week. And you had nothing to do with what happened to what's-her-name—Aurora Jamison—back in Kansas City. Why you?"

"Someone obviously thinks she knows something she doesn't," Derek said. Kate nodded.

"But I don't! I have no idea what someone thinks I know, or what I know that I don't realize that I know."

"Who have you talked to today?" Wayne asked. He had pulled out his little notebook and pencil stub by now and was taking notes.

I shook my head, exasperated. "Everyone on the crew, plus Melissa. You two, Josh and Shannon. All the usual people."

"And no one said anything to make you think they felt threatened by you?"

"I don't think so. I told you about Nina's letters, and about Aurora Jamison. I told you about Fae and Wilson. I was there when Nina figured out that Ted is Fae's father—did I remember to tell you that? I ratted out a whole lot of people and spilled a whole bunch of secrets, and any one of them might have been upset by that, at least theoretically, but no one seemed more upset than anyone else. No one seemed murderous."

We sat in silence for another few seconds.

"Maybe we can arrange a trap," Derek said eventually.

Wayne arched his brows. "Being on TV must have gone to your head. What do you think this is, an episode of *Scooby-Doo*?"

I hid a grin. There was a certain resemblance, actually: the four of us and the cat. Derek would be the industrious Fred, always ready to ensnare the bad guy. Kate was the redheaded Daphne and Wayne the lanky Shaggy. If Mischa was Scooby-Doo, I guess that meant I was Velma, the brainy one. Could be worse.

"I'm serious," Derek said. "Tomorrow morning, I'll go to the house on Cabot and tell everyone what happened tonight. I'll explain that Avery still isn't able to talk because of the damage the smoke did to her throat, and that she doesn't feel well enough to come to work; she's just going to rest at home all day. Alone. I bet at some point, one of them will break free from the group and come over here to finish the job. All we have to do is wait."

Wayne blinked. "That's not actually a bad plan."

"Told ya."

"Wait a minute," I said. "You're not the one who'll be staked out here like a goat, waiting for the wolves to descend."

Derek turned to me. "You won't actually *be* alone, Avery. That's just something I'll say to make whoever is behind this feel safe. Wayne will be here. Or Brandon. Maybe Josh."

"Definitely Josh," Kate shot in. "If this is the person who cut the brake cables on the car and hurt Shannon, Josh is going to want a piece of him or her. I wouldn't mind that myself."

Wayne shook his head. "If this is to work, we all have to stay away. You have to be at the B and B or the hospital with Shannon. I have to be working. Derek has to be at the house on Cabot. This yahoo—whoever he or she is—has to believe that Avery is alone and unprotected. We can't put a whole battalion of people in the house. Just one."

Derek and I exchanged a look. We both wanted that one person to be him, but we also knew it couldn't be. Of everyone, he had to be at the house on Cabot.

"Brandon," I said. Derek nodded.

"I'll arrange it." Wayne got to his feet. "Coming, Kate?"

"Coming." Kate got to her feet, too, and came around the table to give me a hug. "I'm glad you're OK," she whispered in my ear.

"I'm glad I'm OK, too," I croaked back.

She turned to Derek. "You take care of her tonight."

He nodded. "I'm not going anywhere."

He followed them to the front door and made sure it was securely locked behind them before he came back into the kitchen again. "Time for bed. Big day tomorrow."

I nodded and let him carry me up the stairs to bed.

—23—

The next morning at seven, I found myself alone in the house. Derek had spent the night, ostensibly to make sure I was all right and that my coughing didn't get worse, but more, I think, just to be next to me and to know that I was still alive and breathing. I didn't complain; I wanted to be next to him, too. I had that near-fatal accident response that Josh and Shannon probably had, where they realized how close they'd come to losing everything, and they wanted to keep the other person as close as possible every second.

He headed out at a few minutes before seven, and I got ready for the day, and for Brandon. Wayne would be meeting Derek at the house on Cabot to tell the television crew what had happened last night and that I'd be staying home today. He'd also be making comments about how busy he himself was and how he'd have to go to Portland for a few hours in the morning to testify in court. That way, whoever the guilty party was would think the chief of police was safely out of the way. When the whole crew was present at

Cabot Street, Wayne would give Brandon the signal to come to my house, since he'd know that none of them would be watching. Cora and Beatrice had agreed to spend the morning at Cabot Street with Derek to get the last of the work done and also so our bad guy or girl would know they weren't with me. Kate had already told everyone she'd be at the hospital with Shannon this morning, getting ready for Shannon's release, and Josh was supposed to have been there for breakfast, too, saying the same thing. For all the arsonist/killer knew, the coast would be clear, and he or she could hightail it over to my house with nobody being the wiser.

All I had to do was wait.

Brandon arrived just before seven thirty through the back door. I let him in and then peered left and right before I closed and locked the door behind him. I knew the whole crew was supposed to be at Cabot Street, but it was automatic.

Not that there were a lot of places left where someone could hide and watch the house. The shed, obviously, was gone, reduced to a still-smoking pile of ashes and debris. A shiver crept down my spine when I realized, again, how close I'd come to being part of that pile.

There were the rows of raspberry bushes and the occasional fruit tree, which may be where the bad guy or gal had hidden last night. I'd walked all around and through the raspberry patch, and no one had been there, but if he or she had been crouched in an apple tree, I might not have noticed. There were several fruit trees within easy striking distance of the shed; luckily none of them had been touched by the fire.

Brandon went straight upstairs and made himself comfortable with a thick book on the history of fingerprinting. I stayed downstairs and made tea with lots of lemon and honey to soothe my throat.

Time dragged by. We had discussed the possibility of

Derek calling me, or texting, when someone slipped away from the house on Cabot, but we'd decided it was too risky. Just in case the first person to leave had a legitimate errand, we didn't want the real culprit to notice Derek's warning to me and to realize that something was up. I was sure the situation was as difficult for Derek as it was for me, but unfortunately, that didn't make it any easier to deal with.

A few minutes after nine, the doorbell rang. I made my slow way down the hallway, pulling my terrycloth robe around me—I was still in my pajamas and robe to make it look like I was resting and not expecting company—and peered out.

And saw . . .

Adam?

Yep, definitely Adam. Wearing a big grin, along with another pair of tight jeans and another formfitting T-shirt, holding a bakery bag aloft.

Well, hell, this wasn't going according to plan at all, was it? Adam wasn't supposed to be here. He had nothing to do with this. And what would happen if the real bad guy showed up while he was here? Would Real Bad Guy kill Adam, too?

But wait . . . Real Bad Guy wouldn't kill anyone, because Brandon was upstairs ready to save the day. I could hear stealthy steps at the top of the stairs, but I didn't think I'd better turn and tell him to stand down because it was just Adam. Instead, I opened the door and smiled.

"Hi, Evie." Adam gave me his trademarked melting grin. It didn't do anything for me this time, either, especially when coupled with the wrong name. "I brought you a scone." He brandished the bag. "Can I come in?"

I hesitated. It'd probably be safer—for Adam—if I said no. Just because Brandon was here to save the day didn't mean that accidents couldn't happen. If the killer showed up and Adam accidentally got hurt in the melee, I'd feel horrible. Although not too horrible, since I didn't really like him that much. And besides, if he went back to the house on Cabot and told everyone I had refused to let him in, they might suspect that something was going on. So I stepped aside and waved him inside.

He walked through the door looking around before turning to me. "Deke told us what happened. You lost your voice, huh?"

I nodded. Couldn't do anything else, since I didn't want him to go back to Cabot Street and tell everyone that Derek had lied.

"Wow, that's too bad. Are you all alone here?" He looked around again. "Where's the cat?"

Jemmy and Inky had left earlier for their usual amble through the neighborhood, and Mischa was, in fact, upstairs where he could keep an eye on Brandon. He—Mischa— had attacked Brandon when he walked in, the same way that Mischa used to attack Derek. At the moment, he was crouched halfway up the stairs, tail twitching while he thought about attacking Adam. Poor kitty, he couldn't seem to make up his mind which was the bigger threat to me at the moment: Brandon or Adam.

I pointed to him. Adam looked in the direction of the stairs just as Mischa hissed and launched himself from the fifth step. Adam stumbled back with Mischa attached to his leg, and dropped the bakery bag, which landed on the floor with a *thunk*.

I was tempted to giggle, but I remembered I wasn't supposed to be able to use my voice. So when Adam grabbed Mischa and yanked him off his leg, and then sent him skidding down the slick hardwood floor of the hallway, I managed to hold back an outraged scream. Mischa didn't; he squealed in pain and anger at the rough treatment. He landed on his feet, though, and hit the wall with a slap, before he did an about-turn and came running back for more. Obviously he hadn't been hurt by Adam's callousness. I scooped him out of the air in midleap and cradled him to my chest. Adam couldn't be trusted to treat him with consideration.

"Damn cat," Adam grumbled, pulling up his jeans leg to look at the damage. "Shit, I'm bleeding."

He was. Mischa had sunk those little claws straight through Adam's jeans and into the skin below, and tiny trickles of blood were running down Adam's muscular leg. Right next to—my eyes popped—a pawful of tiny puncture marks, partially scabbed over. As if he'd gotten them earlier. Say . . . yesterday?

"Damn," I said.

Adam narrowed his eyes at me. "Oh, you *can* talk."

"A little. My voice is hoarse and my throat hurts."

"You should have been dead," Adam said, dropping the pants again.

"You should have hit me instead of just pushing me inside the shed. I broke a hole in the wall and got out."

Adam smiled unpleasantly. "Deke said he rescued you."

"I would have made it out on my own," I said, since it was true. Although being dragged through the door was a whole lot more pleasant than having to squeeze through the tiny hole surrounded by flames would have been, so I wasn't complaining.

"You won't make it out this time." Adam scooped up the bakery bag, which I should have realized didn't have a scone in it as soon as it hit the floor. Scones don't *thunk*. Adam pulled out a gun instead.

I stared at it. "Where did you get that?"

"It's Wilson's," Adam said. "The big boob supports the NRA." He shrugged. "You don't seem surprised."

"About the gun? Oh, I'm surprised." Not to say shaking in my boots. It was the third time someone had held a gun on me in the past six months, and I'd survived the other two times, but there was something about staring into that black hole that still gave me the jitters. "But I'm more surprised it's you. You're the only person I didn't suspect."

"Of course you didn't," Adam said.

"So why did you kill Tony? And try to kill me?"

He stared at me. "You mean you don't know?"

"Of course I don't know," I said. Duh. Would I really be asking if I did?

"You threatened me yesterday."

"What? No, I didn't!"

"Sure you did," Adam said. "When we were talking about Nina and Tony and Ted and Fae and that girl who died. You said, 'You've done things you don't want anyone to know about.'"

Or something like it. I remembered the gist of the remark if not the exact wording. I was pretty sure I hadn't put it quite that strongly, but it didn't seem worth arguing about.

"So?" I said. "Hasn't everyone? You looked like you were thinking of blackmailing Nina into letting you keep your job, and . . ." I trailed off.

"I need this job," Adam said. "I've tried theater, and movies, and now TV. If this doesn't work out, I'll have to go back to valet parking. This is my last chance to be somebody!" His eyes gleamed fanatically.

"So was it you who put Stuart in the hospital? You turned the electricity back on and electrocuted him?"

Adam nodded. "I figured if he was out of the way, Nina would give me a chance."

"I guess she didn't realize you wouldn't be able to do the job."

"I can do the job!"

"You can't even remember my name!" I said. "It's Avery, Adam! Not Ivory, not Ivy, not Evie. Avery!"

"I would have gotten it right," Adam said sulkily.

Maybe not soon enough for Nina, I thought. "So you got rid of Stuart. I guess it was just pure, dumb luck that he didn't die. Did you even care one way or the other?"

Adam shrugged. Probably not.

"What about Tony? Why did you kill him? He wasn't a threat to you."

"Nina was having dinner with him," Adam said. "She told me to stay home and practice, to write down everything I wanted to say on camera the next day and memorize it all while she went to dinner with Tony. I thought she was going to offer him my job. She kept talking about how great he was on camera."

"So you killed him?"

"It made sense at the time," Adam said.

"What were you even doing at the house that night? You couldn't have known that Tony would be there."

"I waited," Adam said, "outside the B and B until he'd dropped Nina off after dinner. And then I flagged him down. I made nice-nice and asked him to help me out. Asked him if he'd mind driving over to the house and going through it with me to help me come up with some patter that would impress Nina. I laid it on thick and told him how great he was and how much I admired him. He lapped it all up. When we got there, I used the key to open the door and then, when we got into the kitchen, I stabbed him with the screwdriver that was lying there."

His voice was chillingly indifferent, as if he were talking about swatting an insect that was buzzing around his head. It was as if the only thing Adam cared about was what happened to Adam; everyone else was of lesser importance. A lot lesser.

"And then you took the tools because you thought it'd make it look like someone had broken in to steal them?"

Adam nodded.

"Where are they? Surely you didn't carry them all the way back to the B and B on foot. Did you?"

"They're in the Dumpster," Adam said. "Under some wood. I figured nobody'd think to look there."

And no one had that I knew about. The old "Purloined

Letter" trick; hide something in—almost—plain view and watch everyone ignore it.

"What about Melissa? Did you text her? Or was that Tony?"

"Thought she might go down for it," Adam said with a shrug.

Right. So Adam had texted Melissa. I focused on keeping my voice steady. "What about Shannon and Josh? The car accident? What happened there?"

"I thought he'd be going out with Fae again," Adam said.

"And why would you want to get rid of Fae? Did she know that you'd killed Tony? Did she see you go outside that night or something?" She might have, since her room was downstairs close to the back door.

He looked incredulous. "Of course not. Wilson was filming her goofing around for the camera and saying how great she was, and I thought maybe he'd tell Nina to let Fae do my job instead."

"So you almost killed two innocent people because you thought Wilson might suggest that Fae take over your job? She's a summer intern, Adam! In another month, she'll be back in college."

"If she got my job, she might not go back to college," Adam said stubbornly. "Who would?"

It was clearly a rhetorical question, so I didn't bother answering. He was way beyond reasoning with, anyway. Through all this, the gun in his hand hadn't wavered, and I hadn't heard a sound from upstairs, either, where I was pretty sure Brandon was hanging over the railing, waiting for an opportunity to fell Adam. But it was a tough situation. Adam had a gun, too, and if Brandon shot him, Adam might shoot me. If Brandon so much as made a sound, Adam might shoot me.

Hell, Adam might shoot me for any reason, or no reason at all, anytime he wanted. So far, his reasons for killing, or almost killing, everyone else hadn't exactly been well considered.

So I tried to keep him talking, hoping that something would happen to tip the scales in our favor. "And yesterday you decided to get rid of me. Because you thought I knew that you'd killed Tony."

"It made sense at the time," Adam said again. "You know, Evie, you shouldn't go around threatening people if you don't want them to come after you."

"I didn't threaten you, you dipstick! You were the one person I absolutely didn't think could be guilty. Until I saw the scratch marks on your leg just now."

"Stupid cat," Adam growled, scowling at Mischa still cradled in my arms. Mischa hissed, the hairs on the back of his neck standing straight up. "I should shoot the damn thing right now." Adam raised the gun and aimed it at Mischa's head.

"It wasn't his fault," I said, covering the cat, who took the opportunity to bite my finger. "Ouch. Dammit! He was just protecting his house. You're the one who came in here and started messing with him. How come he didn't scratch your hands, too?"

"Gloves," Adam said, lowering the gun again. Just enough to point it at my stomach instead of at the cat. Which was something of a relief. Not just because I didn't want Mischa to get shot, but because if he shot Mischa, the bullet would probably go straight through the tiny cat and into my chest. If he shot me in the stomach, we both stood a better chance of surviving.

"So you took him outside and put him in the shed, and then you waited for me to go looking for him?"

Adam nodded, a pleased smile on his glossily too-handsome face.

"And when I got there, you pushed me in and bolted the door and set fire to the shed. And then I guess you ran away, since you thought the fire truck might show up."

"I figured it would," Adam agreed, "but I thought it'd be too late to save you."

If it hadn't been for the spade, and for Derek, it would have been.

"So you thought I was dead?"

"Until this morning," Adam said, and his bottom lip jutted out in a sulky pout. "When Deke said you'd survived. But he said you couldn't talk, so I thought there was still time to fix things, if I got to you before you could tell anyone what you knew about me. And now I guess it's time."

He lifted the gun, and time slowed down while everything around me became very sharp and clear. I threw the cat at him, watching everything unfold in slow motion. Mischa sailed through the air with a drawn-out scream, legs stiff and claws extended. He landed square in Adam's face, exactly where I'd aimed him. Adam yanked the gun up and pulled the trigger, his own scream muffled by seven pounds of fur, and I swear I could feel the bullet part my hair as I dropped to the floor. A second later, Brandon Thomas had dropped, too, straight out of the sky. Or more accurately, over the railing from the second floor. It took him a few seconds to orient himself once he'd touched down, but then he threw himself at Adam and knocked him down. Adam fell with a crash, the back of his head making a very satisfying crack against the hardwood floor. The gun went flying, and so did Mischa, in another arc through the air. He landed on all fours, the way cats do, before he straightened himself, shook, and turned to survey the scene. I scooped him up and cradled him, my hands shaking.

"My hero."

• • •

That was the scene that met Wayne's eyes a few minutes later when he walked through the front door with Derek right behind him.

The latter quirked a brow, surveying the carnage. "This brings back memories, huh?"

Just a few weeks after I'd moved into Aunt Inga's house, just over a year ago now, someone else had tried to kill me. It had been on the top of the stairs rather than the bottom, but I'd been wearing this same terrycloth robe. A cat had been involved then, too: Inky had tripped the bad guy and sent him tumbling down the flight of stairs to end up in a heap on the hall floor, just a few feet from where Adam was laid out now.

"This time it wasn't me," I said. "Brandon landed on him and sent him flying. He's still out."

Derek looked in that direction. "Breathing, right?"

I nodded. "Brandon checked. Twice. We want him to survive to stand trial."

"Definitely." Derek turned back to me, obviously more concerned with my well-being than with Adam's. His eyes were searching. "You all right, Tink?"

"I'm fine," I said hoarsely.

"You don't look fine."

"I will be, once I've had time to rest. And once the TV crew leaves tomorrow."

"I can't wait," Derek said, wrapping me in his arms. "Remind me never to do this again."

I put my head on his shoulder. "No worries. This isn't something I ever want to do again, either."

"Let's get you upstairs and to bed." He picked me up.

"But the house—"

"Between Cora and Beatrice and Kate and I, we'll get it done. You rest. I'll come get you this afternoon so you can be part of the final filming. Until then, I want you to sleep."

He skirted Adam's recumbent body and started up the stairs.

"I will," I said, since rest sounded pretty good right then.

—Epilogue—

"Good riddance," Derek said, sotto voce, the next morning, as we stood outside the Waterfield Inn and waved good-bye to the television crew and the white van.

I'd spent the previous day in bed, until Derek came and picked me up late in the afternoon so I could be there for when Wilson shot the "after" footage of the cottage.

Yes, Wilson was still on the crew. As Nina had explained when I evinced surprise, he was the best, and she wasn't about to lose him over something so silly as a string of poison-pen letters. They'd worked together for years with no problems, and she was fully prepared to forgive and for-get. She was prepared to forgive Fae, too, although Fae was being dispatched back to Kansas City tout de suite. Which seemed fine with Fae, since the only reason she'd signed on to the crew in the first place was to torment Nina. She'd never planned to work for *Flipped Out!* past the summer in any case.

It was her grandmother—Aurora's mother, Wilson's

mother-in-law—who had mailed the letters, after writing them on her old-fashioned typewriter. Once the crew got to Waterfield, and Fae realized that our Tony was the same Tony who had been in Kansas City when her mother died, she'd decided to include him in the mailings. She had called her grandmother, and Grandma had put a letter in the mail to Tony within the hour; that was how it had gotten to us so fast. Of course, by the time it arrived, Tony was dead, and Fae swore up and down she'd had no intention of actually harming anyone. She knew Nina and Tony hadn't done anything criminal, that Aurora herself was ultimately to blame for what happened; she just wanted them to feel bad about their part in it.

My cheeks were still pink and my throat sore on Saturday morning, but I felt a lot better from resting so much. The shed was a total loss, though. The insurance company had come and gone. They had agreed to pay me for it, however, and Derek had promised to build me a new one. Bigger and better. With a real potting bench and maybe even a sink, if we could figure out how to bring water to the shed. That'd be useful the next time someone locked me in there and tried to burn me alive, too, as Derek said.

Adam would be staying in Maine for the time being, and most likely for the foreseeable future. He'd be standing trial for killing Tony and for attempted murder of Josh and Shannon—or Fae—not to mention attempted murder of me, along with arson. It'd be a while until he got to go anywhere else, but once he did, Kentucky wanted him, so they could try him for attempted murder of Stuart, as well.

Once Fae figured out that Adam had damned near killed Stuart just to get his job, I thought she might blow a gasket. She was so mad she was practically spitting nails, and Adam should consider himself lucky he was in police custody at that point, since I think Fae might have tried to kill him herself.

We managed to get enough of the work on the house done

by evening—with the help of Bea and Cora, Kate and Josh, and even Ted and Fae and Nina—that the shoot wrapped on time, and Wilson said he had enough footage for the editing person to piece together a decent show. It would air in a few months, and someone would let us know to look for it. And then we all went to our various homes—temporary and permanent—and got a better night's sleep than the night before. In the morning, Derek and I dragged ourselves over to Kate's B&B in time to wave the crew on their way, precipitating Derek's remark.

I snuggled into his side. "It wasn't that bad."

He stared down at me, incredulous. "Not that bad? Tony died, Shannon and Josh almost died, and you almost burned to a crisp. Plus, Melissa spent two nights in jail. How can you call that not so bad?"

I shrugged. "I thought you meant the renovation and the TV taping. And it could have been worse, you know. We all survived. Well, except Tony. But even Melissa seemed a lot more concerned with saving her skin than with mourning him. And the fact that she had to spend two nights in jail was actually a sort of bonus. Plus, I did prove that she didn't do it. Maybe she'll be nicer to me after this."

"I wouldn't count on it," Kate said. She was standing there with us, waving good-bye, as well, and probably feeling the same way Derek was. "So what are you two up to today?" She looked from one to the other of us.

Derek shrugged. "There's still a lot of work to do on the house. But I think Avery could use another day off. We both could. And it's not like we're in a hurry anymore. How about we take the ferry out to Rowanberry, Tink, and spend the day out there? Pack a picnic, lay on the beach? It's still our house; Melissa hasn't sold it yet. And it's plenty warm enough to go in the water. What do you say?"

"That sounds great. You wanna come, Kate?"

But Kate shook her head. "I've got a lot of work to do, too, and mine can't wait until next week. I've got new guests coming in tonight. But you two go and have a good time. You deserve it. I'll see you later."

"That you will," Derek said, and turned to me. "Ready, Tink?"

"Ready."

I took his hand, and we wandered down the road toward the harbor, side by side.

—Home-Renovation—
and Design Tips

One Chance to Make a
First Impression . . .

Whether you're thinking of selling your house or you just want to a do a few updates while you're living there, put some thought into your home's curb appeal: what someone sees when they walk or drive up to your place. There are easy, inexpensive DIY fixes that can pump up the volume of an otherwise ho-hum exterior for little or no money.

Here are eight easy and inexpensive ideas to get you started.

1. First things first: Mow grass and tidy up landscaping
It costs little to nothing (except for time clocked) to trim overgrown hedges, edge walkways, pull up weeds, and cut out dead growth. Transplanting is free, too: Move those gorgeous dahlias from the back- to the front yard, where they're

sure to be noticed. Mulch is another winner: Spread a layer of grass clippings (free, collected from a lawn mower), straw, or tree bark–based mulch at the bases of trees and flower beds. Doing so not only protects plantings and improves soil quality, but beautifies your yard. Use an online calculator to figure out how much you'll need.

2. Wash dirty siding and dingy decking
You can pressure wash any type of siding (save for wood shingles) quickly and easily with a rented power washer. Or you can use some good old-fashioned elbow grease, your garden hose (on a medium spray setting), a long-handled scrub brush, and a bucketful of water mixed with a few squirts of dish soap. For wood porches and decks, oxygen bleach is the way to go. It's nontoxic to you and to pets and vegetation. Mix a few scoops into a bucketful of water, dip the brush, and scrub away.

3. Invest in some cool house numbers
Switch out those tired old digits and give your address a makeover. House numbers can be screwed in or easily glued on with adhesive—and there's a vast array of styles and materials available. For even more oomph, paint or stain a tall newel post the same color as your front door or shutters, then attach some new, stylized numbers and sink it into the ground either at the end of your driveway or near your home's entry. (Best to expect some neighborly copy-catting on that one.)

4. Upgrade the mailbox
Wobbly, dented mailboxes are unsightly. Changing the box is a great way to add personality. Installation of a bold door-side mailbox requires only some simple drilling. A good-looking, durable freestanding mailbox just needs a hole dug for the post. Or if your existing mailbox is serviceable but drab, you can paint it or buy a seasonal wrap.

5. Repaint or stain a wood door

If you're not ready to spring for a new door, this is the way to go. There's no excuse for the front door looking anything but shipshape because paint and stain are so inexpensive (and potentially free if you have some paint or stain sitting around from another job). Remove any hardware first (or you can tape around hinges and knobs if you're feeling confident and have a steady hand). Surfaces need sanding (fine, 180-grit sandpaper should suffice), dusting, priming, and two to three coats of paint. Go with the grain; follow the same procedure with stain and varnish.

6. Upgrade the front door hardware

Basic front door hardware is easy to replace. You'll find a wide array of bells, door knockers, and escutcheons (plates surrounding bells, keyholes, knobs) at hardware stores and flea markets. A doorbell upgrade is also easy, as there's often no need to replace the actual chime, just the hardware surrounding it. (If you do want to switch out the entire doorbell, there's minor rewiring involved.) A kick plate, typically made of polished metals like rustic pewter, aged bronze, or satin nickel, boosts a door's wow factor while shielding it from stains and scuff marks. Switching the lock set is the most costly change you'll make to the entry. Protection is your first priority: Choose a lock set that isn't just pretty, but that will protect your home from intruders. For a cohesive, stylized look, choose accents with the same finishes, and be sure they're stylistically similar to your home's design.

7. Replace old light fixtures

Match the style and finish of new lights to other elements in your entry and you're generally good to go. For lighting the yard, you can opt for solar-powered lights, which have three significant advantages over their hardwired electric counterparts: there's no assembly required, they save energy, and you can move them around with little effort. Sink a few attractive lantern-style lights into the soil that flanks walkways and the driveway. You'll be amazed at how good this actually makes a home look.

8. Clean and dress up windows

Mullions, moldings, and decorative brackets can really make your exterior pop, and installation is as easy as clicking in a PVC grid over existing windows, or screwing wooden brackets into existing structures. Sometimes, the act of simply cleaning the windows—inside and out—is all you'll need to massively improve the view. Dish detergent (or plain old vinegar) and a microfiber rag (or a piece of newspaper!) should do the trick. For hard-to-reach windows, use a cleaner formulated for outdoor use that attaches to your garden hose. It should dry to a smudge-free finish, and there's no need to remove screens. Just wash on a cloudy, nonwindy day, as breezes and sunlight dry panes too quickly, leaving unsightly streaks behind.

And on that note:

Make Your Own Batten Board Shutters

Shutters are available in several different styles and one of the most popular is batten board, which is sometimes referred to as board-and-batten. Typically, these shutters consist of three vertical boards held in place by two horizontal boards. They're one of the easiest types of shutters to build on your own.

TOOLS AND MATERIALS
- Tape measure
- Wood

- Waterproof wood glue
- Nail gun or a hammer and nails
- Wood stain or paint

DIRECTIONS

1. Measure the height and width of your windows with a tape measure. Your shutters should be as tall as the window, but half as wide as the window.
2. Purchase the wood. You can choose any type of wood you like, but cedar is a popular choice because it is durable. Each shutter will usually consist of three vertical pieces and two horizontal pieces, for a total of six vertical pieces and four horizontal pieces per window. If you have larger-than-normal windows, you might need additional pieces. Use the measurements of your windows as a guide. You can get the wood cut to the appropriate size at a home-improvement store or do it yourself.
3. Lay out your boards, the vertical pieces, next to each other on a flat surface. Only put the boards together for one shutter at a time, not the entire set. Lay them side by side so that they are even and together. Connect them to each other with waterproof wood glue.
4. Attach the battens. Measure between 8 and 12 inches from the top and bottom to place your battens on the boards. Apply some waterproof wood glue to secure the battens to the boards. Then use a nail gun to attach the battens more securely. Be sure to drive the nails through the outward-facing side of the shutter. Apply nails every 4 to 6 inches.
5. To complete your batten board shutters, apply some waterproof outdoor wood stain or paint. Once they are dry you can attach the shutters to your home with four 2.75-inches-long screws, one in each corner, and a drill. Attach with screws no matter what the exterior of the home is, such as brick or siding.

Make Your Own Window Boxes

TOOLS AND MATERIALS
- Wood in appropriate lengths, widths, and heights for project
- Table saw or manual saw
- Tape measure
- Paper and pencil
- Clamps
- Drill
- 16 3-inch wood screws
- Screwdriver
- Wood putty
- Putty knife
- Sandpaper
- Paint
- Paintbrush

DIRECTIONS
1. Decide on the dimensions of the flower box. A hanging box is typically as long as the window it hangs below, including the window frame.
2. Draw your flower box, labeling the size of each board. The longest piece will be the front piece. The two end pieces will be much smaller and will both measure the same length. These will be set to the inside of the long piece. The last side piece (back) will take the dimension of the longest piece minus the two widths of the side pieces. Finally, the bottom will be as long as the front piece and as wide as the sides.
3. Cut all pieces according to your dimensions using the table saw or manual saw. You can make the sides square or angled; if this is your first time, square is much easier. Alternatively, give only the front piece angled sides, and hide the square box behind.

4. Clamp the boards together. Do this for all the sides but not the bottom piece.

5. Screw each board to the adjoining board with 3-inch wood screws. Put a screw at the top and bottom of the adjoining board.

6. Unclamp the four sides that are now screwed together.

7. Turn the box upside down, place the bottom piece on, and screw in with 2 screws per board (8 screws total). This might be a good time to drill holes through the bottom of the flower box to allow water to drain.

8. Make sure to subset the screws into the wood, or, in other words, screw the screws below the wood surface.

9. Putty over the screw holes and allow the wood putty to dry according to package directions.

10. Sand the putty after it has dried. Sand any rough edges as well.

11. Paint the flower box. For a little extra oomph, you can decorate the box with ornate trim pieces or wood cuts of animals, hearts, or flowers, or paint it in a pattern.

Make Your Own Stenciled Doormat

Welcome guests—and let them know they're at the right house—with a custom stenciled doormat that displays your monogram, name, or street number, or one that says anything else your heart desires.

TOOLS AND MATERIALS
- Acrylic or house paint in your colors of choice
- Round stencil paint brush
- 2- and 3-inch paintbrushes
- Painters tape in various widths
- Stenciled numbers or letters (or any other kind of stencil you'd like)

- Store-bought doormat (those stiff fiber mats work well)
- Craft knife (if making your own stencils)
- Tacks

DIRECTIONS

1. Decide on the width of the border you want and where you want it to be, and then measure and lay tape on both sides of the area you want to paint. You can be as creative as you want with this, and make any kind of pattern or border by using tape of various lengths in various directions.
2. Use the straight paintbrush to brush paint between the lines of tape.
3. Let the border dry thoroughly—at least two hours—before carefully removing tape.
4. Pin the stencil—your own or store-bought—to the center of the mat with large tacks, and then paint the stencil using the round stencil brush.
5. If you want to give your stenciled numbers or letters a three-dimensional look, wait for the first coat of paint to dry, then put the same (washed) stencils down, a little to the right or left, and paint with a lighter or darker complementary color to give the letters or numbers a shadowed look.

Make Your Own Twine-Pendant Light Fixture

These are great for parties, as well, hung on a string with a temporary light stick inside. They don't cost much and are easy to make and use until the light stick runs out of juice.

TOOLS AND MATERIALS
- Thin rubber gloves
- Pendant light kit (available from home improvement stores)
- Lightbulb
- Balloon(s)
- Twine
- Elmer's glue
- Water
- Bowl for glue mixture
- Needle (to pop balloon)

DIRECTIONS
1. Hang one or more pendant light kit(s) and oversize bulb(s) from the porch ceiling.
2. Blow up a round or oblong balloon to the size you want your twine pendant to be, and attach it to the light kit assembly.
3. Fill a bowl with Elmer's glue and a few drops of water.
4. Coat long lengths of twine in the glue mixture.
5. Guide twine around the circumference of the balloon.
6. Be sure to apply twine to every area of the balloon, leaving enough spaces for light to shine through, and ensure that the pendant is securely fastened around the cord.
7. Make sure to leave enough room on the bottom of the pendant to allow for hand and bulb to pass through when bulb needs to be replaced.
8. When dry, pop and remove the balloon, and turn on the light.

NEW FROM ANTHONY AND BARRY AWARD WINNER

JULIE HYZY

GRACE UNDER PRESSURE

Everyone wants a piece of millionaire Bennett Marshfield, owner of Marshfield Manor, but now it's up to the new curator, Grace Wheaton, and handsome groundskeeper Jack Embers to protect their dear old Marshfield. But to do this, they'll have to investigate a botched Ponzi scheme, some torrid Wheaton family secrets—and sour grapes out for revenge.

M762T0810